FINAL
SESSION

FINAL SESSION

A MYSTERY
BY MARY MORELL

spinsters book company
SAN FRANCISCO

First edition.
10-9-8-7-6-5-4-3

Spinsters Book Company
P.O. Box 410687
San Francisco, CA 94141

Cover art by Hillary Mosberg
Cover and text design by Pamela Wilson Design Studio
Copy editing by Jennifer Hamilton
Production by: Nancy Fishman   Margaret Livingston
                 Kathleen Wilkinson
Typeset by Joan Meyers in Cheltenham

Printed in the U.S.A. on acid-free paper.

Library of Congress Cataloging-in-Publication Data:

Morell, Mary
    Final session : a mystery / by Mary Morell. — 1st ed.
       p.   cm.
    ISBN: 0-933216-78-5 : $9.95
    I. Title.
PS3563.0773F56   1991
813'.54—dc20   91-2066
                                                     CIP

Fiction is a type of literary work based on imagination rather than reality. This book is an act of fiction. A few places such as San Antonio are real. Two people are based on my friends Jan and Becky, who have given their amused permission. Everything and everyone else is totally without basis in reality. If they seem to resemble any real person, place or thing, it is sheer coincidence, like a cloud resembling a birthday cake. For the record, I have never seen a dog of the Rhodesian Ridgeback breed, but if I owned one I would name it Zimbabwe.

We are pleased to announce that *Final Session*
by Mary Morell is the first winner of the annual

Spinsters Book Company

Lesbian
Fiction
Contest

1990

DEDICATION

This book is dedicated to the memory of Sabina Spielrein, who was seduced by her therapist Carl Jung, and to the thousands of women who have shared her kind of pain in the last hundred years.

ACKNOWLEDGMENTS

This book was written in cahoots with Anne Grey Frost, my partner. Enough can never be said. This book is hers too.

My particular thanks go to the Wislen family, Luke and his two mothers, for their patience, advice and enthusiasm. Luke named the murderer. Also to Gina for loaning me Darcie and Gala, who could turn my yellow handwritten pages into a lovely manuscript. My thanks to them too, of course.

I would also like to acknowledge the help of Ms. Gonzales, Gutierez, Sanchez and Cohen who made many helpful suggestions. To sweet Emma, who helped with the police procedure and forensics, I want to say, "I couldn't have done it without you." Jan and Becky, who make their own appearance in the book (and they know where), have continued their pattern of fine advice.

I am tempted to thank all the strong loving women who have shared bits and pieces of their lives with me from Susana and Karen through Connie, Alice and Donna, but the task of naming the thousands of ways they have helped me is too overwhelming to contemplate, so I'll let the thought stand for the deed. But I must thank Barbara who has always been there. Thanks, B.J., for twenty-five years of just being you, which is quite enough.

My thanks also go to my family in San Antonio for answering lots of dumb questions, especially my brother Jerry, who told me about the new court house and how the defense of indigents accused of crime works, just in time to fix my errors.

Any errors left are my own and exist despite the diligent and talented efforts of my editor, Sherry Thomas. If they bother you too much, consider them intentional fictions, which they are.

FINAL
SESSION

WEDNESDAY

Dr. Elizabeth Freeman lay quite peacefully on the Navajo rug next to her desk. Her strong face and open green eyes showed no pain. The grey and auburn curls were scarcely disarrayed despite her obvious fall. What she did not look was alive.

When the cleaning lady saw the entire picture, she began to scream.

Detective Lucia Ramos ducked under the yellow tape thirty-five minutes later. Her chocolate brown eyes saw much the same scene as the cleaning lady. The body had fallen forward out of a leather desk chair. The apparent weapon was a bottle of expensive vodka. There was a large puddle on the Saltillo tile floor where the bottle had been dropped and broken. By the murderer. With luck there would be clear prints and a quick wrap-up of the case. But somehow the situation did not feel like luck or quickness. Already it was too messy. What were a liter of vodka and two glasses doing in the office of a psychotherapist? "Messy, very messy," Lucia thought.

"A prosperous psychotherapist," Lucia's mind amended, noting the Indian pots, kachina dolls, the ambience of Santa Fe brought to San Antonio. "Possibly a colleague was the perpetrator. A difficult case, a difference of opinion, heated words, a blow...no, not likely!" Lucia took out a small tape recorder and began her notes while she waited for forensics.

"9:25 a.m., Wednesday, April 7, 1315 Lagrima del Oro, office D. Apparent murder victim is white female, age in early fifties. Body appears to have rigor. Victim is about five foot five, perhaps one hundred and forty-five pounds in weight, looks to be in good physical shape. Wearing grey ostrich cowboy boots, black slacks, grey silk shirt, several heavy silver and turquoise necklaces, large diamond engagement ring. Obviously not a robbery. No signs of struggle. Murder weapon may be a vodka bottle, now broken. There appears to have been drinks shared, implying perpetrator probably not a client but not a stranger. No sign of forced entry."

For a moment, Lucia thought about erasing the last part, then let it stand. First impressions were important, even if somewhat prejudicial. She nodded to the police photographer as he ducked under the tape. "Hi, Dave. Tell forensics I want the purse, the glasses, all of the bottle and anything else that strikes their fancy. Thanks. I'll be out talking to the woman who found her." She went out to the hallway of the small office complex where the cleaning lady was waiting and sobbing.

"She was such a good lady. She talked to my Julio every week even though we can't pay. She lets me clean instead of taking money. She was a very good lady. Who would want to kill Dr. Freeman? He must be crazy. He must be a crazy man. Who else would do such a thing?"

"Who else indeed," thought Lucia, running through the list of murderers she had met in the last month—a couple of angry husbands, a cheated business partner, a couple of drug addicts, an abused son and several complete strangers wanting pocket change from all-night businesses. None of whom she considered crazy. Or perhaps all of them. Lucia pushed a lock of her short black hair behind her ear and began the standard interview questions.

"How long have you known Dr. Freeman?" She turned on her tape again and considered her possible approaches to the interrogation while the cleaning lady responded.

None of the answers were very helpful. Dr. Freeman had rented the office three years before. She worked as

4

a consulting psychologist to Northside Schools where ten-year-old Julio Martinez had become a client due to truancy and petty larceny. On Wednesdays Dr. Freeman consulted at the Cerebral Palsy Clinic which left the office free for a morning cleaning. The cleaning lady was Pita Martinez "Spanish female, age forty-one, married, five children." She felt that the late Dr. Freeman, now being safely dead, was on her way to canonization. No clients or colleagues of the victim were known to the informant. There was no secretary. Not much to go on. Playing bingo with her sister provided Mrs. Martinez with an alibi for the evening before.

In the meantime the victim's office was off limits while forensics dusted for prints and took pictures. Lucia tried to recall where she'd seen the closest pay phone. There had been a Lone Star Ice House on Bandera Road only a couple of blocks south of Lagrima del Oro. She waved to the patrol officer assigned to interview the neighboring offices as she left. "Later," she yelled over her shoulder.

The day was going to be a hot one, despite the wispy clouds. Lucia was glad she had left the windows cracked. Otherwise, the car would be an oven. She opened the door to her maroon Sentra and paused for a few seconds to let the hot air out. She tossed the remains of a sausage and muffin into the paper bag in the back seat. She hated to mess it up, but the car had proven sturdy and Lucia looked forward to the possibility that it would outlast the car loan. She had considered upping her payments since her promotion to homicide, but the extra pay seemed to disappear into higher deductions. She sighed as she approached Bandera Road. It would be difficult to turn left without a light. She waited several minutes for a break in traffic before she gave up and turned right then made a U turn. There were times having a police ID was very useful.

The Ice House was empty of customers. Lucia had no competition for the pay phone in the parking lot. She got $5.00 in quarters from the clerk and went back outside to begin her calls. The phone booth was new enough to possess an intact phone book. Lucia marveled at it. Not even the restaurant section had been ripped out.

5

She flipped to Cerebral Palsy and found the number for the clinic. A friendly, chatty man answered the phone.

"Oh, you'll need to talk to Suzy. She'll know all about that," he said when Lucia finally had a chance to make clear she was calling in regard to Dr. Freeman's absence. He put her on hold. A few moments later, a woman came on the line.

"Suzy O'Keefe, here. How may I help you?" she said.

"I'm Lucia Ramos from the Police Department. I'm afraid Dr. Freeman won't be in today," Lucia said.

"Is she hurt? Did she have an accident? I knew I should have worried when she wasn't here at ten, but she's so often late, I really didn't think about it." Lucia felt the concern in the woman's voice was genuine.

"I'm afraid she's dead." Lucia listened to Suzy express the usual shock and concern, then asked, "How well did you know her?"

"Fairly well, I suppose," Suzy replied. "She had been acting as a consultant for over six months and we were meeting every week for a couple of hours. She would go over the cases I presented and make recommendations."

"Did she ever speak of her personal life?" Lucia asked.

"Not that I recall. But I'm rather shaken, so at the moment I'm not sure I trust my memory. I suppose you need to contact her family."

"Yes, of course. By the way, do you know any of her friends, colleagues or patients?" Lucia readied her notebook.

"Yes, we've referred several families to her. Why?"

"She did not die in an accident. She was murdered," Lucia said. "We're trying to talk to anyone who might have known her. Could you give me the names of her clients?"

"Oh, yes. Let me get them."

Lucia was put on hold again. She thought it probably would have been better to tell Suzy O'Keefe in person, but she didn't sound like a suspect and it certainly sped up the process to do some questioning by phone. Suzy came on the line somewhat breathless.

"The only two who are seeing her now are Carl Jarvis and the Andrews family." She gave Lucia the names, addresses and phone numbers of the patients.

6

"Do you have an employee information sheet on her that might list whom to notify in case of emergency?"

"No. She was a consultant, not an employee."

"Do you know how she came to be hired at the clinic? Was she a friend of someone there who might know how to contact her family?"

"I really don't know. She never mentioned anyone."

"By the way, could you tell me where you were yesterday evening?"

"I was at a support group and dinner for mothers. It started at five-thirty right after I got off work and lasted until about ten. It's a long one because it only happens once a month. Why? You can't think I had..." Her voice was rising in outrage.

"No, no. Of course not," Lucia soothed. "It's just standard procedure to ascertain the whereabouts of everyone who knew the victim until we have some solid suspects. Please don't take it personally, Ms. O'Keefe."

"Mrs. O'Keefe," she said in a very cool voice.

"Thank you very much for your cooperation, Mrs. O'Keefe. It certainly helps us arrive at the truth more quickly when citizens are as forthcoming as you have been. Please think about anything regarding Dr. Freeman that might shed light on her death. If you do remember anything, please give me a call." Lucia gave her both home and office phone numbers and Suzy said good-bye quite cordially.

Lucia jotted down her impressions in her notebook. Then she went to her car to get an address book out of her briefcase. Fortunately, the one person she knew in the Northside School System was likely to be helpful. She knew the director of counselling services from her time in the juvenile sex crimes division. She dropped the coins into the phone and consulted her address book for this number.

"Northside Schools Counselling Services Office. May I help you?"

"This is the police. I need to speak to Ron Gillette."

"One moment, I'll see if he is available."

Lucia waited on hold long enough to have to deposit additional coins twice. That meant Ron was in. If he was out, the secretary would have said so immediately. She wondered if he was stalling for time to make up an alibi.

7

But that would have meant he knew about the murder. Which, given its current lack of publicity, would be indicative of involvement. "Not likely," she thought. "More likely that he was, once again, compensating for his short stature by making people wait."

"Director Gillette will be with you in a moment."

Lucia slipped more coins into the phone and turned her attention back to Bandera Road. The Toys R Us across the street was just opening up. A red BMW turned into its parking lot. Then a yellow Celica. "Do people buying toys for children drive cars in primary colors?" she thought idly. A brown Acura turned into the lot and spoiled her hypothesis.

"This is Ron Gillette."

"Lucia Ramos, Ron."

"Lucia, I thought you had been promoted out of Juvenile."

"Yes, I'm working homicide now. Dr. Elizabeth Freeman has been killed."

There was a long silence.

"So," he replied. "I'm very sorry, but why are you calling me?" Lucia was somewhat taken aback. Indifference was not a typical response to murder.

"I thought that perhaps you might be able to help us track down some of her clients since she worked with some program of yours."

"Freeman? Frankly, Lucia, that name doesn't ring a bell. Hang on, let me ask Nancy." Lucia could hear him yelling, "Nancy, do you know a Dr. Freeman who's worked with us?" There was a response Lucia couldn't decipher from the female voice. "Okay, yeah, that program." she could hear Ron say away from the receiver. Then his voice came in clearly again. "She worked through an early intervention program funded through the brewery. They have this ten point scale, things like truancy, stealing and so on. When a school counselor identifies a kid she thinks will listen but still has six of the ten points, this program pays a private therapist to intervene."

"And Dr. Freeman was paid to see clients through this program? It wasn't volunteer or anything?" Lucia thought of Mrs. Martinez cleaning the therapist's office for months. She felt anger begin to rise.

8

"Not hardly, although the program only pays 85 percent of prevailing office fees. The way those therapists squawk about losing 15 percent you'd think we had asked them to do it for free." Lucia could hear him yelling away from the phone again. "You got that file yet, Nancy?" He returned to the receiver. "We've got fifteen kids in the program. Maybe twelve now. They're winding down. Out of money. I don't know any of the kids or the therapists. Nancy'll have the list in a minute."

Lucia tore the page out of her notebook that she'd been doodling on. She wrote on a clean sheet, "paid twice for Martinez" while she asked, "How were the therapists chosen for this program?"

"Just a minute, here's the file. It's all in here. They got a listing from the Texas Association of Psychologists of all the shrinks in San Antonio who work with kids. Then they sent them all a letter asking if they wanted to participate. The ones that responded formed a pool and were chosen at random. Actually, Nancy went down the list alphabetically. Freeman was number seven. One client to each therapist. None of us met her. Nancy set up the appointments. Freeman has been seeing Julio Martinez for three years. Note in Julio's file says the family got him to the appointments. No cab needed. The program pays for a cab if that's the only way the kid can get there. That's it, Ramos. Nada mas."

"Did she see any other students?" Lucia asked.

"Not that I show."

"Do the records show that Dr. Freeman was paid?"

"Yeah," Gillette replied, "once a month. I got the check numbers if you need them."

"No, that's okay. Thanks, Ron. You are a real help." Lucia said good-bye and hung up. She sat down for a moment on the phone booth's hot metal seat to let the rage flow through her. Cheating Mrs. Martinez who thought Freeman hung the moon. "What a slime," Lucia thought. Then she locked her feelings away for further examination when she was off duty. Lieutenant Reynolds was right: business and anger didn't mix when you're a cop. Lucia took a deep breath and exhaled slowly. For a moment she felt a certain sympathy with the murderer. Then she caught herself. Death was too stiff a sentence for petty chiseling.

She made a note to call Amy Traeger. This case was shaping up as a real mess. Amy had been a big help with the psychological side of dealing with the juvenile victims of sex crimes. There was steadiness about Amy that drew Lucia. It didn't hurt that Amy was very attractive in her understated way. Lucia thought with appreciation of Amy's generous figure and honey brown hair. Yes, she would definitely need a psychologist to consult with on this case. She dialed Amy's number from memory, despite not having dialed it for six months.

"Dr. Traeger's office."

"This is Officer Lucia Ramos. Would you tell Dr. Traeger that I need to consult with her on a case."

The voice became much friendlier. "Hi, Lucia. This is Connie. She's with a client now, but if you can call back at, well, let's see, eleven forty-five, she'll be free. Or can she call you?"

"As usual, Connie, I'm not going to be at a phone. I'll try to call between eleven forty-five and noon. It's important."

Connie chuckled. "In this office, there is nothing mundane. Everything is important. But from you, it carries more weight. Nice to hear your voice again. Drop by for coffee sometime." Lucia could hear the typewriter begin to clack as the connection broke off.

It was ten-thirty. "Forensics should be finished," Lucia thought. She left the phone booth and sat in her car to make a few notes. Then she drove up Bandera back toward the murder scene.

She scanned the neighborhood for possible witnesses. Small office complexes were on all sides. There were no houses that might hide nosy neighbors. Lucia sighed. An eyewitness was too much to hope for. The business directory would give her most of the phone numbers she would need but not many offices were open after 5 p.m. And Lucia thought it very likely that the autopsy would place the time of death after usual office hours.

"Otherwise the next client would have discovered the body—or just knocked loudly, then given up when there was no answer," she countered her own imaginings. "How about the drinks," she came back. "Stop arguing with yourself," Lucia thought. "There's insufficient data for a hypothesis."

She got out of the car and went into office C. The patrol officer was just finishing his final futile interview. He was very willing to step outside for a conference. Like the attorney in A and the optometrist in B, the chiropractor in C had seen nothing and heard nothing. None of them had exchanged anything beyond a casual hello with Dr. Freeman in the year and a half that they had been neighbors. The patrol officer gave Lucia the key to D that Forensics had left with him.

"Thanks..." She paused to read his name tag, "Patrolman Cowley. Check all the offices in sight of this complex and its parking lot. I wish there were houses close by with some nosy neighbors like I grew up with over on Zarzamora."

"Hey, I'm a South San Antonio kid myself," Cowley replied, "We always beat the pants off Lanier. That was your high school, wasn't it?"

"Yeah. You always beat us at football, but we had a better marching band," Lucia smiled at him.

"So, would you rather go to U.T. Austin with a football scholarship or a band scholarship?" he bantered.

"Band. Easier on the knees." She could see Cowley eyeing her for linebacker possibilities. "I'll get your reports late this afternoon. Be sure to find the landlord. We might get some info off the lease."

He broke into a grin. "I get to eat lunch. Hooray for an officer that doesn't need it typed yesterday. You're a decent person for a white lady."

Lucia grinned back, "Watch the racial slurs, turkey. I'm Chicana and damn proud of it. Now march your big beautiful black body back in there and finish up. Forget that it's probably pointless."

"You're right on two counts, Chicana lady. Beautiful and pointless. But I get paid by the hour, so back I go. Catch you later."

Lucia tossed him a left-handed upside-down salute and went into D. The body was gone. The broken glass was gone. The glasses were gone. Everything else seemed the same. "No," she thought, "something else is missing." She recreated the original scene in her mind. The huge purse in Guatemalan fabric that was in the kneehole of

11

the desk was also gone. Of course, forensics had taken that too. Lucia walked across the room and sat on the sofa.

She pondered the office. The sofa was comfortable, about six feet long. "Do patients lie down?" she wrote in her notebook. The thick butcher block ends were sturdy. The beige coarse weave was unobtrusive.

She ran her hands in the cracks at the edge of the cushions. They were clean. Her fingers touched a bit of fabric that was out of place. She tugged on it. A lavender bandana emerged. Lucia got up and took the cushions off the sofa. There was nothing else hidden in the sofa. It was extremely clean. If Mrs. Martinez cleaned the sofa every week, it meant that the bandana had become lodged there recently. She made a note of her observation and put the bandana in her briefcase.

The Ficus tree in the corner was real. Lucia leaned over and felt the soil. It was dry. The window shade above it was wood woven with yarn in shades of blue and turquoise.

There were no books anywhere, which seemed odd. Amy's office was cluttered with books and journals. "Don't psychologists have to read constantly to keep up?" Lucia wondered. There was no file cabinet either. Perhaps both books and files were at home or another office. Lucia closed her eyes for a moment. No sounds filtered in from the outside. "Which means probably no sounds go out of the office either," Lucia thought. With the door closed, no one would have heard a scream, if there had been a scream.

Lucia opened her eyes and let them linger for a moment on the print by Amado Peña on the opposite wall. It showed red rock formations in the background and an Indian holding a pot in the foreground. She wondered for a moment if Peña was an Indian, then mentally scolded herself for indulging in a diversion.

In the spot where Lucia thought there should be books, the shelves held decorated pots and kachinas. She identified the odor of the room. It was cedar. All the room lacked to complete the Santa Fe look were vigas and a kiva fireplace. Lucia moved to the chair on the other side of the desk. "This," she thought, "is where I would sit if I were a client."

The chair was a recliner covered in tan leather. Lucia fixed her eyes on the elaborate pattern of the Navajo rug that hung above the couch. It reminded her of the oriental rug in her grandmother's hallway in the house in Hidalgo. The rug on the floor was much simpler, although the basic colors were the same earth tones with red. The pattern of the floor rug was spoiled by the reddish brown stain of blood.

Satisfied with her examination of the rest of the room, Lucia moved on to the main object of her search, the cherry desk. She pulled the desk chair back to an upright position and seated herself at the desk.

On the wall she was facing hung a framed diploma. Lucia copied the information from it—"University of Maryland, Ph.D." and the date almost twenty years ago. There were no pictures of family on the wall or the desk. There was a wooden card holder with Dr. Freeman's business cards in it. The address and phone were of this office. If she had another office, its number was not on the card.

The desktop was free of clutter. There was a lamp of distressed mesquite and a blue trimline phone. And an appointment book which lay open to yesterday's date. It was a standard "Week At a Glance" slipped inside a soft brown leather cover. None of the corners were torn off on the dotted line. There was nothing on Tuesday's schedule except initials. She copied them into her notebook. "4/7—8:00 S.C., 9:30 H.G., 11:00 R.F., 3:00 N.K., 4:30 J.M." "Julio was the last client to see her alive? Did that mean anything?" she wondered.

Lucia checked the note section in both front and back of the calendar. Both were blank. She flipped through January, February and March. There were nothing but initials written in the book. Lucia compared Tuesday's initials in the last few weeks to April 7. They were identical. She sighed. "It probably means no new patients," she thought. Mondays, Wednesday, Fridays were all blank, as were both weekend days. Only Thursdays also had initials on the calendar. Lucia flipped back a few weeks to check for changes. In the 11 a.m. slot. "C.J." did not appear two weeks earlier. She copied the Thursday initials also. "4/9—8:00 S.C.B., 9:30 A., 11:00 C.J. (*new), 3:00 V.L., 4:30 S.C.*." She starred "S.C." on both days to

13

remind herself that it was a repetition. She closed the book and put it in her briefcase.

The ashtray was large, cut glass. In it were several stubs of thin pastel cigarettes. One had burned completely down and fallen out of the ashtray, leaving a spot on the desk. Since there were no other marks on the desk, Lucia assumed the cigarette had been Dr. Freeman's last, left to burn after her death.

The desk drawer above the kneehole was the next focus of Lucia's attention. Unlike the top of the desk, the drawer was very cluttered. There were seven felt tip, fine point pens, all in different colors. Lucia picked up a gold Cross pen and examined it. On it were the initials "E.F.W." She noted them in her notebook and pulled the drawer all the way open, moving the chair backward from the desk to give herself room. Inside were used tissues, crumpled candy wrappers, a bottle of aspirin and a red shirt button in the farthest corner, as well as four opened packs of TicTac breath fresheners. There were two unopened packages of L'Chic pastel cigarettes and one open package near the front of the drawer. She also found a small jar of lip gloss, a comb, an opened package of picture hangers, a grocery list with "milk, bread—not raisin, lettuce, [undecipherable], and t.p." written on it.

Lucia shook her head to clear it of tangents and closed the top drawer. On the right side of the desk were three drawers of equal size. She opened the top one first. It was fitted with a wooden stationery organizer. There were sheets of lavender parchment with and without letterhead and envelopes in both business and personal length. There was also a yellow legal pad. Lucia examined it carefully. It seemed to be the same paper as the grocery list. She put it in her briefcase hoping forensics could raise some interesting information from the missing top pages. In her heart of hearts, though, she knew the most likely information was the grocery list. She sighed and opened the middle drawer. It held a box of tissues and a box of condoms, both almost full. There was also a large bottle of aspirin. And...Lucia broke into a nervous laugh ...in the back of the drawer was a sex toy.

"Well," Lucia thought, "perhaps more than therapy and drinking go on in this office." Messier and messier. She thought for a moment of her own desk. "No," she thought, "nothing too incriminating." Except the syringe she had gotten to inject melted butter into roasting chickens. Yes, perhaps there were things in her own drawers that a stranger might not understand.

Perhaps sex education was part of Dr. Freeman's therapy. Certainly it made sense in the age of AIDS for a professional to be able to demonstrate the correct use of condoms. "Still," Lucia thought, "it does look funny." She went to the bottom drawer. In it was a thick white book titled *Urantia*. She thumbed through it, noticing occasional underlining and then put it in her briefcase, grateful that she had selected the widest briefcase in the discount store. Also in the drawer was a paperback copy of *The New Testament in Modern English*. There was no underlining so she left it in the drawer, but noted its presence in her records. "Vodka, condoms, sex toys and a Bible. Strange paraphernalia for therapy," she thought.

She turned to the other side of the desk. The bottom drawer was large enough for files and the top one correspondingly smaller. She opened the top drawer. It was quite full except for an empty space at the front where the two glasses probably fit. In the back of the drawer was the familiar blue of a box of tampons and along the left side was an open carton of L'Chic cigarettes. On its side on the right side of the drawer was a paperback copy of one of the few science fiction books Lucia had read—*City of Sorcery*. "Was the good doctor a Bradley fan or was the lady a lesbian?" Lucia wondered. Too bad it wasn't *Daughters of the Coral Dawn*, which would have answered the question clearly. But then it wouldn't have fit in the drawer. "She could have put it in another drawer," her mind immediately retorted. "Too bad victims don't arrange their lives for the convenience of investigating officers," she thought. Lucia noted the possibilities and continued her search. There were no marks in the book. A bookmark suggested that the book was purchased at the Bookstop. An orange price discount sticker confirmed it. Between the book and the front corner of the desk drawer was a bottle of eye drops.

Much of the center of the drawer was taken up by an open bag of small Tootsie Rolls and a coffee sack from Barney's with "Chocolate Expresso 3/21" scribbled across the label in handwriting different from the grocery list. Lucia opened the package, curious why coffee would be kept in a desk drawer. Inside were chocolate candies the size of small grapes. Lucia caught herself looking around the office before she tasted one. She wouldn't want to be seen eating what might turn out to be evidence. But it was almost lunchtime, and it was hard to believe that one piece of chocolate out of dozens would be missed. Lucia was surprised at the crunchy center. The bittersweet chocolate covered an expresso coffee bean. "This," thought Lucia, "is candy to kill for." Then she shuddered at the macabre turn of phrase. "Surely," she thought, "no one killed for candy." Anger, yes; greed, yes; but gluttony seemed very improbable.

Lucia looked at the final drawer with anticipation. Surely there lay the files that would answer her questions and begin the real investigation. It came as a considerable shock when the drawer was empty except the phone book, a bottle of expensive bourbon, a bottle of mineral water and a hole about the size of a liter bottle of vodka. There were no files. "Well," Lucia thought, "she would have had more room in the drawer above if she had kept the carton of cigarettes in this drawer. What am I doing reorganizing her drawers when I haven't a scrap of a lead?"

"Yes, yes, I do," she assured herself. "I have scraps. Not likely to go anywhere, but there's still her purse at forensics. At least that will tell me where she lives."

Lucia picked up the phone and punched in the phone number for forensics. Judy answered on the fourth ring.

"Hi, what have you got on the Freeman murder?"

"Hang on, let me pull it up on the screen. Let's see. You were there so you don't need the physical description of the victim. No autopsy yet, but guesstimate on time of death is between 4 and 10 p.m. Oh, that's your comment."

"Just give me the purse contents, home address and phone on her driver's license. Any family, that sort of thing," Lucia said.

There was genuine pity in Judy's voice as she relayed the bad news.

"Sorry, Ramos. We came up dry. All the addresses she lists are the office she was killed in. What we got is a

16

Day Runner calendar with nothing but initials on Tuesdays and Thursdays. No phone numbers at all. She had American Express, two Visas and a Neiman's card. Electric bill at the office. The rest is the usual junk you can find in a purse, you know, keys, tampons, eye drops, make up. The only unusuals at all are a Swiss Army knife, Camper model; and a silver Cross pen set with the initials E.F.D on them." Lucia noted the initials in her notebook.

"Come on, there's got to be something. A husband, a lover, a kid, a brother, some name written in her purse somewhere," Lucia winced. "How," she thought, "can I do an investigation with nothing to go on? Two calendars with nothing but initials."

"Don't kill the messenger, Ramos, just because she bears bad news," Judy cautioned.

"Well, I'm at her office now and it's dry too. I know it's not your fault. Excuse the snarling dog imitation." Lucia chatted a moment longer before hanging up. It did not pay to anger anyone in forensics. You never knew when you might need big favors from them.

Next, Lucia called Cowley but he had gone to lunch. She left a message for him to run the license through Motor Vehicles for a cross match on car registration, to check with the credit card companies and utilities for home address or phone and to remember to check out the landlord of her office.

She checked her watch. Almost time to call Amy. She read over her notes to have them fresh in her mind, then dialed Amy's number.

"Dr. Amy Traeger, may I help you?" The warmth of her voice carried surprisingly well over the phone, Lucia thought.

"You're answering your own phone now? This is Lucia Ramos."

"Oh, good, Lucia. Connie's already gone to lunch and I didn't want to put my phone on the answering machine until after your call. Connie said it was important so I waited for it. I have a luncheon engagement, so we need to be quick," she replied.

"Did you know a therapist named Elizabeth Freeman?" Lucia asked.

"No."

"She was killed last night and I need some help with the investigation."

"Oh, no. Do you know who did it? Her family must be devastated." Amy's voice was concerned. Lucia could picture her warm brown eyes widening as she took in the fact of death.

"We can't track her family yet. No home phone. That's why I need your help. Who should I contact to find out about her? Would there be some sort of file on her somewhere?" Lucia took out her notebook.

"Try Oliver Whitney. He's the local member of the licensing board and also on the Ethics Committee. If anyone is likely to have a file on her, it's Dr. Whitney. I'm not sure he would have anything about her family though. It would probably all be professional data." Her voice sounded quizzical.

"I need anything I can get. One other quick question. Do therapists have drinks with their clients in therapy?"

"Good grief, no. It would be totally unprofessional and unethical too. Why?" Amy questioned.

"She probably had a drink in the office with her murderer and it would help a lot if that meant I could eliminate her clients as suspects."

"Well, I certainly hope it does. I can't imagine having a drink with a client," Amy said, her voice heavy with disapproval at the faintest possibility of unethical behavior.

"Thanks for the help, Amy. I really appreciate it," Lucia said.

"Call anytime, even at home if you think I can help, Lucia. Bye." Amy broke off the call before Lucia could respond.

The abruptness of the phone call disheartened Lucia who had been hoping for more contact. She realized that her hoping had little or nothing to do with professional needs. She simply missed her almost weekly meetings with Amy.

Lucia pulled out the phone book and looked up Oliver Whitney in the business white pages. Her bad luck held; he had just gone to lunch. But the receptionist scheduled Lucia for 2 p.m., a slot held open for emergencies. Lucia agreed to being superseded if a bona fide psychological emergency walked in the door. She jotted down the time in her notebook. "This is promising to be a long, frustrating day," she thought.

She sighed and gave office D one more cursory glance before she left. She didn't think she had missed anything. As she left, her eyes caught the blood stain that spoiled the pattern of the Navajo rug. It somehow seemed wrong that this was the only sign that a life had ended. The wails that had met her grandfather's death seemed more appropriate. "Death should not be so quiet, so unnoticed," Lucia thought closing and locking the door to Dr. Freeman's office.

Lucia stopped at the Taco Rosita at Bandera and the Loop for flautas. The crunchy tortillas with their highly seasoned chicken filling were perfect for munching in traffic. "Fast, tasty and not nearly as messy as burgers," Lucia thought, wiping her slightly oily fingers on the generous pink napkins that the taco stand provided. What she really wanted to go with her lunch was Wink, but the carbonated grapefruit drink was no longer marketed in the U.S. She would stock up with six or seven cases the next time she went to Laredo. "Well," she thought, "I know what I'm going to do in Laredo. What on earth am I going to do in San Antonio?" All she'd gotten so far were some phone numbers for clients and Amy had said it wasn't too likely she was drinking with clients. Too many pieces were missing. There was nothing real to go on. "Well," she thought, "maybe Cowley will find me something." She leaned over to turn on KLTN for some salsa music, but hit the noon news on the neighboring station instead.

"...no leads in the brutal murder of prominent San Antonio psychologist Elizabeth Freeman. Police spokesmen refuse to answer questions about the possibility of this being the start of a new serial sex killing spree. Are women therapists the target of a sex crazed killer? Tune in at one for the latest update."

"Big help," Lucia thought, angrily punching off the radio. "Sometimes the media is a royal pain. So much for keeping things quiet to aid the investigation." She cut her next turn too sharply and mentally apologized to her Sentra for taking her anger out in her driving.

She strode up to her desk still in a nasty mood. The keyboard bounced as she punched in "Freeman: Homo"

19

and yesterday's date into her terminal to pull up what Cowley and forensics had already reported. The pressure from the media was already having an effect. The autopsy was finished. The video was in Evidence. That was about five hours before the estimate. There was nothing new from Cowley, but he had apparently gotten her message about the credit cards and utilities. No lease was on file yet. Motor Vehicles had come through with a match. The blue Volvo in the office parking lot was Dr. Freeman's. Lucia typed a request for an impound. It wasn't likely to provide evidence, but possible. "Besides," she thought, "that will protect it until we can get in touch with the family who have probably just heard about it on the radio or TV. But if they have, why haven't they called us?" Lucia wondered. "Maybe she has no family."

Lucia sat staring at the green words in front of her. They made less and less sense. The victim was not a street person. This woman came from somewhere. She lived somewhere. Someone had killed her. Somehow the answers had to be found. Lucia began the laborious and odious task of typing in her report. She cursed her inattention in high school typing every time she hit an "i" instead of an "e." "Next they'd add a typing test to the police force screening exams," she thought.

Several times she put aside her notebook for her recorder, until it was finally done. She hit "save," then sent the whole report to the printer. She grabbed a Dr. Pepper from the machine in the hall while the report was printing. When it still wasn't finished, she went down to evidence to watch the autopsy video. The carbonation would help settle her stomach. Nothing turned up that she hadn't already guessed. She dropped the yellow pad from the victim's office off at forensics and asked them to bring up any latent writing it might have. The report had finished by the time she got back. Lucia tore off the half dozen or so pages and tossed them in her briefcase. She double checked the address she had written down for Dr. Whitney. It checked with the phone book. Cowley was coming in just as she left.

"Check for an unlisted phone. Catch you later," she said as she dashed past.

"Done. There's none," he shouted back to her.

20

It was too late for the 1 p.m. news. Lucia wondered if the autopsy had been made public yet, so women therapists could stop worrying about sex crazed murders. Whatever the motive, it didn't appear to be sexual violence. There was no sign of sexual assault on Dr. Freeman's corpse. Of course, that did not totally rule out random violence of a serial nature but the M.O. was wrong. What it looked like and felt like in her gut was that someone got mad and hit the doctor with whatever came to hand. In this case, a liter bottle of vodka.

Lucia pulled into the parking garage next to the Palacio Plaza. It was too close to her appointment time to hunt for a parking place outside. She parked as close to the elevator as she could. The small Sentra fit into a tiny space that the larger cars passed by. She didn't quite run the entire way, but she was still breathing a little hard when she reached Dr. Whitney's office on the twenty-first floor.

The receptionist barely nodded when she announced herself. "Dr. Whitney will be with you in a moment. Please make yourself comfortable."

Lucia sat in the mauve suede armchair and waited. At two-ten she opened the briefcase and reviewed the report. At two twenty-five she trimmed off the computer edges, tore the pages apart and paper clipped them in the proper order. At two forty-five she circled pertinent words and phrases in the report. By the time the solid brass workings of the grandfather clock in the corner chimed three, Lucia was reading back issues of *Omni*. No clients joined Lucia in her wait. The receptionist took two calls, one for an appointment and one that was notice of a meeting. Since she apparently repeated what was said to her verbatim, it required no imagination or piecing together of fragments to deduce the content of the conversations. The receptionist's long raspberry fingernails seemed out of place with her grey hair and motherly demeanor. The main purpose of the fingernails seemed to be occupying time. Each was carefully filed. Then the receptionist brought out a bottle of nail polish. It swiftly disappeared as a very handsome middle-aged man swept into the reception area from an inside office.

"I'm very sorry to have kept you waiting, Officer Ramirez. A call from London about a fellow at Oxford."

He brushed his well-groomed moustache, then extended a hand.

"It's Ramos, Dr. Whitney, Officer Lucia Ramos." Both hands were firm in the handshake and Lucia's grip did not relax until a moment after Dr. Whitney's. "Thank you for seeing me on such short notice."

"Of course. When a therapist is murdered we want to pull out all of the stops to help the authorities." He opened a solid mahogany door and escorted Lucia into a side room. The floor was wood in a very complex parquet pattern, but the sound of their entry was absorbed by the grey carpeting on the walls. Dr. Whitney gestured toward two chrome and mauve suede director chairs, which proved to be as uncomfortable as they looked.

Dr. Whitney tapped the manila file on the glass and chrome table between them. "I had her professional file copied. Everything we know about her is in there except, of course, confidential information."

"What do you mean, confidential information? Can you give me an idea of what has been deleted?"

"Certainly, Officer Ramirez. Things like evaluations of her professional competency made during her year of licensure. That kind of thing."

"It's Ramos, not Ramirez. Now that Dr. Freeman is dead, I see no reason for keeping that information confidential. Has any other information been deleted?"

Dr. Whitney again brushed his trim dark brown moustache. "We also deleted a complaint from a patient alleging inappropriate sexual behavior." Lucia stared at his grey-brown eyes and held them.

"The police will need all that information, Dr. Whitney. It may prove to be evidence."

"I'm sure you'll understand that we will need a court order before we would consider compromising client confidentiality." Dr. Whitney smiled.

Lucia mentally gritted her teeth. It would take days, endless pieces of paper and hours of waiting for the judge to get what this pompous—"Stop right there," she thought. "This line of thinking will get you in trouble." Lucia smiled up at him.

"It's gratifying to encounter such professionalism. Can you at least tell me the disposition of the complaint?"

"Yes, as a matter of fact, I served on the review board. There was nothing substantive offered in evidence, so it was dismissed. These things happen. An unhappy client seeking to strike out.... Well, most of us end up with a complaint or two in our files. It doesn't mean much." He gestured in obvious dismissal. "If there is nothing further...."

Lucia took out her tape recorder. "Yes, I do have further questions. Do you mind if I record our conversation?"

His mouth set in a thin, unflattering line. "I do mind," he said.

She put away the recorder and took out a small spiral notebook, "How well did you know Dr. Freeman?"

"This is outrageous," he exploded. "How dare you question me like some sort of criminal! I will answer nothing without my lawyer present."

Lucia took her time putting away the notebook. "Okay, Dr. Whitney, no recorder, no notebook. But let's take a minute before you call your lawyer. I have absolutely no reason to think you might be a suspect in Dr. Freeman's murder. I just want to find out what I can about her. Quietly. No publicity." She noticed him wince at the word. "Just you being helpful and me keeping private information private. That gets a whole lot harder when lawyers and formal questions are involved. So, can we work together? Okay? I gather from your reaction that you did know her."

She watched the tiny beads of perspiration form just above his moustache as the seconds of silence turned to minutes. He did not move a muscle. Lucia examined the grey shark skin suit, the mauve silk kerchief in the pocket, his gold and diamond Rolex watch, the plain gold wedding band. She left her eyes on the ring for a moment, then met his eyes.

"I don't believe your wife would need to know anything we discuss, Dr. Whitney," Lucia said, hoping she'd guessed right.

"She already does." His laugh was short and hard. "She thought it was amusing. No, it's not my wife I want this kept from, it's my colleagues."

"Surely," Lucia said, "it can't be that unusual for two therapists to become involved emotionally."

23

"Sexually. There was not a lot of emotion about it. I would rather it not become general knowledge because it happened the first year she was here. I was supervising her licensure. It would be considered inappropriate."

"How long did your liaison last?"

"A couple of months. It didn't work sexually. We parted friends."

"Did she talk about her friends, her family?" The standard questions began to flow and Dr. Whitney answered. He was not talkative, but he did answer. Dr. Freeman was a private person. Spoke little of her life. Her stepfather was dead. Her mother in a home. Her brother, a lawyer. Nothing else. He did not know her home address. They would meet at her office for a drink, then go to a motel. She liked the illicitness of motels. He did not know any of her friends. She was associated with an informal group of women psychotherapists; primarily to get their referrals. She didn't seem a feminist. He did not have her home phone. He called her at the office. Her mailing address was the office. He had not seen her since the end of her licensing year.

Lucia tried one more time to get the file on the complaint before she left. Dr. Whitney would not budge. She thanked him for his cooperation and left. Her badge got her out of the parking garage without a charge. When she got to her desk, she checked the file in the computer. Still no leads. The landlord was out of town. The address for the phone bill was the office. All electric bills were sent to the office. Her checking account listed only the office address. Had there been a closet full of clothes at the office, Lucia would have come to believe that Dr. Freeman lived there. There seemed to be no trace of another address. "Well," Lucia thought, "maybe we'll have more luck with the credit cards." She called the only leads left, the two clients from the Cerebral Palsy Clinic. One didn't answer. The other, Carl Jarvis, was out. His wife invited Lucia to come to the house to see Mr. Jarvis that evening. She sounded lonely. Lucia set the time at seven-thirty. With luck she could be home in time for the reruns of *Cagney & Lacey*. She always wished for a partner like either of them. Cowley interrupted her before she got too far into fantasy or into finishing her report.

"Hello," he said, "we didn't have much time for introductions this morning. I'm Jake Cowley, three years in traffic patrol and damn happy to be out of it. I was offered homicide or vice. I figured murder is cleaner so here I am, all yours, Officer Ramos." Her new and very temporary assistant grinned at her. Lucia smiled back.

"What do you think, Cowley? I'm lost. Nothing, but nothing, turning up. I can't even get her home address." Lucia pulled out her bottom drawer to prop her feet on and gestured Cowley into the Army Surplus chair next to her desk. "So far all we've got is a weak suspect that may have a grudge."

"Who's that?"

"Some client who filed a complaint against her. The file is 'confidential' and I need a court order to see it."

Cowley beamed a huge smile at her. "Here is where you come to love my being on your team, Ramos."

"How come?" she said surprised. She had never heard of an officer who liked getting court orders.

"I've got a cousin that's bailiff in Reasoner's court. Saved the judge when some wacko husband pulled a gun in divorce proceedings. We'll have no trouble at all with that court order. If I hurry I might have it before dinner. Can you authorize overtime?" he asked hopefully.

"Fat chance on this budget, Cowley. If you work late, take a long lunch tomorrow." Lucia snickered at the thought of overtime. It had been over a year and a half since anybody had gotten overtime and no one she knew was working only forty hours a week. "Get on it, and thanks, Cowley. We could use a break."

He rose gracefully out of his chair and moved swiftly out the door. "Nice moves," she thought. "Too bad they're wasted on me." She dialed Lieutenant Reynolds' office.

"Lieutenant Reynolds, this is Officer Ramos. I'd like to talk about the case I'm on if you have a few minutes." When he said he was free, Lucia gathered up all her case notes and dumped them in the briefcase. Her report could wait. Reynolds started talking as she walked in his office.

"Okay, Ramos, let's talk about what you have. Only first let me tell you a little story about the first time my father took me deer hunting. 'Bob,' he says to me, 'look

25

at that tree. See how all the limbs pretty much grow vertical, maybe at an incline, but pretty much they go up. What we're going to look hard for is a horizontal line. Because that's a whole lot more likely to be a deer than a vertical line.' So that's what we're looking for, Ramos. The horizontals. The things that don't fit just anybody. The things that made her different from the forest of people around her. Why did she stand out? Tell me about her." He sat back in his chair and put his feet in the middle of his desk. "Not stuff in the report. I've read that. Find the horizontal." Lucia furrowed her brow, not quite sure what he meant.

"She didn't have her home address anywhere. That seems odd."

"Good," he replied.

"Sex seemed larger in her life than for most people. She slept with a therapist who was supervising her, had condoms and a sex toy in her desk, had a complaint from a client that she may have slept with."

"Good," Reynolds said. "Most of us talk about sex a lot more than we do it. What else?"

"Her initials have changed more than once. No, that's not so good. Everybody gets divorced these days. That's a tree, right?" she asked, trying to get into the framework of the unfamiliar metaphor.

"Maybe, yes. Maybe, no. Keep an eye on it and if it moves shoot it." he laughed.

"I've got to say that kind of phrase always sounded funnier before I got into homicide."

"Don't take this job too serious, Ramos, or it'll kill you," he laughed again. "What else?"

"She had booze in her file drawer. She was killed with a bottle of vodka that probably came out of the drawer. I didn't think a therapist would drink in her office. It seems unprofessional."

"Good. Find out about the drinking. Alcoholics can make lots of people very angry. It's a talent they have. I know. Been sober five years now, but never lost the talent for making people mad. I'm still good at that. Anyway, what else was out of pattern for this shrink?"

Reynolds reached in his coat pocket and took out a cigar. He unwrapped it with loving care and rolled it between his fingers. Then he put it in his mouth. He didn't light it. He never did. No one had the courage to ask him why he didn't. Lucia looked away from his cigar to her notes.

"On the surface, her office was very clean. But inside the drawers it was messy. Her clothes were very neat and attractive, but her purse was full of junk. I bet her car and her house will be the same way."

"I don't know where that may lead. It may be important. You're getting the idea. Look for what's different. What else?"

"Nothing yet."

"Think harder," he pressed. Then he waited in silence while Lucia reread her notes.

"She moved here from New Jersey about three years ago. Why?"

"Very good. Now you're thinking like a detective. You don't need me. Go track down your deer, Ramos." He gestured her out of his office.

"But I..."

"It's five o'clock, Ramos. Ask me tomorrow."

Lucia gritted her teeth. "So put in for overtime, Reynolds."

He laughed loudly. "I like you, Ramos. You're spunky. Now get out." She did.

Lucia sat at her desk with the hard copy of her finished report in front of her. She took a legal pad out of her file drawer and began to outline what she did not know about Dr. Freeman. It was a long list. The more she looked at it, the more she realized that she had focused on Dr. Freeman, the person, as the victim. "What if," she thought, "the media was right? What if Freeman had been killed because she was a therapist, any therapist? Or had been killed as a woman professional?" She made a note to get a list of therapists from Whitney and run it through the computer to see if any had been victims of violence in the last six months or so. Maybe there was a crazy loose who hated shrinks. She added to her notes: "Have Cowley get list of women killed in last six months and check for pattern." She tucked everything pertinent back in her briefcase. There was just enough time for a quick meal before the long drive out to Alamo Heights and the Carl Jarvis interview.

All the way over there she kept thinking about the murder weapon. No prints on the bottle or the glasses. The leather chair and the doorknob had been wiped clean also, according to the forensics report. That only meant the murderer watched TV and wasn't totally panicked. Even five-year-olds knew enough to wipe off prints these days. But what was a bottle of vodka doing in a therapist's office in the first place? That thought was still in her mind as she pulled off Powhatten into Jarvis' driveway.

It was a ranch-style duplex with a nicely fenced yard and a carport. A Chevy station wagon was parked in the carport. "Solid middle class," Lucia thought, "probably 2.3 children. One with cerebral palsy," she reminded herself. "Be very nice to this family; they've probably been through a lot."

She pushed the doorbell and it responded with a chime version of "The Eyes of Texas." The door swung open to display a thin woman in her late twenties with dark circles under her eyes. Her dark brown hair was clean but uncombed. She wore a flowered house dress covered by an apron which was covered with food. She looked down at it following Lucia's gaze.

"I'm Annette Jarvis. Excuse the mess. Betty gets pretty wild with her dinner. Make yourself comfortable." She gestured to the couch behind her. "Carl is changing clothes. He'll be out in a minute." Annette Jarvis disappeared into the rest of the house. "Carl, the police-woman is here, honey."

Lucia sat on the couch alone for a few minutes. The furniture was too large for the small living room. The duplex was smaller than it had seemed from the outside. Carl Jarvis walked into the room in uniform. He nervously extended his freckled hand and introduced himself. He sat next to Lucia on the couch.

"I only have a few minutes, Officer Ramos. I work from eight to midnight as a security guard at the country club. Pretty big come down for a guy who thought he would belong someday. So I guess you're here about Dr. Freeman, right?" Lucia nodded. "I don't think I can help you much. I had only seen her a couple of times. I don't know anything much about her except that she seemed to be a pretty good shrink."

28

Lucia took out her tape recorder. "Do you mind?" She gestured with it.

"No, go ahead. I hate taking notes myself. I don't know how I thought I would get through medical school. But I don't have to worry about that now. There's no money. I got in. Did you know that? I did get in." Lucia shook her head no. "But it's so expensive. We want the best for Betty. To give her some sort of a shot at life. So I work two jobs and Annette stays home to take care of her. We're doing our best." Suddenly, surprisingly, he began to sob.

"I did it. Betty has CP because of me. That's why I was wasting money on a therapist. I've just got to live with the guilt."

"I didn't know CP was hereditary," Lucia said puzzled.

"It's not," Annette said, carrying in a beautiful blonde child. "This is Officer Ramos, Betty. Say hello." The child seemed to be spasming, but her "hello" was clear and strong for a two-year-old. "Carl thinks it happened because he dropped acid in high school. My mother thinks it happened because we slept together before we were married. Ancient Romans thought it was divinely inspired. Me, I just think Betty chose us because she knew we would love her more than any other people on this earth."

She held the sturdy child tightly and kissed her on the head, then held her out to Carl. "Kiss Daddy good-night, baby."

Carl took her in his arms and sang her a little song. She tried to sing, too. Then he kissed her and got up with her. "I'll tuck her in. It won't take a minute, Officer." He took Betty out of the living room.

"Why did this have to happen?" said Annette bitterly.

"I don't know why babies get CP," Lucia responded.

"I don't either. No one does. But I mean the doctor dying. It took a year to talk Carl into therapy. Thank god his x-ray tech job has insurance to cover it. He gets so depressed. Now he feels like some sort of curse. He just walks into her office and something terrible happens." She paused for a moment. "That's terrible. The doctor is

29

murdered and all I can think about is what it means to us."

"Most people react that way. It's pretty normal."

"What's normal?" Carl said as he re-entered the room.

"I'll let you two talk while I finish the dishes," Annette said, leaving.

"To think about someone else's death as an event in your life," Lucia said.

"Yeah, I guess we do. What else do you want to know? I'm kind of in a hurry." Carl had obviously used his moments with Betty to regain his composure.

"What time were your appointments with Dr. Freeman?" Lucia asked.

"Eleven on Thursday mornings. I took an early lunch," Carl replied.

"Did you know any of Dr. Freeman's friends, colleagues or other patients?"

"No," he answered, "just the Andrews family. They had the appointment right before mine. They have a CP kid too, a teenager."

"Did Dr. Freeman talk to you about her life?"

"No," he said. "Not at all."

"Did she give you her home phone so you could reach her in an emergency?" Lucia crossed her fingers.

"No, she said to call the office number and I'd be referred to some service."

"Did you ever see a bottle of alcoholic beverage in her office?" Lucia asked.

"Yeah, she offered me a drink once when I was really upset. It helped calm me down, but it kind of surprised me. I didn't expect it." He checked his watch. "I've got to go now. I'm sorry."

"Just one more question. Can you tell me where you were last night?" Carl looked shocked.

"I was at work till six. I came home, changed clothes and went to work at the club at 8 p.m., just like every night. Why?"

"I'm asking everyone who knew her. It's just a standard question." Lucia turned off the tape recorder. "If you think of anything that might help, please give me a call." She handed him her card. "Please say good-bye to

Annette and Betty. Thank you for your cooperation, Carl. You've been very helpful."

Her mind was buzzing on the drive home. "What a bombshell," she thought. "The doctor offered her clients drinks. What was going on here? The petty chiseling of Mrs. Martinez was only the tip of this shrink's iceberg." Questions ran circles in her mind.

Her apartment was dark when she drove up. Her neighbor, Cayetano, had left the outside lights on for her. Both of the tiny houses were on the same circuit for outdoor lights. Hers had been the studio for an eccentric sculptor who had built both buildings with his own hands. Both had floor plans resembling a small house trailer and both were solidly built out of cinder block. There the resemblances ended. Carmen and Cayetano had Saltillo tile floors and hand-hewn mesquite paneling for interior walls. They also had a hand-sculpted sink in each of the four rooms. Their windows were tiny, though. Carmen kept her house plants at Lucia's.

The studio Lucia lived in had been converted after the sculptor's death. It was the smaller of the buildings. There was a small kitchen at one end of the living room. The bedroom was cozy and the bathroom was enormous to accommodate the hand-sculpted marble tub. It was only one of several pieces that had been left behind at the sale of the property. It was simply cheaper to leave them than move them. The new owner agreed and designed the remodeling around the pieces where they were. The wall between the living room and bedroom contained a massive granite frame for a rose window, half of it in each room. Lucia had filled it with paper flowers on the living room side and left it empty in the bedroom.

In her living room sat a piece that had been started but never finished. She used it for a coffee table. A teal and brown carpet covered the concrete slab that had been the floor. The bathroom floor was done in tile. But the best thing about her tiny house were the huge windows. They were large enough to catch any breeze. She had hung lace table cloths from Mexico as curtains in the living room and had the bedroom shuttered. Carmen's plants hung everywhere, somctimes giving Lucia the feeling that she lived on the edge of a jungle.

Lucia went over to the roll-top desk that had been a graduation present from her entire family. They had all worked on the sanding and staining. Her cousin Felicia wrote a beautiful note of congratulations on the bottom of the drawer and everyone signed it. Lucia loved the desk immoderately. She caressed its smooth edges whenever she passed and sometimes, like tonight, spoke to it as if it were a person. It seemed slightly healthier than talking out loud to herself.

"So," she said to it, "Where do I go from here?" When it offered no suggestions, she opened her briefcase and took out all her case notes. She reviewed them and put in a call to Amy Traeger's answering machine.

"This is Lucia Ramos. It is 8:10 p.m. There has been a new angle in the Freeman murder that I would like to discuss with you. Please call me tonight even if it's late so we can set up an appointment. Thanks." Lucia hung up and flipped back to the case notes where she had listed the initials of what she suspected were client appointments.

If "C.J." was Carl Jarvis at 11 a.m. on Thursday, then "A." was probably the Andrews family. She called the phone number she had gotten for them from O'Keefe at the Cerebral Palsy Clinic. This time a man answered. She identified herself and set up a meeting at nine-thirty the next day to talk with the whole family, since they were all seeing Freeman. He said their appointment was 9:30 a.m. Thursday, so Celeste was already missing school anyway. They were "A." in the appointment book, but they did not have the doctor's home phone.

Lucia made a list of the initials from the appointment book and filled in the two names that she knew. Only eight to go. She listed the days in the week before Freeman's murder and filled in Tuesday and Thursday with the word "Clients" and Wednesday with "CP Clinic." That only left four days and all evenings. She took a second sheet and wrote "People she knew" at the top. She listed parents, brothers, sisters, husbands, children, lovers, friends, colleagues, old clients, client's families, clubs, church, hobbies, sports, hairdresser, employees, car repairman.

"That's it!" she thought. There were very few car repair places that worked on Volvos. Surely one of them would remember working on Dr. Freeman's car. She made a note to have Cowley check on it.

The list was empty of names. Lucia checked her notes and put the initials of the Cross pens in the space by husband (E.F.W., E.F.D.) with a question mark next to them. Then she wrote "Oliver Whitney" in the space by lovers. She went over the notes she made after talking to Whitney and crossed out "sisters." She wrote "lawyer" next to "brother" and "deceased stepfather" next to parents. It was tedious, but it would get filled in. If the victim's family was in another state (perhaps Maryland where she got her degree) they would not have heard of her murder. That would explain why they had not contacted the police. She made a note to have Cowley contact the University of Maryland alumni office to see if they had a home address for her. It was a long shot, but everything was a long shot at this point.

She looked again at the notebook page with the contents of the purse listed on it. With a red pen she starred "single key—house type." That might lead to something. She could just have Cowley start at one end of San Antonio with a copy of the key and she could start at the other and in two or three decades they could meet in the middle having tried every lock in the city. "Talk about long shots," she thought.

Her head was no longer functioning in a useful manner. She took the book *Urantia* out of her briefcase and resettled on the sofa in front of the TV. Cagney and Lacy were confronting a drug lord. It was the third time she had seen it. The first time she had agonized over Cagney's lie to the judge. The second time she focused on Lacey's loyalty and her lie to the judge. "Ethics," she thought, "at the heart is ethics." She opened the book and groaned. It did not look like a book she would enjoy as much as the latest Naiad romance.

She settled into reading it despite the book having a very different spiritual outlook than she was used to. After a few pages she had to admit it was interesting. She was much deeper in the book when the phone rang. As she rose to get it, Lucia noticed that the detective show was over and the news was on. The phone call was from Amy. Lucia felt her pulse pick up.

"What's up?" Amy asked.

"My murder victim offered her clients drinks. I think I need some help on what all this means. Do you have any time tomorrow?"

"Let me check." There was a pause. "I have about thirty minutes at eight-thirty. Will that do?"

"Great!" Lucia said.

"Is this pro bono or on the department's tab?" Amy asked hopefully.

"Still no money in the budget, sorry. Does that make a difference?"

"Of course not." Amy said. "I know my civic duty, Officer. But I would love getting paid for doing it. See you tomorrow." Amy hung up.

Lucia felt warm. Something at least had gotten accomplished in this frustrating day. That night Lucia dreamed that she was frozen, unable to move as a giant faceless figure swung a huge bottle at Amy's unsuspecting head. It replayed over and over. Lucia did not sleep well.

THURSDAY

The dream still clung to Lucia as she drove to work. Her subconscious certainly knew how to personalize her job, she thought. It was very unlikely that this was some sort of serial killing. But the worried voice inside her kept murmuring, "Who's next, Lucia?"

Fortunately, traffic was light on Interstate 10 and she made it to the station by 7:30 a.m. Cowley had been as good as his word. The subpoena for Whitney's file was sitting on her desk. She pulled up the Freeman file on her terminal. The credit card information was back. The American Express and one of the Visas listed her office address. The Neiman's card and the other Visa were listed under Christian Melons, Inc. and a post office box in Freer, Texas. The landlord listed the same post office box on the lease. The legal pad from Freeman's desk drawer yielded a grocery list that matched the original in the upper drawer. She updated the report with the Jarvis interview and ran a new copy. She made a note to Cowley listing his tasks for the day.

    Check answering service for home number
    Copy pages from previous month in Day Runner
       (at forensics)
    Check on impound of Freeman's car

Check for prescription on sunglasses. Trace-
able?
Check liquor stores in area of office. Who bought
that brand of vodka?
Check Volvo repair places. Any worked on
Freeman's car?
Check alumni office, U. of Maryland—Baltimore
for home address
Check registrar's office at same U. for old files
Where born? Family?
Check on Christian Melons angle. Who owns
it? What is it?
Keep working on pattern of women murdered
Get list of psychologists to match with crime
victims

"That should keep him busy until lunch," she thought,
putting the subpoena in her briefcase. She checked her
watch. She had time for coffee and a quick breakfast
before she was due at Amy's office, and the Pancake
House was only about a block from her destination.

Amy's office was just off McCullough Avenue in an
older section that had gotten run down but was on its
way back up. The office was in an huge old house with a
wide porch now covered in geraniums. It was really
too early for flowers, but a few brave buds were just
beginning to show red. The tulips and jonquils along the
sidewalk were in full bloom. Lucia was still a little early
so she would have time for a cup of coffee with Connie.

"Your coffee is famous world wide, Connie. Truly it
is. Only last week when I was in Beijing I overheard two
guides talking about it."

Connie laughed. "If you had been born Irish, as I am
sure you were intended to be, I'd say you had kissed the
Blarney Stone. Where did a nice Mexican girl like you
learn such flattery?"

"*Echar flores*—to throw flowers. It's an old Mexican
custom. Men stand on street corners and say flattering
things about the women who pass by." She took the refill
that Connie offered. "Where do you get this wonderful
coffee, at Barney's?"

"Yes. It's the Swiss Water Process Decaf Expresso. I
grind it with a teaspoon of cinnamon."

"Delicious. Ever had their chocolate-covered expresso beans?" Lucia realized she could not keep her mind off the case.

"No. I've seen them there once or twice, but they're frighteningly expensive. Besides, I try to stay away from chocolate. It's a worse addiction than heroin. At least heroin doesn't leap at you from every store counter." She made leaping motions with her hands just as the client came out of Amy's office. He seemed offended at such levity and stomped out without speaking. "My, aren't we in a foul mood today?" Connie said to the slammed door.

Connie and Lucia chatted for a few minutes before Amy came out of her office. "Look," Connie said, "the prodigal detective has returned."

"Come on in, Lucia. Sorry to keep you waiting." Amy held the door open for her and closed it behind Lucia. "Can I read the report before we talk?"

Lucia took the report out of her briefcase and gave it to Amy. "Thanks for your help," she said.

It took Amy seven minutes to read through the twenty pages. Lucia knew from experience that Amy had missed nothing in her quick read.

"I'm ashamed to be associated with her in any way." Amy sat back in her arm chair.

"Who do you think killed her?" Lucia asked. "More important, do you think they'll kill again."

"I don't know that much about murder, Lucia. It isn't my field. Let's start with the doctor herself. She fits the profile for a perpetrator of seductive child sexual assault. She seemed charming, self-centered, amoral and possibly alcoholic. People like that make other people mad but they rarely get killed. They rarely even get confronted. I'm surprised she had a complaint filed against her. They usually talk their way out of confrontations. They're very glib on the whole. How does that fit with your picture of the late therapist?"

"I pretty much agree. You think the complaint that she slept with a client was valid?"

Amy shrugged. "Who knows? Given what I've just read, I'd say probably."

"Do you think having the complaint dismissed could cause someone to murder her?" Lucia took out her notebook.

"Don't quote me on this, Detective Ramos, but I'd say no, not by itself. If it fit into some larger pattern in the murderer's personality, yes, it could."

"So the complainant is a possible suspect?" Lucia's pen remained poised over her notebook.

"Yes," Amy said. "So are all her clients. Her husband, if she has one, has been cheated on. She may have more than one lover. Any of them could be subject to jealous rage. Then we have the motives that lie in other areas of her lack of ethics. Did she break confidentiality? That could prove to be terribly frightening to some clients. Was she even blackmailing someone? I don't see her going that far, but only because she might be afraid of a criminal charge. The neat conventional surface is a clue. She tried to maintain respectability. If you find evidence of drug use, though, all bets are off."

Lucia sighed. "Anyone."

Amy agreed. "Anyone."

Lucia looked hard at Amy, then smiled, "So where were you Tuesday night between 7 and 10 p.m., Dr. Traeger?"

Amy, caught by surprise, blushed. "With a friend."

Lucia laughed. "One suspect eliminated. Millions to go. Let's get back to the murderer. Do you think he will kill again?"

"No way to know, Lucia. No way." Amy shook her head sadly.

Lucia spent a moment collecting her thoughts. The two spider plants on either side of the window made her feel at home. In fact the whole office was very comfortable. Very different from Freeman's office, which had an almost sterile feel to it. She let her eyes rest on the vibrant floral calendar on the wall. It looked like one she had almost bought at Bookwoman in Austin last December. Did Dr. Traeger shop at Bookwoman too? If she did, what did that mean? In the two years she had known Amy, she had never heard a word about any man except Dr. Pharris with whom she shared an office. Did that mean Amy was a lesbian too? Lucia certainly hoped so. Sternly she brought her mind back to the topic at hand. "This is no time to play 'come out, come out, whoever you are,' " she thought.

"Dr. Whitney mentioned a group of women psychologists who met informally," Lucia said. "He thought Dr. Freeman might have met with them. Do you know who they might be?"

"It's probably Marsha Prado's group. Would you like me to give her a call?"

Lucia beamed. That was exactly what she had in mind.

"Great. See if anyone in the group knows where she lives or her home phone. That would really help. I'd like you to look over the complaint file too. If it wouldn't take too much of your time." Lucia smiled her most winning smile. "Please, as a good citizen."

"No money is what you mean. This is a commitment on my part to help on the case. Give me a minute to think this through, Lucia." Amy closed her eyes and retreated to a place deep inside herself. Lucia focused her attention on a photograph of an old woman that hung to the right of Amy's desk. She silently asked the old woman's help in convincing Amy to take on the case. "You must be friends," she thought. "Please use your friendship to intercede for me." The old woman seemed to be smiling a small secret smile.

"I don't like this case, Lucia. I don't like Dr. Freeman. In fact, I think I despise her. She reminds me too much of my father. I don't like the fact that she has disgraced a profession I am very proud to be a part of. There were moments, reading that report, when I could have killed her myself." Amy paused, watching Lucia's face fall to a frown. "Despite all this, I want in on it."

"But why if you dislike her so?"

"My own agenda, Lucia. I want to clean my own house. Therapy is my house. I live in it. She has made a mess of it and you can bet the messes you've already found are going to be the least of them. I don't want clients hurt any more than they already have been. So I'll help you because that helps me. But you are going to have to pay. No more conferences in my office. I get paid to work here. You can call me here in an emergency, but most of my consulting will be done over dinner. And..." she looked triumphantly at Lucia, "you provide dinner."

"Is that all?" Lucia asked.

"I'm not sure. For now, it's all. Is it a deal?" They stood shaking hands and made a date for dinner that night at around seven. Lucia gave Amy her home address.

"Oh, I almost forgot," Lucia said, "I need the report back. I'll bring you your own copy tonight. And here, for your kids, for the sandbox." She took a plastic package out of her briefcase. Inside were a dozen inch high green clay monsters.

"Oh, they're wonderful." Amy opened the door. "Connie, look what Lucia bought us for the sand table. Aren't they wonderful? And they break. That's perfect. You remembered when I said it was hard to find monsters that would break."

She scattered them in the child level sandbox along the opposite wall. Connie came in to see and promptly stuck them head down in the sand.

"We'll show those bastards, won't we?" Connie said.

"I saw them in Laredo on my last trip and thought they might be useful. I have to run now to make my nine-thirty appointment up in Castle Hills. Can I use your phone to check in with the station before I go?" Lucia asked.

"Sure," Connie said. "Better use mine. Amy has a nine o'clock to get ready for." She shooed Lucia toward the outer office.

Lucia reached Cowley on the first try.

"I don't think there's a pattern with women murder victims," he said. "We only have eight unsolved in six months and the M.O.s are different. I ran a hard copy on those eight. They're on your desk. You want me to go back another six months?" he asked.

"Sure. How about the match with therapists?"

"All I need is the list which Dr. Whitney's receptionist tells me I can get from Austin. It'll take a couple of days."

Lucia felt her temper rise.

"I'll see if I can't get the list out of Whitney. You work on the other stuff. Have they brought the car in?"

"Yeah, I'm trying to get forensics over there now. They don't see it as a priority. But for the price of six hamburgers I think I can get them to spend lunch at the car. Will you cover it?"

"Sure, but why six? Are we feeding the whole forensics team?"

"No," he said, "just two, but they are really big." Lucia laughed. She knew the two he meant. She heard rumors that they were semi-pro wrestlers on the weekends.

"I'll even spring for a pound of fries and a liter of coke. Thanks for the subpoena, Cowley. I like your style and your hard work."

"I want to be your boss someday. It takes hard work. By the way, the court date was set on the Marchan case. They need you at 8 a.m. tomorrow. Later Ramos."

Lucia hung up and looked at her watch. She hated to be late to the Andrews appointment, but she didn't want another hour and a half wait at Dr. Whitney's office. She was irritated enough with him already. No point in setting up more irritation. She dialed his number and waited on hold for several minutes before he came on the line.

"I don't want to deal with you this morning, Officer Ramirez. I'm very busy." He hung up on her.

Furious, Lucia hung up and dashed for her car. The Andrews home was not difficult to find. All the houses in Castle Hills were clearly marked with house numbers. All the lawns were neatly trimmed. The wide driveways were clean and most had a basketball standard on the garage. The Andrews' house did not. There were, however, two cars in the driveway. The front door was opened as soon as Lucia's finger touched the doorbell. A harried woman in her forties opened the door. She stuck out a plump, pale hand.

"I'm Candy Andrews. You must be the policeman. It's just terrible what happened to Dr. Freeman. Did you catch the murderer yet?"

Lucia shook her head "no" and introduced herself. Candy kept shaking her hand the entire time. Gently, Lucia extricated her hand and asked to see the rest of the family.

"Joe and Celeste are in the den. I hope you don't mind. We just had the living room carpet shampooed. White is so hard to keep clean. I wish we had chosen another color, but it's too late now." Candy explained the importance of the carpet being clean for the big party

41

Saturday night. Joe's boss would be there as well as his fellow engineers. "In these days of layoffs, it's important to make a good impression," she said. "And Joe isn't getting any younger. They save all that pension money when they fire an older engineer and hire some kid fresh out of college."

They reached the den at the back of the house. There was a swimming pool just outside the sliding glass doors. Joe was a nice looking man in his early forties. His brown hair had a bit of grey. He had a great smile that distracted people from his nose which had been broken. "Does he have violent tendencies?" Lucia mused. They shook hands and went through introductions. Lucia turned her attention to the blonde teenager with a sullen pout. She seemed unable to remain still, her movements seemed almost writhing. Her handshake was limp and odd-feeling.

"I'm Celeste. I'm glad she's dead so we won't have to go back and see her. It was so embarrassing going to a shrink. No one goes to shrinks. It's weird."

Lucia glanced back at Candy. Candy shrugged hopelessly.

"You can't pin the murder on any of us," Celeste continued, "because we were at a dumb church meeting with tons of witnesses." Celeste regarded Lucia hostilely.

"Excuse my daughter," Joe said. "She's operating with her gears stuck on brat. We were trying to get them unstuck."

Lucia smothered an involuntary giggle. With a little editing, this family could star in a sit-com on TV. She sat in a rocker and took out her tape recorder.

"I just have a few questions about Dr. Freeman. Had you known her very long?"

"We had been seeing her since last August," Joe said.

"Because I wanted to go on one little date. I'm fourteen. Everybody dates when they're fourteen. Except me. Daddy doesn't want me to have babies. He's afraid I'll have sex and then have babies with CP. Mom just doesn't want me to have sex at all ever. I'm living in a prison." Celeste looked quite pleased with her own diatribe.

Joe's face had turned an alarming shade of red. Candy rushed into the silence.

42

"Celeste, dear, don't say such things. It's very impolite."

"Go to your room," Joe said angrily.

Celeste gave a satisfied smile. It was the response she had obviously wanted. Lucia took the attention away from her grand exit with the next question.

"Did you know any of Dr. Freeman's colleagues, friends or family?"

"No one." Joe's answer was terse.

"Did she ever talk about herself to you?" Lucia asked.

"No."

"Did you ever see a bottle of alcohol of any sort in her office?"

"No," Joe said again.

"Did you consider her a good therapist?"

"I don't know. I don't have a standard to judge by. We didn't seem to be making any progress. Celeste still wants to date." Joe's face was still red.

"Thank you for your cooperation. If you think of anything that may help the investigation, please give me a call." Lucia rose giving them her card.

"That's it?" Joe said "I took off work for this? You could have asked these questions on the phone."

"Now, honey, you would have taken off anyway. This is when our appointment was," Candy said.

"That's how we conduct interviews in a murder investigation, Mr. Andrews." "Besides," Lucia thought, "I never would have guessed at your anger over the phone."

Her next stop was the nearest pay phone for another call to Dr. Oliver Whitney. The receptionist attempted to take a message, then tried to put Lucia on hold. Finally, she said the doctor was out. Lucia pointed out that lying to a police officer during the course of a murder investigation could easily be construed as obstructing justice and she might just want to double check before saying the doctor was out. Lucia was put on hold. The next voice was Dr. Whitney's.

"I don't appreciate your threats to my staff, Ramirez."

"And I'm getting very impatient with your attitude, Dr. Whitney. You have tried to make my job difficult. You refuse to cooperate with my assistant. That's both unnecessary and unprofessional. You don't like it that I know one of your dirty little secrets. Too bad. I have my

43

subpoena. I will be in your office in fifteen minutes. I want everything. That last file didn't have anything in it, not even her date of birth. I got more information from her driver's license. I want every scrap of paper you own that pertains to Dr. Elizabeth Freeman and the complaint filed against her."

Lucia listened to Whitney sputter and fume about her harassment for a few minutes. Then she interrupted him.

"You now have thirteen minutes. If I get there and I am not satisfied that I have the original and complete information, you will not be happy with my next step." She hung up on his outrage. It was very clear to her that Dr. Whitney had information he wanted to hold back. She couldn't tell what his motives were. Was it simple spite or something more sinister? She really hoped her firmness would convince him to cooperate.

About twenty minutes later she entered his office. There were no clients waiting, but things were considerably livelier than on her first visit. The receptionist was at the copy machine, hurriedly making copies. Whitney was rummaging through file drawers. The grandfather clock was striking half-past ten.

"There you are, Ramirez. It's almost ready. I hope you're happy. You have disrupted my entire morning."

"I am Officer Lucia Ramos, Dr. Whitney. You might want to keep my card," she handed him a business card, "in case you remember something else that might help the investigation. I do have a few questions...."

Whitney, obviously distressed, grabbed her by the shoulder and pulled her into his office.

"I wouldn't advise you to lay hands on an officer of the law again, Dr. Whitney. It could be construed as assault on a police officer during the performance of her duties. A very nasty charge, let me assure you."

"Oh, shut up. I don't want to talk in front of the receptionist. She's a terrible gossip." He seemed shaken by his own behavior. He kept dabbing his moustache with his kerchief. "Get it over with and get the hell out of here, Ramos." He pronounced her name with exaggerated care.

"On what days and at what times did you usually schedule your liaisons with Dr. Freeman?" Lucia asked.

"Wednesday afternoons. Always. What else?" His hand shook.

"What hotels did you go to?" She wrote his answers in her notebook.

"La Quinta near the airport."

"Who paid for the room?"

"I did."

"When do you allege this relationship ended?"

"Two years ago. Two years ago. I told you that." Dr. Whitney wiped his forehead. His eyes were red.

"Where were you Tuesday night between 7 and 10 p.m.?"

"I was playing bridge like I have every first Tuesday of the month for several years. Why are you treating me like a criminal? I resent this whole line of questioning."

Lucia continued as if the last few words had not been spoken. "Give me the names and phone numbers of the other bridge players." While he was writing them down she continued her interrogation. "Did you ever have drinks with Dr. Freeman in her office?"

"Yes, two or three times. Why?"

"Did you bring the drinks in with you or were they already there?"

"She had a couple of bottles in her desk drawer. Why?"

"How many other therapists do you know who keep liquor in their offices?"

"None. Where is this leading, Ramos? I have work to do." His frustration was obvious. Lucia remembered Reynolds' earliest advice; never let the suspect control the interview.

"Do you have liquor of any sort in your office, Dr. Whitney?"

"No, why should I?" He spat out the words.

"Why should Dr. Freeman?" Lucia retorted.

"I've no idea. I never thought about it."

"Obviously," Lucia said. "Did you give a list of licensed psychotherapists in Bexar County to my colleague Patrolman Cowley?"

"I told him to ask the State Licensing Board in Austin." Whitney smiled in triumph.

"Are you a member of the board?"

"Yes," he replied.

"Good. Do you have such a list?"

"Yes. But you'll have to get it from Austin because I'm tired of dealing with you." He turned and stomped out.

"You supercilious, arrogant, anal orifice," Lucia thought. She followed him out into the reception area and walked over to the reception desk. She picked up the phone and punched an outside line.

"Vic," she barked into the phone as soon as her number connected. "Send me over half a dozen uniforms to this address—Office 2331, Palacio Plaza, Maltzberger and Wurzbach Road. I've got a warrant that I'm having some trouble executing. We are going to have to take this office apart piece by piece to get what we need."

Whitney opened the file nearest him and took out a sheaf of papers and threw it on the floor in front of Lucia.

"Call off your dogs," he screamed at her. "Here's the damn list. The receptionist will give you the file. The originals. I hope to god I never see another policeman in my life." He slammed his office door behind him.

"Good-bye, Dr. Whitney, and thank you very much for your cooperation." Lucia said to the door. "Cancel the backup, Vic." she said into the phone.

The receptionist bent over and picked the list up off the floor and gave it to Lucia. Then she put all the papers she had copied into a new folder and gave that to Lucia. She put the copies in the old folders. Lucia sat for a moment and checked over the papers. They seemed complete, but how could you ever know?

"He isn't usually such an idiot," the receptionist said. "Dr. Freeman's murder really hit him. He cared deeply for her."

"You knew about their relationship?" Lucia was taken aback.

"There's very little my son does that I don't know about. But he's a good boy. Too full of pride, though. Don't judge him too harshly. He really isn't himself. He canceled all his appointments this week. He's probably in there crying. He would die if anybody knew. He'd much rather pretend to be angry than let anyone know he's grieving. It makes him act like a royal idiot, but what can we women do?" She showed Lucia the door and patted her on the shoulder. "Now, please don't let on that I said

46

any of this. He would just die. Bye, now." She closed the door.

Lucia stood in the hallway with her mouth open. She had thought that nothing would ever surprise her again, but here she stood utterly astounded. "Life is a great deal stranger than fiction," she thought. "Now if I read this in a book I wouldn't believe a word of it. Never." She shook her head and walked toward the elevators. "Never," she thought.

Cowley was gone by the time she got back to the office. His response to her list of questions was on her desk along with eight files of unsolved murders of women in the last year and copies of pages from Freeman's Day Runner. His note read:

1) Sunglasses—no prescription. Corpse had contacts on. Common type—common prescription.
2) Vince's Volvo sold her the car last year. Title held by Christian Melons, Inc. Company owned by F.J. Christian, sole stockholder, CEO and president. Address listed as P.O. Box 14, Freer, Texas. Dun & Bradstreet lists local attorney, J. Morales, as vice-president. I have an appointment with him at three o'clock today.
3) Women murdered. See files.
4) Copies done on Day Runner. Station charged twenty-five cents a page for copying by forensics. It's a crime. Petty larceny.
5) Nearest liquor store—two miles away, never heard of Freeman. No regular customer fits description. Want me to go two and a half mile radius?
6) No address in U.M.B.C. alumni office. Maureen in registrar's office will FAX, Express Mail or mail records. Will bill department for postage. Call her at 301-752-6000, extension 412 before 2 p.m., our time.
7) Answering service sends bill to her office. No home phone on file.

Lucia looked over the files of unsolved murders. Cowley was right. There was no pattern she could see either. She stuck them in a file to return to records when the case was closed. Next she looked at the copies of the Day Runner calendar. No new information there either, since it matched the Week at a Glance exactly. She called Maureen at University of Maryland-Baltimore Campus and asked her to Express Mail the records. Maureen promised to get them out that afternoon. She was excited to be a part of a murder investigation in Texas. Lucia thanked her and hung up. She called two of the names on Dr. Whitney's list of bridge players. Both recalled him being present from 6:30 to 9:30 p.m. on Tuesday evening.

Lucia looked at her watch. If she hurried she could beat the lunch crowd. She grabbed the complaint file that Whitney had given her and walked briskly out and across the street to Juan's Hamburger Heaven.

She sat in the single seat booth at the very back of the diner. The river was barely visible from the angle she had, but it reminded Lucia that there was life outside police work. Even a glimpse was a window into a slower pace of life. "Someday," she thought, "I'll pack myself sandwiches and eat by the river." She thought of her hectic dash to be out of the house before 7 a.m. that very morning and sighed. Maybe if she made lieutenant she would have more time.

Lucia opened the file and began to read. The first sheet was titled "Evaluation of Pending License: Psychotherapy." It listed eighteen categories to be evaluated as "Competent, Unable to Assess, Unacceptable." Dr. Freeman's name was entered at the top. "Competent" was circled in all categories, and it was signed by Dr. Oliver Whitney. In the blank for comments was written, "I strongly recommend licensure." There were copies of certificates of licensure for several other states. The oldest was Maryland, then Pennsylvania in the name of Elizabeth Freeman Drinell, followed by Virginia and, finally, the most recent was New Jersey in the name of Elizabeth Freeman Welter. The file also contained a copy of her transcript. The grades were primarily A's with a clustering of B's in the more technical courses like statistics.

Surprisingly, a course in music appeared each semester on a pass/fail basis. All were passes. Lucia made a note to check with the symphony office to see if Freeman or F. Christian had season tickets.

The next section of papers appeared to be related to the complaint against Dr. Freeman. The first document was a letter making the complaint. The body of the letter read:

"I would like to bring a complaint against Dr. Elizabeth Freeman, a psychotherapist, for behavior I believe is unethical. For a period of six months she had a sexual relationship with me when I was a client. Now she is having sex with another client. I have talked with her about it and she denies everything. I believe someone should stop her as a sexual relationship with clients can be damaging."

It was signed M. Peterson. "Short and to the point," thought Lucia.

The next letter was a copy of a letter from the Board of Licensure to M. Peterson. It sounded like a form letter as it asked the complainant to read through the enclosed "Rules Governing the Practice of Psychotherapy in the State of Texas," determine which rules the therapist was alleged to have violated and give specific dates and description of the alleged violation. Lucia noted that it took the Board about six weeks to answer the original complaint. The rules were also enclosed in the file given to Lucia. It would take at least twelve hours in college level psychology to fully understand the wording of them. Most of the rules (seven out of ten) dealt with plagiarism. One paragraph dealt with "dual relationships with clients." Three paragraphs dealt with handling fees. "Interesting set of priorities," Lucia thought.

M. Peterson's response was brief. It cited the appropriate section, sub-section and paragraph numbers, the dates which spanned almost six months, and stated, "Dr. Freeman and I had sex during this period almost every Wednesday and sometimes on Thursday evening during my therapy appointment. That seems like a dual relationship to me. She was also having sex with another client, but I do not know the dates of that relationship."

There was a handwritten note next in the file. "I talked to Peterson on the phone. She offered no

49

corroboration. She said the other client was not able to come forth. She refused to give me the name of the other client. Allegation seems weak to me." It was signed "Oliver Whitney."

A letter of response from Dr. Freeman was next in the file.

"The client, Marita Peterson, exhibited an unusually strong transference. As we tried to work through it, she increasingly projected her sexual fantasies into the therapeutic relationship. She began to believe the fantasies were reality to the point where she became somewhat delusional. Unfortunately, I was unable to affect change in this pattern. When her behavior changed from simple seductiveness to becoming physically insistent on acting out these fantasies, I suggested that perhaps another therapist might be more helpful to her. She became very agitated, saying that I had obviously found another lover and terminated therapy. I regret that I was not more effective with this patient. Her complaint is apparently based on her feelings of rejection when I would not act out her transference-based sexual fantasies. I hope she will seek out another therapist who will be able to be more helpful than I was."

The waitress was ready for Lucia's order. "A rare burger with cheese. A coke. An order of potato skins and a jalapeno." Lucia closed the file for a moment and looked at the little piece of river. The tall buildings reduced the view to one similar to an arrow slit in a medieval castle. She could barely see the deep green water. "If the complaint is true," Lucia thought, "the doctor was bisexual. So what?" It might be pertinent to her murder; more likely it wasn't. She reopened the file. "This is getting too complex," she thought. "Entirely too many diversions." She flipped to the last part of the file. There was a copy of the minutes of a meeting of the Board of Licensure where the complaint was brought up and dismissed with no discussion. Next in the file was a copy of a letter to Marita Peterson.

Ben Etly
Chairman
Texas Board of Psychologist Examiners
P.O. Drawer 508
Austin, Texas 73105
November 10, 1990

Marita Peterson
1051 New Braunfels
San Antonio, Texas 87048

Dear Ms. Peterson:

I am writing to you as chair of the Texas Board of Psychologist Examiners. The Board carefully considered your letter of September 22 at its regularly scheduled meeting on December 2. Your letter contained allegations of actions by a certified psychologist which, if proven to be true, would be violations of the Professional Psychology Act and the Board's regulations and would be grounds for the Board to suspend or revoke the psychologist's certificate. However, lacking any corroborative evidence, the Board finds insufficient grounds for any action. Furthermore, should corroborative evidence become available, please be aware that the Board can take action on a certificate only in compliance with the Uniform Licensing Act, Sections 61-1-1 TSA 1978, et seq. Section 61-1-3.1 of the Act states, in part: "No action ...may be initiated by a board later than two years after the conduct which would be the basis for the action." The Texas Supreme Court recently has defined the Act's limitation period as beginning to run from the date of the certificate holder's culpable conduct. Jimenez v. Bd. of Opthamology, 104 Tex 454, 722 S.W.2d 1176. When the date of the last alleged incident is more than two years past, the Board will be barred by the two year statute of limitations from taking any action against the psychologist. The Board asked that I extend its appreciation to you for bringing this matter to its attention in the interest of protecting other individuals.

Sincerely,
Ben Etly
Texas Board of Psychologist Examiners

The last item in the file was a letter from Marita Peterson to the Board. It was simple and to the point.

"I'm disappointed but not surprised that you covered Dr. Freeman's ass. I expected that. But somebody needs to stop her. If you won't, maybe somebody else will. Thanks for nothing."

"Well," Lucia thought as her hamburger arrived, "at last, a real live suspect with a motive and even a threat." She ate with her left hand while she made notes with her right. She carefully wiped her fingers while turning pages in the file. "It wouldn't do to get grease on what may turn out to be evidence," she thought. She finished her lunch and went back to the station. Cowley walked in just as she sat at her desk.

"Great," he said, " I finally catch you. The car is all yours. Forensics has finished their magic rituals on it. So fill me in."

Lucia gave him a summary of her morning.

"A dyke with a gripe. Hot suspect, Ramos. Maybe this will be a break. We can use one."

Lucia flinched inside at his crack. "So Cowley thinks queers are better murder suspects than hets," she thought. "That just put him in the homophobic majority." A slight coolness crept into her voice as she answered.

"Yes, we can. Let's try her number and see if she's home." Lucia checked the white pages. "Peterson, M." was listed at the address in the complaint letter. When she dialed the number, though, she got a recording, "This number has been disconnected. There is no new listing."

"The phone's disconnected. No other number given. Check with the phone company. I want to track her down today." She turned on her terminal. "Got to get my report in."

Cowley copied the name and address out of the file. "Did you call Maryland?" he asked.

"Yes. The records should be here tomorrow. Oh, would you check with the symphony office and see if

52

Freeman or Christian had season tickets?" Lucia said without looking up from her keyboard.

"Sure thing," Cowley said.

"And run the list of therapists for a match as crime victims on any violent crime in the last year," Lucia added.

"Done," said Cowley as he left.

When her report was finished, Lucia went out to the impound yard to check out Freeman's blue Volvo. She opened the door. A wave of hot air rushed out. "Dr. Freeman should have chosen a light color interior," Lucia thought, reaching inside to crank down the windows.

In the back seat there appeared to be a hole above the center arm rest. Protruding from the hole was the tip of a black leather horse whip. Lucia unlocked the back door and reached over to pull the whip out. It was quite long. Lucia's eyebrows raised quizzically. The more Lucia knew about Dr. Freeman, the less she understood her. There was a small silver tag high on the handle with the initials E.E.F. on it. Lucia recorded it all in her notebook and turned her attention back to the front seat.

There were three pieces of paper in plain sight. The first was an expired coupon for a car wash dated March 23. On the dash was a folded piece of paper that turned out to be an social security check for $244 made out to Sarah Carter and endorsed over to Dr. Elizabeth Freeman. Lucia checked her notes. There was an "S.C." who saw Freeman Tuesday morning and Thursday afternoon. The check was dated April 1.

The other piece of paper was lying on the passenger seat. Lucia unfolded it. "I need you desperately. Tonight at 6:15. Please. M.P." "Marita Peterson is looking better, or worse, as a suspect," Lucia thought. The handwriting was similar to the letters in the complaint file. Lucia took notes on the SSI check and the note, then put them in an evidence bag in her briefcase.

A Patsy Cline tape was in the tape deck. Lucia turned on the ignition and pushed the cassette in. Patsy was singing *I Fall To Pieces.* "Eerie to have your voice go on singing after you're dead," Lucia thought. She opened the box of tapes on the floor of the passenger side. There were several Rampal flute tapes. Three of Kay Gardener ("Kay Gardener?"), Ferron, Crystal Gayle, ("I got rid of mine when she sang for George Bush," Lucia thought), Linda Ronstadt, Billie Holiday and three homemade tapes.

Lucia pulled out Patsy and popped in the first homemade tape which was labeled "Flute '64." It was a lovely flute solo. There was another labeled just "flute." It was another flute solo. Lucia put them in her briefcase to play later.

The final tape was labeled "R.F. Session." Lucia checked Freeman's list of appointments. R.F. was in the 11:30 a.m. Tuesday slot. She put the cassette into the tape deck.

"...Right, Bobbie, you're safe here." The voice in the speakers was strong and soothing. A child's voice responded something inaudible. Then started crying. The crying went on for a while. Lucia pulled the tape out and put it in her briefcase too.

She opened the glove compartment which had been locked. On the top was a San Antonio map then other maps. Lucia opened them all. There were no routes marked or circles drawn nor were they auto club maps. "No clues here," she thought, refolding them. The owner's manual had the car registration and insurance card in it. She copied the policy number. "Maybe the company will have her home address," Lucia thought.

At this level she ran into the trash: three cheap pens (all dry), two tampons, an open box of Freeman's cigarettes with several gone, a couple of melted Tootsie Rolls, a cork screw, a yellow comb (dirty), a crumpled piece of blue wrapping paper, a bottle opener, a small white jewelry box with a quartz crystal inside. A gift enclosure card was stuck in the top of the box. "Our love will sing with the Universal Harmony. Sarah."

The "Sarah" matched the signature on the government check. Lucia sighed, put the note and the crystal in her briefcase with the other evidence. She replaced the contents of the glove compartment and closed it. "This is like swimming with your eyes closed," she thought. "You feel like you're getting somewhere, but you've no idea where you're headed."

She noticed the map pocket on the passenger side. It was empty. She turned back to the one on the driver's side. This pocket held a silver hip flask. She unscrewed the top and sniffed. Then she tasted. Vodka. Lucia shook her head. It was too late to charge someone under the open container law when they were dead. It certainly scored a large point for Amy's theory that the doctor was an alcoholic. Lucia entered the new information in her notebook.

The ashtray was the next focus of her investigation. It held a dozen or so butts of Dr. Freeman's brand of cigarettes, two crumpled marijuana butts and three Camel Filter Lights. Lucia put the roaches and the Camels in a plastic bag and tossed them in her briefcase.

The back seat was empty except for a paperback book. *Northern Girl,* more lesbian science fiction. "Score another point for bisexual and add a point to believing the complaint is valid," Lucia thought. The floor of the back seat had several small sacks full of trash from fast food chains. A Taco Rosita bag, a Wendy's, a Top Dog and one plain one without label. Each seemed to contain the trash appropriate to one meal.

Only the trunk was left. She went to the back of the car and unlocked it. "Bingo," Lucia thought, "now I'm getting somewhere." On the floor of the trunk was a cardboard box with a dozen or so files in it. The files were unlabeled. She pulled out the first one. It had travel brochures for Acapulco. None of the brochures came from the same travel agency. The next file had brochures for the Bahamas; the one after, Cartagena. There were only travel brochures in all of the files. A brochure for the Hotel del Prado, Isla Mujeres in the Yucatan had the word "yes" written on the front. Lucia copied the name of the travel agency into her notes and put the brochure in her briefcase. "So much for bingo," she thought.

There was a small stack of turquoise flyers beside the box. Lucia picked one up and read it. It announced the beginning of several martial arts classes for women on April 15. The instructor was Nya Kyle. Lucia checked her notes. "N.K." was listed Tuesday at 3 p.m. The flyer went on at great length praising the background of Nya Kyle as a superb instructor in the ungentle arts of the Orient.

The picture of Nya on the flyer showed a young woman in a martial arts stance with something tied around her forehead. "Perhaps a lavender bandana," Lucia thought. She put one of the flyers in her briefcase.

Lucia tugged at the wool blanket under the box. It was in a green tartan weave. She opened it. It was queen size. It had been covering a brown paper sack near the wheel well. In the bag were four hand-dipped candles that had melted into grotesque shapes. Two were lavender, two were light blue. The rest of the trunk was empty. Lucia closed the trunk and the windows and locked the doors.

Back at her desk, she plugged earphones into her portable cassette recorder and set the "R.F. Session" tape to rewind. Then she played it.

After twenty minutes, she took the headset off and shut off the cassette. There seemed to be a patient named Bekka, a young child, Bobby, whose voice did not register well, and an older child who spoke German. Lucia decided to put the tape away and listen to it at home where she could concentrate on it better. She went down to evidence to see the autopsy again.

Watching the video of the autopsy was grim but necessary. At least CamCorders had made her physical presence optional. The two autopsies she had attended were gruesome and her presence had added nothing to the proceedings. Only the police cameraman and the chief forensics investigator on the scene had to attend, now. She watched them interact on the screen with the medical examiner. His assistant, who hovered in the background had tagged the body and supervised its removal.

The murder itself was straightforward. Dr. Freeman had leaned forward apparently to get something out of her purse. The murderer had struck her a blow to the head which landed, either by bad luck or design, on one of the few spots on the skull fragile enough to prove fatal. Simple cranial hemorrhage was the cause of death. The body did not appear to have been moved after the blow was struck. The bottle had broken on the floor, not on the victim's head. It was exactly as it looked at the scene. Further examination found the lungs damaged by smoking and the liver by drinking. The victim had not yet gone through menopause. Everything else was normal. It was a routine "blow by a blunt object" death. Even the second viewing brought no new light on the case.

Back at her desk, Lucia put in a call to a case worker she knew might help her track Sarah Carter from the SSI check. He was "in the field." She left a message asking him to call back. She called the phone number on the martial arts flyer. The message on the answering machine said that Nya Kyle was out of town, but would return calls on Saturday. She left a message.

It was two forty-five. Cowley would be on his way to F.J. Christian's attorney's office. Lucia pulled up the file. No season tickets to the symphony. Marita Peterson's phone was disconnected without a forwarding number. Her file had been purged as non-current by the phone company. Cowley had requested a copy of her last three phone bills. "Good," Lucia thought, "we might get a lead from a long distance call or something." She softened a little toward Cowley.

Lucia took out her notebook and updated the report. Then she went to the aging copier and copied the files from Whitney. She took an evidence bag and placed the files from Whitney in it, noting the date, time and source of the evidence on the label. She did the same for the items she had taken out of Dr. Freeman's Volvo, except the cassettes. She wondered if the whip would prove to be evidence. She walked the bags down to the evidence room and checked the items in.

"Time to see Reynolds," she decided.

He was sitting with his shoes on the desk. The heels were worn down to the leather, but they were very good shoes. She thought about what he had said in the patrol training class—"Don't be stingy with your feet. Be stingy with your wife and kids. They'll forgive you, your feet won't." He obviously took his own advice on some occasions.

"Got your deer yet?" he chuckled. She shook her head no. "You don't get up early enough. You're not there when they're moving. Where were you at roll call?"

"Early interview."

"What you got so far?"

"Prime suspect at the moment is an ex-patient and ex- lover with a gripe, " she answered.

"I thought shrinks weren't supposed to do that sort of thing. It's not a crime, though. Murder is. You may have a deer in your sights after all, Ramos. Have you brought

57

him in?" He rolled his unlit cigar between his thumb and fingers.

"Her."

"Too bad. Not likely your murderer. Hit someone on the head with a bottle, it's almost always a guy. Wrong style for a lady."

"Murder isn't very ladylike," Lucia retorted.

"Equal opportunity killing," Reynolds guffawed. "You got me there, Ramos."

"I think you were right about the alcohol. I found a flask in her car in the map pocket on the driver's side and the autopsy found evidence of liver damage."

"Good. We've got a drunk dyke shrink who diddles her clients. Hell of a deer." He smiled.

"Lieutenant Reynolds, just who is the deer? The victim or the murderer? I'm confused."

"Both, Ramos. Both. What else you got? Witnesses? Hard evidence?"

"Maybe. I've got a note that may be from my suspect, setting up an appointment. Could be for the night of the murder. It doesn't have a date."

"Good. Very good. I'll make a detective out of you yet. What else?" He nodded approvingly.

"The names of a few people. Cowley is helping me track them down. And a corporation named Christian Melons that owned her car."

"Sounds like monks and cantaloupes, like that California wine." Reynolds chuckled. "I like this case, Ramos. It's very entertaining."

"Yeah, entertaining. I guess you'll like the whip in the car." Lucia sounded faintly disgusted.

"Whips, huh? Great. This shrink is a winner. You're likely to end up with more suspects than you'll need."

"I finally get one and I'm supposed to worry about having too many? I should be so lucky."

"So, go nail the perp. What are you sitting here chatting with me for? Bring her in and book her." He pointed his cigar at her face.

"I don't have the evidence or even her address."

"Get it, Ramos. Get it before the public information department decides to serve you up to the press. The trail is getting cold." He motioned her out. He began to hum "Back in the Saddle Again" and reached over his knees to pick up one of the file folders off his desk.

"So much for getting more time with Reynolds," she thought as she left.

When Lucia got back to her desk there was a message from the case worker returning her call. She got him on the first try. He agreed to track down an address on Sarah Carter. She crossed that off her list. Next was the insurance company for the Volvo. She pulled out the yellow pages. There were thirty to forty agents for the company listed in San Antonio starting with Allison ending with Zepeda. None of the names listed matched the agent's name on the insurance card.

Lucia called the main office. Several clerks later she reached someone who could give her an answer. The agent was based in Freer, Texas. The insurance was held by Christian Melons. Dr. Elizabeth Freeman was listed as driver. Bills were sent to a post office box in Freer. There had been one claim; a bit of gravel had cracked the windshield. It was described as having happened just north of the cement plants on I-10. The claimant insisted on having the windshield fixed at Vince's Volvo and paid the difference between the standard adjustment and the dealership's charges.

The phone company liaison was easy to deal with. He immediately produced Nya Kyle's address. It was not too far from Freeman's office. Kyle was trained to act violently and lived fairly close to the murder scene. "Definitely a person to check out," Lucia thought as she added the new information to Freeman's computer file.

Cowley sauntered up as she hit the "save" button.

"Get a load off," Lucia said, gesturing to the empty chair next to her desk.

"You've been talking to Reynolds, haven't you?" Cowley grinned.

"Yeah, I guess it rubs off. What did you get from the lawyer?"

"He is a she. Juanita Morales." Cowley opened his notebook. "Very cool, very professional, not as good-looking as you." Lucia looked at him.

"Okay, forget the last comment, Ramos. It was uncalled for." Cowley looked back down at his notes. "F.J. Christian lives in a development north of the cement plant on I-10 called the Paddock. Against the advice of attorney, Christian is willing to speak with you at one-thirty tomorrow afternoon. Here are the directions and the phone number in case you get lost." He handed Lucia a sheet with letterhead from J. Morales' office. The typed instructions were very precise.

"That's it?" Lucia said.

"I was out of there in five minutes." Cowley looked chagrined. "I tried chatting up the secretary. No luck."

"Well, I guess I go see F.J. Christian at 1:30 p.m. tomorrow. How did the match go on the list of psychotherapists?"

Cowley smiled. "We may have something there. Let me get the file."

While he was gone, Lucia concentrated on the Christian angle. Did Freeman have a "sugar daddy" who paid the bills? Was she a kept woman of a rich older man? Were they business partners? Why was Christian Melons paying her bills? Was F.J. Christian married and having a secret affair on the side? Did he kill his lover to keep her quiet, out of jealousy or over money? Were they even lovers? Could this be a relative of Freeman's? "I'll know soon enough," Lucia thought. She brought up the file to review all the information that related to Christian and made notes for the next day's interview.

There were only a couple of pages in the file Cowley brought. The first match was a domestic violence case. An attorney stabbed his fiancée who was a psychotherapist. He was serving an eighteen month term for aggravated battery. The second was a report of an auto accident of a Dr. Milton Demer. The brake line had been cut by persons unknown. The last case was arson. A building had been torched that housed an abortion clinic. Also burned was the office of Dr. Gail Miller, a psychotherapist and abortion counselor.

Lucia pulled out her file of murdered women that had been run the day before. Halfway through the list she found a case that seemed to fit. Ms. Phillips, a social worker, had been beaten to death a block from her job at an alcohol rehab center. The assumed motive was robbery since her purse was missing. But three persons as targets of violence within three months might be more than coincidence. Four, if you counted Freeman. Three

60

were women. Two were beaten to death. Perhaps there was more to the serial killer theory than it seemed.

The list of murdered women yielded one more possible tie-in. Ester Washington, a pastoral counselor at Robert B. Green Hospital, had been found stabbed and raped next to her car about five months ago. That was a lot of women mental health professionals to be victims of violence in less than half a year. Lucia remembered her dream with a shudder. Even if it was a long shot, she wasn't going to ignore the possibility that there was a serial killer loose who hated women in mental health professions. "Women like Amy," Lucia thought.

"Cowley, it's a real long shot, but I think we should look into a possible connection between these cases." She handed him the print outs on Phillips and Washington. "Check out their clients. See if there is any cross over. I don't have all the names of Freeman's clients yet, but here's what I have." She copied the list from her notes. "See what you can find out. And keep your mouth closed. The media would love to have the story that we're investigating a possible serial murder."

"Give me a break, Ramos. I want to make detective someday. Even if my mother was a reporter, I know enough to keep my mouth shut." He scowled at Lucia.

"Right. I just wanted to be clear."

Cowley put the print outs in his manila file and saluted. "You're the boss. See you tomorrow."

Lucia grimaced. She was not working well with Cowley since his crack about dykes. She needed to relax and get easy. One thing she definitely did not need was the reputation of a ball-buster who threw her weight around. "This situation needs attention but it could wait for tomorrow," she decided. She called the travel agency named on the Isla Mujeres brochure. Neither Freeman nor Christian were listed in their files. The brochure had been distributed at a travel show in February. Over twenty-five hundred had been distributed. Another dead end.

Lucia pushed her chair back from her desk and concentrated on dinner for Amy. There was no time to cook. Carry out seemed a graceless idea. What if Amy was a vegetarian? It was too risky to serve chicken or beef.

Would cheese be okay? Did Amy take cream in her coffee? Yes! Dairy was definitely okay. Lucia was ready to shop.

L'Fromage had eighty-seven varieties of cheese to choose from. Lucia picked four and a baguette. The upscale farmer's market next door had fresh crisp vegetables and unblemished fruit. Lucia picked out broccoli, baby carrots and zucchini. She passed up the tomatoes. It had been years since tomatoes from stores resembled anything other than damp red sawdust. The Granny Smith apples looked wonderful. Lucia took a small bite. She always bought the bitten apple, but the practice had saved her from many dozens of mushy apples. This batch was crisp and tart. Lucia took a half dozen.

The red grapes would be perfect, but Lucia could not bring herself to buy them. The California boycott had focused attention on the desperate plight of the farm workers. Thirty years wasn't so far from the cotton fields of Hidalgo County that she could forget the grinding poverty the migrants lived in. Buying grapes would be a betrayal both of her earliest childhood and of the sympathy she felt for the fieldworkers. Two ripe pears finished the menu in Lucia's subconscious. No, not quite finished. She reached impulsively for a can of black olives.

Lucia got home with fifteen minutes to spare. She changed into jeans and a teal turtleneck. She picked up her glass from the night before and her morning's coffee cup and washed them out. She rinsed off the fruits and vegetables and dried them. The platter she arranged them on had a turquoise glaze. Lucia got out a bowl with a rose glaze for the dip, then remembered that she had no dip. She shrugged and poured half a bottle of Garlic Lover's salad dressing in the bowl.

She had just opened the can of olives to drain them when she heard a knock on the door. She dumped the juice out and left the can upside down in the sink to finish draining. She was wiping her hands on the dish towel as she opened the door.

"Hi," said Amy. "Am I early?"

Lucia looked at her watch and nodded.

"I knew I should have driven around the block again," Amy said. "I hate to be late, so when I'm going to a new place I leave early so if I get lost, I won't be late. But when

I don't get lost I just drive around and around until it's time. Sorry. I know it's better to be late than early."

"It's okay. I'm a little late. You'll just have to watch me cut up vegetables while we talk. Let me get your copy of the report. Then you'll know what I know and we can start from there." Lucia got the print out from her briefcase. Amy settled on the sofa with it.

"Would you like anything to drink?" Lucia asked.

"I'd love a glass of milk if you have it."

"Sure," said Lucia. "Do you mind if I have a beer?"

"No. I'm not a temperance freak. I just don't do well with alcohol on an empty stomach." Amy turned her attention to the report. She was so absorbed she didn't notice the glass of milk that Lucia brought.

Lucia finished preparing the vegetables and laid them out in patterns on the platter. She dipped the apple slices in lemon water to keep them from discoloring. The cheeses in various shapes were difficult to work into the overall pattern. It took several tries before she was happy with the result.

"Looks sumptuous," Amy said, admiring the platter from behind Lucia's shoulder.

"Thanks. What did you think of the report?"

"It just gets worse and worse, doesn't it?" Amy tried to sneak an olive out of the can.

"Have a couple," Lucia said pouring them into a glass mug, "then put them on the table."

"I talked to Marsha Prado. Dr. Freeman was in the women psychotherapists' group for about six months when she first came to town. Then she dropped out. Had a client that could see her only on Thursday evenings so she couldn't make the meetings. Marsha didn't think she was close to anyone in the group. I have a list of the women who were members in case you wanted to check them out. I know all but one and she's left town. None of them seem likely candidates for murder suspects."

"Do any of them seem likely candidates for a sexual liaison with Freeman?" said Lucia, trying to sound calm as she carried the conversation into dangerous waters.

"Maybe Greta. She's married to another therapist and I've heard rumors that they are nonmonogamous, but only for same-sex relationships. Just rumor, though. Do you think Dr. Freeman was killed by a lover?"

"Most people are killed for money, rage or jealousy. Money doesn't seem the most likely. Nothing was taken, not even her diamond ring. That doesn't rule money out, but…. Rage is my guess. It seemed a very impulsive murder. But jealousy is definitely in the running as a motive given what we know about Freeman's sex life. She definitely slept with people she shouldn't have." Lucia set the table while they talked.

"I love your dishes," Amy exclaimed examining the bright glazes in various colors. "Did you get them in Mexico?"

Lucia shook her head "No. At the grocery store with coupons. I can only serve seven people soup. They discontinued the sets before I finished."

"They're delightful. Absolutely delightful. I would have felt compelled to get them all the same color. They look so much more joyous being all different colors," Amy said stroking a light yellow bread plate.

"My Aunt Luz calls it my circus table. She thinks it's gaudy. But she smiles when she says it. Are you ready for dinner?"

"Yes" said Amy. "Let me retrieve my milk."

Lucia watched her walk over to the sofa and back. "She handled the lesbian question very professionally," Lucia thought. "I couldn't tell her feelings at all."

"Do you want a break from work at dinner or should we plunge into it?" Amy asked.

"Let's go. Sooner into it, the sooner we get done," Lucia replied.

"What was left out?" Amy said cutting into the Brie and spreading it on a slice of apple. "Mmm. This is wonderful cheese."

"Thanks. The report doesn't include something I'm kind of worried about. There is a very slight chance that the murder may be part of a serial killing of women in the mental health professions."

Amy stopped eating and stared at Lucia. "I think I just lost my appetite," she said.

"No. It's really a long shot. There's no real M.O. It's probably just coincidence," Lucia tried to reassure her.

"Tell me more," Amy demanded.

"There have been two deaths. A social worker beaten and a pastoral counselor stabbed and raped. An abortion clinic arson also destroyed the office of a therapist," Lucia said.

"Gail Miller. I know. We worked together on a teen pregnant by her father. Gail's a good therapist. But she wasn't hurt."

"Right," Lucia said. "The cases are really too different for it to look like the same person. It's probably just coincidence that four women in your field have been the target of violence in less than six months. But I'd feel better if you were aware of it and maybe a little more cautious...."

"You bet. I've no desire to be the statistic that proves the pattern. Caution is the word until the murderer is caught, Detective," said Amy with a bit of irony in her voice. She dipped a bit of broccoli in the garlic dressing. "Great dip."

"Out of a bottle. Really, Amy, I'd feel better if you were cautious for a while. Please."

"Okay, Lucia, I will. It just seems silly. I haven't thought about myself as a target for years. But it's very nice of you to be so solicitous."

"I would hate to lose my favorite pro bono shrink. Let's forget work for the rest of dinner. It was a bad idea. Try some more triple cream. It's a cheese that begins a whole new definition of decadence."

Amy waved a slice of pear with cheese under Lucia's nose. "Wrong again," she said. "It's the Stilchester. Nothing is more decadent than Stilchester."

The dinner proceeded on the lighter vein. Lucia chatted about some of her fellow officer's foibles and Amy added her stories of bureaucratic snafus until the platter was almost empty.

"Down to work now?" asked Lucia.

"Bathroom first. I presume through the only door?"

"And immediately to your left, beyond the book-case," Lucia replied, clearing the table. While Amy was gone she washed the dishes and spread out her papers and tape recorder on the table.

"I see you have *Memory Board*. Did you enjoy it?" Amy asked smiling as she re-entered the living room.

Lucia grinned. "Rule is one of my favorite authors and I think this is her best."

"My favorite too, although I love *Outlander*. Especially..."

" 'Killer Dyke and the Lady,' " they said in unison.

"That answers some questions," Lucia said.

"Let's get the rest out of the way. I'm single."

"Me too," said Lucia.

"And I'm more interested in good conversation than sex," Amy replied.

"I'm partial to both and don't like having to choose."

"Good," Amy said, "that settles a lot of issues. I certainly feel more comfortable. I could have been terribly wrong and you were an ex-nun instead of a lesbian."

Lucia laughed. "I have a good friend, Evie, who's both. But I never got past the two-day vocation retreat stage. I was really tempted by the convent; all of the nuns seemed so serene. But then I found Yolanda and that was the end of any plans for the convent."

"Yolanda was your first lover?"

"The first and only, except for a few short affairs. No one seemed to be what I needed. I think, though, that I was still grieving. Her death was just awful for me." Lucia stopped abruptly.

"It's okay to cry. I don't mind." Amy gently covered Lucia's hand with her own.

"No. I don't want to get into it. I need to talk about the case." She brushed her tears away with the back of her hand.

"So," Amy replied, "we'll go to work. What did you learn from her clients?"

Lucia reviewed her conversations with the Andrewses and the Jarvises with no comments from Amy. Dr. Whitney was another matter.

"There's no question that their relationship was unethical," Amy said. "It makes me furious that a member of the Ethics Committee would do such a thing. Dr. Freeman was victimized by this man. She was not in a position to say no to his sexual demands. He obviously protected her against the complaint because he wanted to avoid examination of his own behavior. And who paid the price? The clients. The protection they should have been able to count on was subverted to protect that slime!"

66

Lucia looked confused. "I thought you would see this as Freeman being unethical, as evidence of her violation of boundaries."

"Sure. But it wasn't her job to maintain boundaries in the relationship with her supervisor. It's like a professor and student. Her entire career in this state depended on Dr. Whitney's assessment. Of course, she wanted to please him!" Amy's voice hit a higher pitch.

"I'm surprised," Lucia said. "I hadn't thought about it like that at all. You're right. I had it in for Freeman from the time I found out she was double charging the Martinez kid."

"I'm not trying to excuse her behavior. I'd be furious at her too if she weren't dead. Her sexual relationship with a client was worse. It's that damnable cycle. People learn abuse as victims and then they become the abusers. Where does it stop, Lucia, where does it stop?" Amy cried out.

"Amy, it has stopped. She's dead. She can't hurt anyone else."

"But my father isn't. Who stops him? I'm sorry, Lucia. That was inappropriate. Sometimes, I lose it. Things get too close to my own pain and I just lose it. I feel like such an idiot."

"If you want to call it quits, Amy, I won't hold it against you. This was a favor. There's no real commitment. I don't want to put you in a bad situation," Lucia said closing her briefcase.

"No. I want in on this. Frankly, I wouldn't be surprised if you'd rather I was out of it. But I want to be of help to the client or clients she damaged. I care about them. I promise, I won't blow up again...please."

"Of course, you're in. If you'll accept the pay, the job is yours. Can you listen to this tape and tell me what's going on? I'm totally lost." Lucia put the tape labeled "R.F. Session" in her tape player.

"Could I have pen and paper?" Amy asked. "I might want to take notes."

Lucia tore several pages out of her notebook and passed them to Amy with a pen. "Do you want something to drink?"

Amy shook her head "no" and pressed the "play" button. They sat listening to the tape for forty-five minutes. Amy took no notes.

"Family therapy?" Lucia asked, her voice very unsure.

"No. Unless I'm mistaken, I think there's only one client present." Amy said very slowly. "I think the client is probably a multiple personality. And I don't think the therapist knew what she was doing. She kept looking for the real person. They're all real." Amy began to write on the paper. "There's a small child. Bobbie. The one that cries. Benji, who speaks German. Bekka, who talks to the other children. And Ricki, who's a whore, but a young one—nine to twelve. The therapist was using hypnosis to bring out the various personalities."

"Oh," said Lucia, stunned.

"I think I'd like a beer," Amy said.

They were both silent for a few moments while Lucia fetched a beer from the refrigerator. "Would you like a glass?"

"Yes, thank you." Amy replied. "I've worked with several multiple personalities. It's not uncommon among incest survivors. Some experts believe that the child develops another new personality as a response to severe abuse. If that new personality can't cope or can't stop the abuse, the child tries a new personality. It sounds reasonable to me. I have seen a lot of clients that have isolated the child who suffered the abuse and then developed a personality that knows nothing about the incest."

Lucia digested that information. "Would one of the child personalities be more likely to act violently," she asked. "I mean the children are likely to be angry, aren't they? And angry children have tantrums."

Amy did not try to hide the disappointment in her voice. "Lucia, how many of the abused children you worked with ever attacked an adult?"

"None. I always wondered why. There were times I wanted to hit some of those perpetrators."

"As a society, we project our emotions onto the powerless. If I were in that situation, we think, I would be in a murderous rage. But the powerless know they would be smashed in a minute if they step out of line. They

68

usually turn that anger inward. The few kids that have fought back with violence usually possess some power in their societal roles. Frankly, they are usually teenage white males.

"The one case I know about where a multiple personality killed someone was a guy in California. He fits your description."

"But," Amy cautioned, "we're dealing with people. And people always break our neat little rules. So I don't think you can rule someone out as a suspect because of being a multiple personality. But they are certainly not more likely than the average person to commit a violent crime."

"When I find out her name, would you be willing to talk to her? I feel a little out of my league."

Amy thought it over. "Okay, Ramos, I'll do a deal with you. I'll interview R.F. if you'll let me talk to the client who filed the complaint, Marita Peterson. And any other clients who Freeman exploited sexually."

"I can't let you do the first interview with any that are high on the suspect list. You know that, Amy. My job comes first."

Amy tapped the paper in front of her with a pen. "Can I suggest that you avoid talking about the sexual relationship itself unless you really have to?"

"What do you suggest I do about it?" Lucia felt a little irritated that Amy was telling her how to do her job.

"Tell her the truth. That you believe her complaint. That you don't have the need or the psychological competence to risk damaging her by discussing it."

"You drive a hard bargain. I'll need a tape of any interview you do, just like it was with the child victims we worked with."

"It's a deal, Officer Ramos." Amy extended her hand across the table and they shook on it. "Give her my card and tell her to call me."

FRIDAY

The address listed for Nya Kyle's telephone was seven minutes from Dr. Freeman's office, Lucia noted. At least it was at 6:30 a.m. when traffic was light. Lucia parked in front of the old warehouse, out of place in the tract neighborhood. It probably had been one of several farm buildings before urban sprawl had consumed the farm. The wood siding was weathered to a lovely grey. Lucia surreptitiously peered through the uncurtained windows before knocking. No one answered.

The first floor appeared to be one big room. There were several Japanese paper screens propped against one wall. In the far corner of the room was an artificial waterfall that wasn't operating. There were mats rolled up against the walls. The shiny wood floor was obviously not the original floor.

Lucia walked around to the back of the building. A small fruit orchard and rock garden filled the surprisingly large yard. Lucia looked through the back windows and saw that the other side of the room was covered with sliding panels. She could not have been sure which panel covered the front door and adjacent window had it not been standing open. Only the staircase to the second floor extended above the top of the panels. Lucia returned to her car. There were no other cars either in the driveway or on the street near the martial arts studio. She shrugged. There was no way to tell what was on the second floor. "It could be Nya Kyle's home," Lucia thought, "but she doesn't seem to be here."

The traffic stayed light all the way to the office. Graveyard shift workers were leaving as Lucia arrived. She updated her report with the information about R.F. and Amy's agreement to do pro bono work on the case. She filled out a request for a transcript from the R.F. tape, addressing the inter-office envelope to clerical support services. Then she sealed the tape in an evidence bag and took it downstairs.

"I hear we got a whip from this case, Ramos," the burly clerk guffawed. "Kinky, very kinky."

"You know what Reynolds will do if a rumor like this hits the press?" Lucia replied.

"Yeah, yeah." He looked considerably subdued.

"He might just lose his sense of humor," Lucia said handing over the evidence bag.

"Midnight foot patrol in the cattle feed lots is what he promised the last guy he caught." The clerk's face fell.

"Don't spread rumors or you'll retire from the evidence room," Lucia cautioned.

"I don't nee d a broad to lecture me, Ramos. Beat it." He turned his back on her.

Lucia shrugged. "Cranky," she thought. "This case is definitely making me cranky. First I growl at Cowley, then at Leander in evidence. I've got to stop this stupidity." She chastised herself all the way back to roll call. She sifted through the sergeant's information while he droned on. "They might pull Cowley for backup on the east side crack bust," she thought. Otherwise nothing was really pertinent to her case. She wondered if roll call wasn't a waste of time, but at least it broke the isolation after the powers that be had done away with partners. Lucia returned to her desk.

The phone company liaison was in his office by 7:15 a.m. He verified that the copies of the last three phone bills of Marita Peterson were ready. Lucia told him she would be there in the time it took to walk the six blocks to the Southwestern Bell office. It took less than ten minutes. The receptionist had the file ready and Lucia was on her way out a minute later.

Barney's was her next stop. All the tables on the river's edge were full so Lucia took a seat inside the coffeehouse. A harried young woman took Lucia's order and brushed aside Lucia's questions about customers. "Even if Dr. Freeman was a regular customer, the waitstaff wouldn't know her, since none of us has been on the job a month," she said.

Lucia opened the envelope from the phone company. In three months, Marita Peterson had not made a single long distance call. She had, however, changed her address. The last bill had been mailed to 31083 Medina Road, a long way out of town. She decided to try to catch Cowley before she left. The sooner she mended that relationship, the better.

Lucia almost choked on her coffee when the tab came—$2.75 for one cup of coffee. She left two quarters for a tip thinking that, with the tip, the cup of coffee cost twice the price of yesterday's entire breakfast. "An expensive waste of time, even if the coffee is great," she thought.

The streets to the new courthouse were clogged with rush hour traffic that also slowed pedestrians. But Lucia still arrived a few minutes before the gavel came down. She put on the most interested look she could come up with. Judges disliked any hint that sitting in their courtrooms might be a bore. Cases had been lost on less and this wasn't a jury trial. Few juries had any sympathy with drug-related murders. And Marchant had been caught with the gun and the speed. Legal technicalities were his only hope.

Marchant's lawyer made all the standard motions to dismiss. Judge Blumberg overruled them all. The witnesses were sworn in and the rule was invoked. The witnesses went into the hall to wait. Lucia was called second, gave her testimony establishing the chain of evidence and was dismissed.

It was well after nine when she got back to her office. She put her briefcase in the middle of the desk. Then she just stared at it. None of the pieces of the Freeman case were falling into place the way she would like. Every detail of the case was hard to extract. The most likely suspect was not really very probable. If the murder had happened within a month of the Board's non-action, Marita Peterson would have been a much likelier suspect.

Waiting over four months to kill someone was definite premeditation. The note on the front seat seemed to set the psychologist up. Strong circumstantial evidence. And a motive. But the murder felt like a spontaneous act.

Lucia took out her list of people in Dr. Freeman's file. Mrs. Martinez was very unlikely as a suspect. Her son was too young to have murdered anyone. Her husband was unknown, but also very unlikely. O'Keefe had a great alibi and no apparent motive. She was out of consideration as a suspect. Whitney had a possible motive, but also a strong alibi. Andrews seemed capable of murder as an impulsive act, but there seemed no motive or opportunity for him. Jarvis did not seem capable. The other clients were total unknowns. So far Marita Peterson had the field of suspects all to herself.

"Sleeping at the office these days?" Cowley's voice broke Lucia's reverie.

"Don't I wish. Then I could save all that rent I pay for an apartment I barely visit," Lucia smiled. "I think the lack of sleep is getting to me. If I don't put in a solid five hours in the sack I get cranky."

"Yeah, I noticed."

"Sorry, Cowley. This is my first big case and it feels like quicksand. Nothing to grab onto. I'm used to walking in to take statements while guys like you lead the murderer out of the room with the gun still warm from his hand."

"Cold trail on this one for sure," said Cowley frowning.

"Now you're sounding like Reynolds and his damn deer. So where are you headed today? Do I get some of your time again?"

"I'm yours until further notice. But there is a bit of investigating I did last night." He shifted his weight in the chair. "The address of that accident that Dr. Miles Demer had sounded real familiar to me. Funny part of town for a therapist to be in at 2:15 a.m. unless he spent the evening a block away at the Assay Mining Company Bar. So what do you think? Maybe we have a gay bashing spree?"

"Could be. Hard to tell though. We don't keep records that code sexual preference. Hard to find a pattern. Long shot, but possible. I've no idea how to follow it up." Lucia screwed her face up while she thought. "Check with Metropolitan Community Church; they may have heard something. Then there's a gay political group you should check. I don't remember the name, but MCC can probably give it to you. And the bartenders. Just phone them. I don't think you need to go by. Do you know which bars are gay?"

He nodded and handed her a list he had already prepared. She read it over quickly.

"Well," Lucia said, "It seems pretty complete. I'm not sure about Old Heidleberg. It may not still be gay. The New Cuntry is missing. Check with Vice to see if there are any new ones. Good work, Cowley. I wish I could get that overtime approved. This is going to eat into your evening."

"Why should tonight be different from any other night?" He pushed his chair back and put his feet on Lucia's desk. "There's no match yet on clients from any of the therapists, but Gail Miller won't give me her list."

"Let her see the other therapists' lists and just say yes or no. That won't compromise confidentiality. There is some good news, though. The phone company came through with a change of address for Peterson. I'm headed out there as soon as I finish my report."

"Great," he said. "Maybe we'll have this wrapped up and I can drop the gay angle."

"It would be nice. Say, would you mind working at my desk while I'm out? I've got a friend in Social Services getting an address for me on one of Freeman's clients, a Sarah Carter. I don't want to lose the message at the switchboard."

"Sure. Let me get my stuff. I'll be right back." Lucia entered the new information and left before he returned. A lot of high hazy clouds had moved in and her car was not as hot to get in as it had been earlier that morning. Lucia turned on the all-news station. Most of it was canned national news, but for a few minutes every hour they covered local stories. Lucia threaded her way through traffic to a background of disasters, wars and violence. The obligatory "good news" item concerned the marriage of Siamese twins in Canada.

75

When the local news finally hit the air, there was no mention of Dr. Freeman's death. The drug raid on Lackland Air Base air traffic controllers had pushed every other story aside. Lucia breathed a sigh of relief. Perhaps the media pressure was off.

She was so distracted by her thoughts, she missed the turn. The ascending numbers on the mail boxes clued her to her error and she found the gravel road next to Ms. Peterson's mail box. It was rutted, but not washed out. Lucia shifted into first for a fairly steep section. At the top of the hill the drive made a circle in front of an old trailer. There was a woman sitting under its awning in a lawn chair. She got up to meet the car.

Marita Peterson was a dyke. Her red t-shirt said so. The rest of her appearance strongly implied it. Her curly hair was about two inches at its longest. Her jeans were old and torn as were her white tennis shoes. Her hands were calloused, her nails bitten. There were dark circles under her deeply sunken eyes. An old scar went from wrist to elbow on her left arm. She did not try to hide it. "I've been expecting you," she said.

"I'm Officer Lucia Ramos, Homicide Department. You have the right to remain silent..." Lucia completed the Miranda warning while activating her tape recorder.

"I'm Marita Peterson Winfield, prime suspect, I suspect. The Winfield is on my birth certificate. I dropped it and all association with the destructive prick who gave it to me." Marita leaned against the post that held up the patio cover. She patted the two large brown dogs who had provided barking escort to Lucia's car. They were quiet now. Marita looked Lucia in the eyes, her light brown eyes holding Lucia's dark ones. "I didn't do it. I have an alibi with lots of witnesses. I was in a pool tournament at Our Place on Tuesday night."

"Sometimes patrons of lesbian bars are not anxious to be witnesses." Lucia sat in a brown and white lawn chair and looked out on a small patch of bluebonnets that had obviously been planted.

"They'll talk to you, Officer Ramos. Will they be safe? Or will you report them to the paper, to their bosses, their families?"

Lucia shook her head no.

"I hoped you wouldn't." Marita reached in her back pocket and pulled out a folded three by five card. She opened it and gave it to Lucia. It was a neat list of women's first names and phone numbers, each one numbered. "Please call the first ones first. Please stop when you are sure I'm telling the truth. If it takes more than these girls to convince you, there are about a dozen others you can call, but they'll be very nervous talking to the police."

"Thanks for doing my work for me. It's not often a suspect is this prepared."

"It's not often the witnesses risk as much. No, I guess that's not true. This isn't a mob hit where witnesses could die. At least I don't think Lizzie was involved with the mob, but with her, who knows."

"Do you mind talking about her?"

"Yes, but I guess I'd better." Marita scratched one dog behind the ear.

"How well did you know her?"

"I was a client for two years. The last six months of it, we were involved sexually. We talked about her life as well as mine. I suppose I knew her as well as you know any friend." Marita stood very still. Her face showed no expression. Her eyes seemed unfocused.

"Ms. Peterson, I'd rather not talk about your relationship to Dr. Freeman right now. Frankly, if you are willing, I'd prefer you talk about that to a psychologist I've been working with."

Marita focused her eyes on Lucia in surprise.

"Why?" she asked.

"I have every reason to believe you. I have the details from your complaint to the review board. I don't feel that I have the need or the psychological competence to bring this up without risking some damage to you." "I hope I said that right, Amy. It's what you said to say," Lucia thought.

Marita's laugh was bitter. She drew herself up to her full five feet, two inches, then relaxed into a lawn chair next to Lucia's.

"Okay, you got me. How come you care? No one else did. Not a single therapist on that damn board. She got off scot free. Now you come along telling me you know I was telling the truth. What gives?"

Lucia paused to think, then said, "Perhaps because I'm investigating her life, not your sanity. Having sex with a client seems very consistent with the character of Dr. Freeman." There was another pause. "Besides, she didn't get off scot free. She's dead."

Marita slumped over, putting her head in her hands. "Yeah," she whispered, "I know." She began to sob quietly. "I really loved her, you know. It was stupid. But I loved her. She made me feel safe. Cared about. Loved. I knew she wasn't perfect. Who is? I wanted to take away her pain. Now she's dead. I hurt her with the complaint. I really hurt her. She felt betrayed. I talked to her before I did it. She didn't understand. She thought it was just between the two of us. But it wasn't. I knew she was having sex with another client. It had to stop. She denied it. I was the only one, she said. She lied. I knew she was lying. I knew the other client. That girl may have had several personalities inside her, but she wasn't crazy like Lizzie said."

"Can you tell me who the other patient was?" Lucia's voice was imperative.

The sobbing girl disappeared into the tough dyke once again. Marita sat up, shaking Lucia's hand off her shoulder.

"No. Just someone I heard about. I don't even know her name." Marita's eyes narrowed.

"Don't push it," Lucia told herself. "Take it easy." "What about Dr. Freeman's personal life? Did you know her outside of her office?"

"And her bed? Not a great deal. I went to a Fourth of July party at her house last summer. I met Freddie and some other people whose names didn't stick. A couple of retired military types: some men, one of them was a bricklayer. I don't remember much. I was drinking pretty heavily and so was everyone else. The fireworks were great. Everyone brought some."

"She lived out in the country then?"

"Yeah, northwest on I-10. I'd've thought you'd've been there already. I may be the prime suspect, but Freddie can't be far behind. A lover that's been cheated on has to at least make the list." All the dogs had flopped between Marita and the driveway. She scratched the belly of one with her toe.

"How much do you know about Freddie?" Lucia asked.

"They met in New York at a party of a mutual friend. Lizzie was up from Jersey for a workshop and Freddie was talking to her publisher."

"Dr. Freeman's publisher?"

"No," Marita chortled, "Lizzie was no writer. She probably would have tried for a professorship, but she had no chance of getting published after her second husband died. He did most of the work on her dissertation, the writing anyway. I think she did the research. I always wondered if she didn't hope Freddie would help her out. But I guess it's a long way from professional journals to murder mysteries. I've read all of Freddie's books. All five set in this little ranch and oil town in southern Texas. Sounded just like Freer. That's where Freddie grew up. They're not bad. You ought to read one."

"Do you happen to have one I might see?" Lucia asked.

"Sure. You want some iced tea while I'm up?" Marita nudged the dogs out of the way as she stood.

"Thank you. Yes." As soon as Marita was in the door of the trailer, Lucia got our her notebook and began taking notes. She was still writing when Marita reappeared with two tall yellow glasses full of ice and weak tea. Marita put a glass on the cement next to Lucia's chair. Then she handed Lucia the paperback book she had tucked under her arm. *The Woman Who Cries at Night* by Fletcher Christi, Lucia copied into her notebook.

"I can't believe Freddie didn't talk your ear off about the books." Marita shook a cigarette out of a pack of Camel Filter Lights. Lucia felt her eyebrows raise slightly. They were the same brand of cigarettes as were found in the Volvo's ashtray.

"I haven't talked to Freddie yet," Lucia admitted.

"I don't want to tell you how to do your job, but I would think you'd phone the person who lived with her first." She wrinkled her mouth like she was eating a lime. "I guess I really am prime suspect."

Lucia brought out her tape recorder again and gestured with it toward the empty chair. "Do you mind going on?"

"No, might as well get it over with." She stared intently at the rim of her glass and answered Lucia's questions in a monotone. Dr. Freeman had outlived three parents and two husbands. Her current lover/partner, Freddie Christian, had heart disease. Lizzie had moved to San Antonio to live with Freddie. She brought money with her from the previous marriages, but nothing like Freddie's money from the ranch. Oil and cantaloupes, an unlikely combination for a fortune.

"When was your last contact with Dr. Freeman?" Lucia asked.

"Probably six months ago. I got a letter from some lawyer threatening me with a lawsuit if I went around saying that Lizzie had sex with her clients. I would go to jail for telling the truth," Marita said bitterly.

"Actually, it would have been a civil suit. The penalties would have been financial," Lucia clarified.

"Oh. As if I hadn't already paid enough. I guess you can never be too rich."

"By the way, how did you expect me to find you? You didn't leave a forwarding address with the post office."

"I figured you would get it out of Lizzie's files. I don't know how she tracked me down, but the third piece of mail I got here was that damn bill for my final session. That's one of the reasons I moved," Marita said. "I hate being reminded of that mess every month."

"We didn't find any files at her office. Do you know where she might have kept them?"

"At home, I guess. I never saw her write anything down. But she had to have something for insurance payments. She had me claim twice the sessions I actually had because the insurance would only pay half. That way I didn't have to pay anything, which was good because Lizzie wasn't cheap." Marita stopped for a swallow of ice tea.

"Did Dr. Freeman ever offer you a drink during a session?" Lucia asked.

"No, but we used to have one before we made love. She liked to mix sex and alcohol. Said it loosened her up. God, she was wild sometimes. She would get to screaming sometimes like you wouldn't believe. I was afraid someone might walk in to see what was going on. But I guess the soundproofing in her office was pretty good."

"What kind of liquor did she have in the office?" Lucia kept writing as she asked questions.

"Vodka and bourbon. She always drank the vodka. Didn't want clients to smell it on her breath. Then she'd eat a handful of little breath mints. She reeked of sex, but she never seemed to think of covering that up. And I guess no one noticed."

"Do you know any of her other patients?" Lucia asked.

A stubborn set appeared around Marita's mouth. "Only one and I'm not going to talk about her," she answered. "Another woman," Lucia thought.

"How about her family? Did she mention the names of relatives at all?"

"The only one left was her brother David. He lived somewhere in New York. State, not city. They became less friendly after he refused to cover for her trips to the city to see Freddie. Wouldn't lie to Lizzie's husband." Marita shook her head. "Lizzie thought he was a prig."

One of the dogs leapt up and began a low vigorous barking. Lucia could hear a strange whooshing sound. All the other dogs joined in the warning. Slowly a hot-air balloon floated into view. Rainbow colors swirled around it. A man stuck his head over the edge of the wicker basket and yelled, "Which way to Boerne?"

Marita pointed beyond her trailer.

"Thanks." The whooshing sound got louder and the balloon rose. The next wind current pushed it east of the right direction and it was soon out of sight.

"Does that happen often?" Lucia asked.

"First time. What a kick. Well, at least I know I'm well protected from balloons." She patted the dogs' heads.

Lucia finished her questioning without finding out anything else that was useful. She handed Marita the book back.

"Why don't you keep it? I don't think I want to read it again. I just bought it because I was curious about Lizzie's lover," Marita said, pushing her hand away. Lucia handed over Amy's card.

"This is the therapist I have arranged to handle the questioning about your intimate relationship with Dr. Freeman. Please call her today and set up an appointment as soon as possible."

Marita frowned at the card. "I guess I don't have much of a choice, do I?" she asked. She walked back to her lawn chair and sat watching Lucia drive away.

As she drove down the calèche driveway from Marita's house, Lucia pondered the question of the note. It seemed likely that Marita had lied about not having any contact with Freeman for over six months. If she had lied about that, she may have lied about other things. Murderers were not always cold blooded. Crimes of passion were often regretted later. Marita's grief could be real and still a reaction to guilt over her own actions.

Truth and falsehood, intertwined. Lucia felt saddened by the need to disbelieve someone she liked as well as Marita. Perhaps the witnesses at the bar would prove Marita's alibi. Then the little lies would be unimportant. And the infidelity would move up as a motive.

"Suppose," Lucia thought, "Marita isn't lying. Where could the note have come from? Could it have been planted to cast suspicion on her? Perhaps Freddie Christian found the note while cleaning out a desk drawer or in a forgotten file. The perfect opportunity for safe revenge."

The Sentra sat at the head of the drive for several minutes while Lucia tried to sort out the new and the old information. Nothing quite meshed. "Not enough data," she thought. Then she wondered if there would ever be enough data or if Dr. Freeman's file would remain permanently "open" along with countless other unsolved murders.

"And if it remains open, does that mean there's a crazy out there murdering women therapists or gay therapists? A crazy with an impulse to kill and a pattern too erratic to be helpful to investigators," Lucia wondered. A crazy who might endanger Amy or who might have been passing through town and is long gone? "No," she thought, "it takes too much time to figure out that some-one is a therapist and gay or female and where her office is. Don't let your affection for Amy send you off on a wild goose chase. You're hunting a deer, not a bolt of lightning. Stick to the greatest probabilities: a family member, lover or friend killed her for money, rage or jealousy." Despite her internal lecture, Lucia made a note to have Cowley check the list of murdered women to see if any were lesbian. And it wouldn't hurt to hang out near Amy's office when she is going to or from work.

"Down girl," Lucia chided herself. "Nobody has appointed you her bodyguard. Get your head on straight. Amy is a grown woman who can take care of herself. Her life is none of your business...yet."

She eased the car into first gear and pulled onto the pavement. Lucia checked her watch. She had over an hour and a half to get to the Christian place. If she cut over on Farm Road 1640 she could make it in forty-five minutes, forty if she was casual with the speed limit. That left plenty of time for lunch. She remembered the afternoons she and Yolanda had explored these hidden back roads in the hills. Curtly she pulled her thoughts back to the present.

She stopped at the next convenience store and parked under the dying elm near the back. The bird droppings were a trade-off for shade on a day that already reached 92°. "At least it sounds cooler in celsius," Lucia thought, smiling at the cool air in the store. She popped a ham and cheese sandwich in the store's microwave and then found a small bottle of grapefruit juice in the cooler.

The sandwich was surprisingly tasty. Lucia held it with her right hand and *The Woman Who Cries at Night* in her left. She skimmed the first chapter, then flipped through the book to get a feel for the plot. And, hopefully, a feel for the author. The book was quite engrossing. Set in the '30s in a small Texas town, it followed the investigation of the murder of the county's district attorney. It ended with the capture and release of a wronged husband who successfully pleaded "the unwritten law." Lucia closed the book with a sigh. If Christian believed "the unwritten law" gave the right to murder unfaithful spouses or their lovers, Christian may have felt a moral backing for murder. Lucia pulled her Sentra onto the slightly soft pavement and headed for I-10.

Lucia turned off the Interstate on the second exit beyond the cement factory. A mile and a half from the exit were the limestone pillars supporting the large sign saying "The Paddock" and in smaller letters "Home owners and guests only. Security strictly enforced."

"I suppose I'm a guest," she thought, "even though I invited myself." She turned into the manicured drive.

Acres of daffodils and bluebonnets stretched in front of her, echoing the yellow and blue colors of the entrance sign. She wondered what successive blooms would echo the motif. She dared not think about the landscaping costs as compared to her annual salary. At least it was beautiful, which was more than she could say for most conspicuous consumption.

As the directions indicated, the second left was Stallion Lane. Lucia turned, admiring the blending of the limestone architecture with the natural landscape. None of the large homes she had passed were intrusive. The developer had displayed rare good taste. Stallion Lane came to an end at a cul de sac with a single driveway. A small blue and yellow sign announced "Critics and Trespassers Will Be Shot." The mile long drive was fenced with limestone pillars and white paddocks. The enclosed horses paid little attention to Lucia's passage. The square limestone house was the largest she had seen yet. The stone path, interspersed with moss, led to a comfortable-looking screened porch. She pulled the rope by the door. An unseen and definitely not electric bell rang.

The person who opened the door was so totally opposite Lucia's preconceptions that for a moment she mistook her for a maid. Gone forever was Lucia's image of a short, balding pot-bellied writer. The person at the door was, to quote Lieutenant Reynolds, "a fine figure of a woman." Lucia sighed mentally. There went the theory that Lizzie Freeman was just in this relationship for the money. If this was Freddie, the doctor was definitely a lesbian.

"I'm Freddie Christian and you must be Officer Ramos. How very nice to meet you." Freddie's whiskey tenor sent shivers down Lucia's spine. Lucia glanced with open admiration at the tall, dark woman who had welcomed her. Freddie's athletic body was enhanced by the white linen slacks and purple crepe blouse. Around her neck hung a squash blossom necklace in gold. She had a ring of turquoise and sugilite set in gold on the third finger of her left hand.

"The pleasure is all mine," Lucia replied in her best flirting voice.

Freddie chuckled a low throaty laugh. "I must admit you are not at all what I expected. No stern minion of the

84

law marching up with military rigidity. My, my, my, Officer Ramos. Are there many like you on the force?"

Lucia was tempted for a moment to continue the banter. "Never," she reminded herself, "mix business and pleasure." "Alas, I appear to be in a very small minority, shall we say one in ten. But my unique perspective does have its uses in police work. In the current case, for example."

"Too abrupt, Ramos. A bit more social chatter to put the suspect at ease. You watch too much TV, where it's all action. You need to read more police procedurals, where the pace is slower." Freddie escorted her through the large foyer. "Let's sit in the patio. It's such a pleasant day." She opened the double glass doors onto a patio of hacienda style proportions. It dawned on Lucia that the East Texas limestone exterior had not dictated the actual floor plan. The house was clearly based on the Spanish courtyard concept. One corner of the open space held a stone waterfall which ended in a large rocky pool. Freddie led Lucia to the cast iron furniture that was under a huge live oak. Obviously the house had been built around the tree.

"I'm afraid real life police work is considerably less polished than mystery novels. It would be wonderful if I could edit and rewrite some of my mistakes, but...." Lucia put her hands out palms up and shrugged.

"Touché. Would you like some lemonade or tea?" Freddie gestured toward the ice filled pitchers on the table.

"Lemonade, please." Lucia watched Freddie lift the heavy glass pitcher smoothly and gracefully. There was no sign of weakness in those sixty-plus-year-old wrists. "I presume that you understand that anything you say can and will..."

"Be used against me in a court of law; that I have a right to an attorney. Should I be unable, et cetera, et cetera. I do, in fact, have several very expensive attorneys on retainer, any of whom would go into cardiac arrest if they were to witness this discussion. They constantly warn me against curiosity and candor. Those are considered two of the seven deadly sins in law. The others probably include whims, generosity and casualness, all of which I am occasionally guilty of—and of ending sentences with prepositions."

Lucia removed her tape recorder from her purse. "Do you mind if I record our conversation?"

"No, I often use them myself when writing. The truth is I write very little. Mostly I dictate. It's one of the many advantages of being filthy rich. Transcription is someone else's work. I can hire it done. One editor suggested that I simply hire out the whole process and put my name on it like that Cartland woman. Dreadful books she doesn't write. Plots like lumbering elephants, some grace, but heavy and predictable. They don't appeal to me at all, do they you?"

"I've never read one. Frankly, the only romance I'm interested in at the moment is Dr. Freeman's. How did you meet?"

Freddie looked displeased. "In New York at a small party of mutual friends. Lizzie used to play in New York. She didn't want her husband to know her interest in women, so she would come up from Jersey for her adventures into sapphistry. She loved the illicitness of it. That was one of the attractions therapy had for her, I suspect, getting to hear all of the secret things people do. She was a terrible gossip at heart. The stories she would tell me! She would come home from the office, pour herself a bourbon and branch and tell me all of the interesting things she had heard that day. She would chain smoke those sexy pastel cigarettes of hers and say 'That multiple from Poteet was in today with the strangest story about her mother.' Then she'd be off. If the story was sexual we'd end up in bed. She was always like that…ready for sex. Had I met her in my youth, I could have kept up with her. But ill as I am…."

Lucia's disbelief registered in her face. Despite Marita's comments about Freddie's health, she would not have been surprised if Freddie turned cartwheels. The woman looked in marvelous condition. "No," she said, "you can't be ill."

"Heart disease. It killed my father and it'll kill me too, in time. I'd like to make it a long time, so I work at slowing it down. I eat my oat bran every morning, avoid eggs, butter and cheese like poison. Tai chi twice a week. Forty minutes of serious walking or swimming daily. That pool's not just for looks. It does look nice though, doesn't it?"

"Yes, but back to Dr. Freeman." Lucia let the information about Freddie's health settle in. Added to Freeman's previous two dead husbands, the money angle took on new interest. "Was she understanding about your illness? Or did she seem, perhaps, restive with your inability to keep up with her sexually?"

Freddie looked at her sharply, then brushed a fly off the rim of the lemonade pitcher. "Damn bugs are so annoying. I'd like to go inside now, if you don't mind." She stood up and walked toward a side door without giving Lucia a backward glance. Lucia picked up her bag and the tape recorder and hurried to catch up. "Hit a nerve there," she thought. She came through the open door several paces behind Freddie who was already seated in a leather arm chair across from a stone fireplace. Above the mantle hung an Impressionist painting of a young girl. The wall adjacent to the fireplace held three massive gun cases with glass doors. The third wall was host to a complex oak desk complete with wooden file cabinets and extensive computer equipment.

"You were saying before, that she was not being sexually fulfilled at home. I have reason to believe that she may have had other sexual outlets."

"She didn't want me to know. But, of course, I did. Like Nya, that's our tai chi instructor. When she decided Lizzie needed extra sessions in private...I'm not blind. I come from the Spanish culture, and you know we understand passion. My first lover was an opera star. No kidding. What that woman taught me about passion! I followed her from city to city. That's how I ended up in New York. She finally made it to the Met. Never past the chorus though. She just didn't have the voice. No real strength in the high notes. But passion. She had passion enough for ten Carmens. It worked in Texas and Oklahoma and Kansas. But at the Met she had to compete with the women who had the passion *and* the high notes. It broke her heart. She finally gave singing up altogether, but by that time we were involved in the 'Sapphic Set' as Andrea called them."

"And what did you call Dr. Freeman's behavior, cheating?"

"Technically we weren't married so…"

"Your ring has no significance?" Lucia raised her eyebrows.

"A gift between lovers. Andrea gave me a Shakespeare folio she found in London. Enchanting Ester gave me a hybrid orchid she herself bred. A beautiful plant. I have one of its descendants in the solarium if you'd like to see it. A truly sensuous color. Almost edible. Succulent. She picked up one of its ancestors in Colombia and had to smuggle it in. Knew it would die in quarantine. They can be very sensitive; too much heat, too little; too much water, too little; too much sun, too little and they die. They can be very fragile."

"Like humans," Lucia thought.

"And what did you give Dr. Freeman? A diamond?"

Freddie looked surprised. "No. That ring she wore was from her first marriage. She really loved it. Never took it off."

Lucia let it be silent for a moment, then she asked, "Why didn't you leave her when you found out she wasn't being faithful?"

"She was mine. I loved her. She was good in bed. She made me think. She was interested in strange spiritual ideas. She had a very good sense of humor. Why should I leave all that simply because I could not satisfy her appetite for sex? Everybody cheats. I had a grandfather from Monterrey who locked his wife up whenever he left the house. She cheated anyway. He came home one night and found them. He shot her lover dead, but he never left her." She noticed Lucia nodding. "Yes, it's the plot for *The Woman Who Cries at Night.* My best plots have come from my crazy family. Or my lovers' crazy families. As a policeman, I'm sure you know the statistic that the person most likely to kill you is a relative."

"Yes." Lucia said looking past Freddie to the three cases of guns.

"Murder fascinates me. Always has. In the blood, I guess. Funny, my grandmother could forgive her husband for murder, but not her daughter for loving a gringo. She never spoke to my mother once after the wedding. Didn't even come to the funeral. Mama died in childbirth when I was eight. Doesn't happen much anymore. But more than fifty years ago…it happened.

Lost my older brother too. Snakebite. The damn fool had about a dozen rattlers in a gunny sack. Three or four bit him and made me a rich woman. I was sorry to lose him, though. We had a lot of fun together, even if he was a fool. He gave me my first horse and my first gun. I still have the gun. In that middle case on the top. That little .22 rifle. I had a little sister too. She died of typhus after Hurricane Dora. Water went bad. We should have boiled it. Didn't learn that 'til later though. Almost lost the ranch too. No cash for taxes during the Depression. Papa gave them cattle. Tax collector bought them just to be nice. Saved the ranch. Strange what people turn out to be kind."

As she paused for a breath, Lucia asked "Could we get back to Dr. Freeman?"

"Yes, I guess that's why you're here, isn't it?" Freddie said. "I'm an old woman. I've lost a lot in this life, but you never get used to it. Never. Excuse me." Freddie walked out of the room. Lucia sat holding her tape recorder and feeling foolish. "Always control the interrogation," she thought. "Fat chance with this wily old dyke." Lucia didn't know whether to follow Freddie or not, so she decided to sit tight for awhile and see what happened. Ten minutes passed. Lucia was getting ready to try to find Freddie when she walked back into the room. Her eyes were red and puffy. Her hands were full of files.

"I know you'll want these. They aren't much. Just insurance papers. Lizzie had a phobia about records. Her first husband had his records subpoenaed in a custody battle. The mother was his client. To get custody, the father used the argument that she was nuts, then the father beat the child to death two years later. Lizzie would never keep anything related to clients in her office. She even used initials on her calendar."

"I know," Lucia said. "How did she keep track of things like billing?"

"The computer." Freddie sat at her desk and turned it on. "I'll get you a print out of all her files." The printer seemed very quiet compared to the ones at the station.

Lucia pulled up a chair near the desk "Can you tell me anything about her clients? You said she talked about them."

"I knew a lot about them. Shoot. Where do you want to start?"

"Marita Peterson."

"Why her? She hasn't seen Lizzie in over a year." Freddie seemed surprised.

"She filed a complaint against Dr. Freeman for inappropriate sexual behavior. She seemed very upset when it was dismissed."

"I thought Lizzie was sleeping with Marita after she stopped sleeping with that psychologist, Whittler or something. He sounded like a real snot."

"Whitney, I believe," Lucia said, then mentally chided herself. Freddie did not need to know that.

"Did Dr. Freeman mention Marita trying to get in touch with her anytime in the last couple of weeks?" Lucia asked.

"Nope. Do you think she did it? She has a temper, that's for sure. She could have taken a swing at Lizzie with a bottle." Freddie cocked one eyebrow and looked at Lucia.

"How did you find that out? Were you there?" Lucia felt breathless.

"Nope. But money can buy information, even from the police."

"I'd like to know who's taking bribes." Lucia's mind began assembling a list of likely people. Then she realized that she was taking Freddie's word as truth. What if Freddie was the murderer? Then she would know all the details. Even if she did bribe the police for information, it could have been an elaborate cover for any slip-ups she might make.

"I'll give you the name as a reward for catching Lizzie's murderer. I'll even go State's evidence if you want to prosecute."

"It's a deal." Lucia kept her facial muscles still. "Now, tell me about Marita?"

Freddie thought for a moment. "Lizzie talked about her all the time. Thought Marita was great. I could tell all the sexual stories from Marita's childhood really turned Lizzie on. I finally made her invite Marita out here for a party. She's a little bitty thing. I wasn't impressed. She got very drunk and insulted the bartender. She called him a macho prick and then she smashed a bunch of his bottles. It did liven up the party, though. Still, it wasn't as good a party as the last one Dad threw. The governor of

90

Texas got drunk at that one. Tried to perform unnatural acts on Dad's favorite hound, a big Ridgeback called Poochie. That governor almost lost his pleasure implement. Old Poochie took great exception..."

"I'd love to hear the story, Freddie, I really would." Lucia interrupted. "But it's very important to me to catch Dr. Freeman's murderer. Can we go on?"

"Sure." Freddie did not sound the least bit chastened. Lucia flipped through the files.

"How about Sarah Carter?"

"Sweet young thing. Totally lost. Has no idea what she's supposed to do in this world. She was becoming a student of Lizzie's spiritual theories."

"Someone with initials R.F.?" Lucia asked.

"Rebecca Field. The multiple personality from Poteet. Nasty, nasty mother. Did terrible ritual abuse stuff to the kid. Now, if that mother had been murdered, you might have to come looking for me. I thought about it. It would certainly make the world a better place. I can't say much specific about Rebecca. Too many different people live there. I never could keep them all straight. She holds down a good job as bookkeeper and general factotum for a strawberry co-op in Poteet. I always wondered how she did it. Amazing woman. Women? People? I'm never sure what's the correct terminology. I read that book *When Rabbit Howls* just to try and understand it. Amazing phenomena."

"Are any of the personalities violent?"

"One young boy. He draws pictures of stabbing and blood. Good drawings. There's a couple in the file. Rebecca's file has the most material in it. Lizzie was considering writing a book about the case."

"Was Lizzie sleeping with her?"

"I don't think so, but who can tell with Lizzie?"

"I have a tape she made of a session with Rebecca. There also were two tapes of flute solos with it. Are they from a client?"

"No, they were Lizzie's. She was quite good." Freddie looked ready to cry.

"How about H.G.?"

"Helen Garcia. Forget her. Agoraphobic. Her daughter drives her to and from appointments. Otherwise, she never leaves the house. It's a major step for her to open the front door to get the mail."

"And N.K.? Nya Kyle?"

"Yes. Her real name is Nancy Kolder. She's our tai chi instructor. Lizzie was sleeping with her. The new Wednesday sex partner. I didn't mind too much. I was sleeping with Nya on Thursdays. I don't think Lizzie knew. You needn't look so disapproving, Officer Ramos. It seemed only fair to me."

"Julio Martinez."

"The kid. She never talked about him."

"S.C.B.?"

"I don't know."

"The Andrews family."

"Lizzie thought they were boring. Typical sexual power struggle with budding teenage daughter."

"Carl Jarvis."

"A new patient. He may kill himself, but not anyone else. A sad, sad boy taking on all the guilt for his baby's CP. He was a referral very recently from the Cerebral Palsy Clinic. Lizzie works there Wednesday mornings. She always told me it was all day. One Wednesday afternoon I tried to call her there. Her little secret was out."

"What did she do on Mondays and Fridays?" Lucia asked.

"Mondays she took off. Fridays she did counseling out at that little college on the west side. Used to be a girls' school. I don't remember the name."

"I know the place," Lucia said.

"Is that all?" Freddie asked. She was beginning to look more her age. The interview had taken its toll.

"Just one more. V.L."

"Tom Van Lander, the attorney. Lizzie would never talk about him. Afraid of being sued. He's a very litigious man." Freddie tore off the print out and handed it to Lucia.

"Thank you. This was all very helpful," Lucia said, "I may have further questions."

"I'm not going anywhere. Just give a call first so I can lock up the dogs."

"The dogs?" Lucia looked at the front door.

"You don't think two women would sleep alone out here without protection, do you? I wouldn't give two sticks for the estate's security patrol. I have my own little patrol. Three Ridgebacks, all descended from Poochie. Lizzie was scared to death of them. She had this long carriage whip to keep them away. I never told her how little good that whip would do if they decided to have her for dinner. But they are sweet, loving dogs. They would never hurt any friend of mine."

"I'm glad I didn't meet them unannounced." Lucia shuddered.

"I'll introduce you if you have the time." Freddie perked up at the thought of showing off her pets.

"Perhaps another visit," Lucia said. "Do you happen to have the address and phone for Dr. Freeman's brother?"

"Sure. It's in the print out too."

"I'd like to talk to you about her husbands."

Freddie shook her head no. "I'm too tired. Perhaps later. Monday afternoon is free." She escorted Lucia toward the front door.

"By the way," Lucia said, hoping to catch Freddie off guard, "where were you Tuesday evening?"

"At home working on my next book. The victim is an old bruja, a Mexican witch. But you would know about brujas, wouldn't you? Anyway, she's in this old folks home and...no. I shouldn't tell you the plot. If you know the plot, you won't buy the book and I'll be out the sixty-five cents in royalties."

"Weren't you concerned when Dr. Freeman didn't come home?"

"Yes, but frankly I wasn't worried about her safety. That didn't occur to me. I was concerned that she was spending the night with another lover. She had never done that before. I was afraid I was going to lose her. But not to death. I never thought of death. I was so very sure that I would die first."

Freddie closed the door quickly.

The dogs were not in evidence. Lucia made very sure of that fact before she stepped off the porch. She had no idea what a Ridgeback looked like, but she suspected, given the grand scale of everything else Freddie owned, that they were very large. Apparently they were still securely penned. She walked to the car with a faster pace than usual. "Of course," she thought, "I'm only assuming they couldn't get in a car."

It did not take long for Lucia to get down the driveway. From that point on, most of her thoughts were on the case. She liked Marita and Freddie. They could be friends of hers. "Lizzie certainly had better taste in women than men," she thought. But one thing working Juvenile had taught her was that charm was not synonymous with virtue.

She mulled over the two conversations. A lot of loose ends had been tied up. The multiple that Marita knew was Rebecca Field. No need to try to badger the name out of Marita who was obviously trying to protect Rebecca. But why was Marita trying to protect her? Were they lovers? Or had jealousy rather than protection been Marita's motive when she wrote the Board? Was there some other link, still hidden that tied these incidents to the murder?

Then there was Freddie, who raised as many questions as she answered. Had one of Lizzie's many affairs proven to be the last straw? Was money somehow an issue? Had Freddie grown tired of Lizzie? Was Lizzie blackmailing Freddie? Lucia felt tired at the thought of all the possibilities. And she had only talked to three of Lizzie's lovers. There was certainly the flavor of soap opera to this case. At least the whip was not going to become evidence. But the note and the cigarette butts were looking very likely.

As was the letter of complaint. The evidence against Marita was piling up. There was no physical evidence against anyone else. Was it that simple? Did you just arrest the person with the most black marks and let the courts sift it out? Somehow that solution felt sloppy. But it could end up being the way it went.

Lucia reached her desk still focused on the case. Cowley was sitting in her chair reading through a large stack of print outs.

"Jesus, Ramos," he said, "you're not going to believe what I've found"

Lucia felt her heart speed up.

"You were right about no computer code for sexual preference of victims," he said. "But I figured out how to get some data anyway. I searched for location using the gay bars as a focus. Two blocks every direction from the center. Six month limit. Violent crimes only. Look at this print out." He waved the thick sheath of papers at her. "Can you believe it?"

Lucia laughed in relief. "Of course. Barroom brawls are hardly rare."

"No, really, Ramos, there's a lot of violence going on around these places." His voice sounded hurt.

"Gay bars are not usually located in quiet residential neighborhoods. But it's a great idea, Cowley, even if it is a real long shot." She motioned him out of her chair.

"So, any luck on your end?"

"I got the client list from Christian with all the addresses and phone numbers. That should keep me busy."

"Too bad. I was hoping you'd come back with an arrest." Cowley did not look sad. He looked rather pleased as he absentmindedly flipped through the edges of the thick print out.

"Well, I did come back with another suspect. Freddie Christian is her lover, she writes murder mysteries, she knew about Freeman's affairs and she has no alibi."

"Sounds good. What about Peterson?"

"She has an alibi I'll check out. What happened here besides your brainstorm? Did we get the address for Carter? Not that we need it since it's in here." Lucia tapped the top of her briefcase.

"Nope. But you got a call from a Dr. Traeger. She wants you to call back. I wrote the phone number on the file." He flipped to the last page and tore off the handwritten message. "And the papers from the University of Maryland came in."

"I see," Lucia said, picking up the thick over-night delivery envelope. "How did you do with the gay organizations, with MCC, with the bartenders?"

"Struck out. That's when I got the bright idea about the locale search."

"What about Dr. Miller?"

"No match on the client lists."

"Too bad. Check the background on the murdered women. See if any were lesbians. And I've got a patient of Dr. Freeman's I want you to interview. She doesn't drive. She doesn't even leave her house if she can help it. Not a likely suspect at all. Check it out. See if she can add anything but, frankly, I doubt it." Lucia rummaged through the files in her briefcase to find the print out on Helen Garcia. She copied the address and handed it to Cowley. "No hurry. Yesterday is fine."

"Thanks, Ramos, you're all heart." Cowley flashed her a grin as he turned to leave.

"Do you know where to find her street?" she asked his departing back.

"Sure," Cowley shot over his shoulder, "your old neighborhood. Just off Zarzamora and Commerce."

Lucia breathed a sigh of relief. The rift with Cowley seemed mended. He seemed genuinely shocked at the level of violence around the gay bars. She wondered if he realized yet that his fellow policemen were contributing to the violence. There was a surprising streak of innocence in Cowley.

Lucia called the dean of students at Our Lady of the Lake College, the little college on the west side. She was out of her office, but the receptionist said she would be working Saturday morning. Lucia made an appointment for 9 a.m.

She went down the list of clients, crossing off the people she had already contacted. She called Rebecca Field first. Ms. Field was extremely reluctant. Lucia asked if she would be willing to be interviewed by a therapist who worked with the police. Ms. Field said she would consider it. Lucia gave her Amy's name and told her to expect Dr. Traeger's call the next morning.

The next phone call was to Nya Kyle. Her answering machine was still on. Sarah Carter's phone number proved to be for the People's Cornucopia Food Bank. According to the person who answered the phone, Sarah lived upstairs and worked at the Food Bank ten hours a week in exchange for rent. This was not one of those ten hours, but a message could be left, which she might get if she happened to check the message board. Lucia left a message.

Thomas Van Lander, attorney at law, was out. He would return Monday at 9 a.m. His home phone number was unlisted and could not be given out, even to people claiming to be with the police force. Lucia gave a polite good-bye, but hung up the phone with considerable force.

"Watch it. That's government property," someone yelled from across the room. Lucia looked around. No one was claiming credit for the comment, but there were several smiles. Lucia shrugged and went back to the phone. There was no answer at the office of David Freeman, attorney at law, which was not too surprising since it was after six in Suffolk, New York. She left a message on the answering machine. She also left a message on his home answering machine.

She flipped on her computer and pulled up the Freeman file. Then she decided to call Amy first. Updating the file was going to take a long time and she didn't want a delay to cause her to miss Amy.

Connie put Lucia through immediately.

"Lucia, how's it going?"

"First I have too little information. Then too much. All the client files, such as they are, were at her home."

"What about the client, Marita Peterson?"

"It doesn't look great for her. She does have an alibi though. She was in a pool tournament at Our Place when the therapist was murdered. I've got a list of witnesses to check out. Maybe she'll be off the suspect list after my visit tonight."

Amy's voice sounded puzzled. "I'm not sure I'm following you."

"Sorry," Lucia said "Our Place is a lesbian bar. I'm going out there tonight to check out Peterson's alibi."

"Oh. I suppose I should have recognized the name, but I don't socialize much in the lesbian community. Too much risk of encountering clients."

"I have a name and address for the client who's a multiple personality, Rebecca Field. Freeman slept with her too."

"Shit! Sorry, Lucia, that wasn't a very professional comment. I was afraid Marita Peterson wasn't the only one. Studies indicate that therapists who sexualize therapy usually do it with multiple clients." Her voice sounded very sad.

"Like child molesters," Lucia said.

"Yeah."

"Well, you called that one right. According to Ms. Freddie Christian, who's Freeman's lover, she was also sleeping with another client, Nya Kyle."

There was a low whistle from Amy's end of the line. "So Dr. Freeman was a lesbian. Were all her victims women?" Amy asked.

"Who knows? Peterson knew about Rebecca Field, but wouldn't name names. Christian knew which one was a multiple, so I could tie a name to the situation Peterson described. She wouldn't talk about how she found out. And Christian knew about Kyle because she was sleeping with Kyle too."

"What?" Amy shouted.

"Both Freeman and her lover Christian were sleeping with Nya Kyle, who was Freeman's client and, get this, their tai chi teacher ."

"This is ridiculous. That woman slept with everything that moved. What a mess! I want to talk, but I have a client in fifteen minutes and I need to prepare. Frankly, I'm shaking with anger and I really need the time to refocus before my next session. Later, okay?"

Lucia made arrangements to drop off the updates of the file and said good-bye. Her computer seemed even more like a TV set as she typed in the new information. This case was shaping up as total soap opera. She was so engrossed with the data, she didn't notice Reynolds standing behind her. She jumped slightly as he spoke.

"Got your deer yet, Ramos? The time limit's running out. If you don't bag a murderer in the first seventy-two hours the odds go way down."

"Do you see antlers on my desk, Lieutenant Reynolds? Zip. Nothing. I've got two hot suspects. One's the ex-client. I've got some physical evidence on her, but it's weak. It all came out of the car, not the murder scene. She has an alibi. I'm checking it tonight. The other one is the lover, the spouse, if you don't mind applying that term to a homosexual union. She has no alibi, but nothing really connects her except motive—possible jealousy. I've also got at least two other clients that the shrink was sleeping with. They also could be jealous. I have just gone from not enough suspects to too many. Frankly, it stinks."

"Either of the clients a man?"

"No, but one of them is a martial arts teacher and the spouse writes murder mysteries. The ex-client has a bad temper." Lucia realized that she was withholding comment on Rebecca Field. If both Marita and Amy wanted her protected, Lucia would do what she could to keep Rebecca's name out of the investigation as long as she could.

"Well, cut one out of the herd and go for it, Ramos. You don't solve cases sitting at a desk. Good night. Have a nice weekend." He sauntered away, not noticing Lucia's clenched teeth.

She opened the envelope from the University of Maryland and input all the information into the victim bio. Freeman had a B.A. in psychology from a college in Newark. Then there was a more than ten year gap. She was in her early thirties when she got her Ph.D. from the University of Maryland. Three years later a transcript was sent to the licensing board in Pennsylvania. Seven years after that a copy was sent to the licensing board in New Jersey; then another seven and one was sent to the licensing board in Texas. Two changes of names were noted: first, to Drinell, then to Welter. "Well, that accounted for all the initials on the Cross pens," she thought.

Lucia stared at the screen for a moment, then printed out two copies of the new material. She threw one in her briefcase and put the other in an envelope. When she got to Amy's office it was almost six. She saw Amy's car next to a station wagon and realized that Amy was driving instead of cycling to work. Some of her warning must of gotten through.

The front door was locked. "The other car must belong to Amy's last patient," Lucia thought as she slid the envelope with the case notes through the mail slot. She checked her watch and decided to eat after checking out Marita's alibi. "Pizza," she decided on the way home. "I'll stop for a Mazio's carry-out after the bar."

Lucia thought carefully about what she should wear to the bar. She put on her black lace underpants. She was sure that black lace underpants were appropriate. That led to black jeans, black socks and plain black boots. "Good," she thought. "Basic black goes anywhere, especially a lesbian bar." She stood in front of her closet,

99

naked from the waist up, trying to decide on a shirt. She rather fancied the gold velour, but it didn't seem quite businesslike. The baby blue satin was definitely out for the same reason. Finally, she settled on the maroon western shirt. It seemed almost sedate compared with her other choices. She thought about a bra and decided that was carrying professionalism too far. She snapped the shirt closed and admired herself in the mirror. It was going to seem very strange—being in a gay bar and not flirting. She sighed and slipped her wallet in her back pocket.

The bar had been open since six, but there were still plenty of parking places near the front door. Lucia pulled in. She took a deep breath. Even if seven-thirty was early for the big crowd, there was a possibility she might run into someone who would recognize her. Lucia could feel her pulse rate increase. There were a lot of lesbians who frequented the bars in both San Antonio and Austin. Someone might recognize her. But she wasn't in uniform so they couldn't know she was with the police unless they had met her on a case. The possibility seemed remote to Lucia, but still made her a little nervous. She took a deep breath and headed toward the entrance of Our Place. It looked like the bar in Austin, but bigger. At least it wasn't mob connected. Lucia had checked. Owned by a retired school teacher. That's coming out of the closet with a vengeance. "Let's see," Lucia thought, "I've got fourteen more years…"

"Your ID, please," the dapper bouncer asked, with a hint of a British accent. She glanced at Lucia's badge. "Business or pleasure, Officer? Pleasure, I hope—we're clean. No minors. No same sex dancing." Lucia watched the bouncer's foot hit the alarm switch on the floor. "No drugs except alcohol and nicotine. A little caffeine for the coffee and cola junkies. So what's the problem?"

"Relax. No problem. I'm homicide, not vice. I'm trying to help one of your customers establish an alibi." Lucia stepped out of the way to let the couple behind her pay the cover and go in. They were a striking Chicana couple in white western suits, white boots and hats.

"You should see them under the ultraviolets," said the bouncer watching Lucia's glance. "Quite charming. I'm Paddy. You must be here about Marita."

"Yes. And Paddy is the first name on my list. Were you working last Tuesday?" Lucia flipped open her notebook.

"No. I only work the door on the weekends. But I never miss a pool tourney. Good noshes, free too. I came in third." Paddy flipped her thumb off her forehead at the short dark woman who walked through the door without smiling. "The owner, Carla Rustino."

"Mmm," Lucia commented. "She's on my list too. Does she play pool too?"

"No, it wouldn't be fair. Her dad owned a pool hall. She can clear the table in about twenty seconds. A real pro."

"How was Marita?"

"Lousy. Out in the second round. But she's a good sport. Always stays around to congratulate the winner."

"So she was here all evening? From what time to what time?"

"About five-thirty to near eleven."

"And you saw her all evening? No dinner, no trips to the facilities, no momentary distractions?"

"Look, mate, we weren't Siamese twins or anything, but I was here all night and I didn't see Mare leave or come back."

"Thanks," Lucia closed her notebook. She started to go into the bar.

"Cover's two bills, mate." Paddy held out her hand. Lucia shrugged and handed her two dollars. "This is one expense item I wouldn't dream of turning in," Lucia thought.

Our Place looked like any neighborhood bar. The theme was Western. A hitching rail surrounded the raised dance floor. The Christmas tree lights were green. The red string had been turned off. A few brave couples were dancing. Lucia admired the fringed leather vest on one woman. She and her vest swayed with the beat. The tiny mirrors on the turning globe scattered bits of light festively over the dance floor and the vest.

Lucia edged her way up to the bar. When the crowd thinned out for a moment, she quickly flashed her badge at the bartender.

"Do you know Marita Peterson?" she asked.

"Sure. She was here Tuesday just like she said." The bartender put a glass of soda water in front of her. "Drink something. Makes people nervous, you standing here just talking. Might be a cop or something. Drink up, Officer. Please."

"No problem. What's your name?" Lucia sipped on the soda. She left her notebook in her pocket.

"Reggie."

"You're on Marita's list of people I should talk to."

"She asked me if it was okay. I said sure. I'm not exactly in the closet, working where I do." An angelic smile made her round cheeks even rounder. A lock of straight blonde hair fell across her forehead. Reggie was very easy to believe.

"Did you see her go in or out at all?"

"No," Reggie said, topping off Lucia's soda before she moved to fill the order for a couple of Pearl Lights. Lucia wondered if the bottle caps still had puzzles on them. It had been years since she had bought a beer as cheap as Pearl. Reggie popped the caps.

"Can I see one?"

"Huh?" Reggie said, very puzzled.

"The bottle caps. Can I see one?"

"Sure," Reggie said, looking at Lucia as if she were slightly demented. She tossed a cap across the bar. There was no puzzle on it.

Lucia looked back at the dance floor.

"Where are the pool tables?"

"To the left." Reggie gestured toward the wall at the end of the bar.

"You can't see it from the bar?"

"No, but that door is the only entrance and I can see it just fine."

"Do you ever go to the bathroom, take any sort of break in an evening?"

"Sure. I get two fifteen minute breaks. Why?"

"Was Marita in your sight the entire time of your breaks?"

"No, but she didn't leave the bar." Reggie was looking worried.

"How do you know, for sure?"

"I just know." Reggie shrugged unable to produce convincing evidence. Lucia sighed. It was much easier to be sure of what people saw than what they didn't see. She waited for Reggie to serve several patrons. During the next lull she showed Reggie the list Marita had prepared.

"Are any of these women here tonight?"

"You met Paddy at the door. Carla's the boss. That door next to the video games is her office. She's in. Anita and Sue are here. You'll know them by their matching white outfits. Beth and Sam are probably back shooting pool. Beth has a very fancy red cue stick. She won the Tuesday tournament. Sam is in a blue turtleneck with a heavy gold chain. They're a couple. I haven't seen the other two." Reggie turned away to flash her smile at the very young woman ordering two vodka tonics. "You sure you have an ID? I think I'll need to see it. I'm running short of new names for my little black book." Lucia moved away from the bar before the ID was produced. If the young woman had an ID, it was probably fake. "Not my problem tonight," she thought.

Her interviews of the other women on the list were inconclusive. No one could swear that they had seen Marita for the entire time. But no one had seen her leave or re-enter. Lucia sat at a table in the back of the bar where it was dark. Patsy Cline was singing *Leavin' On Your Mind*. The bubbles from the soda tickled Lucia's upper lip. She let herself drift into the music enough that she was startled when a woman put a hand on her shoulder.

"Would you like to dance?" she said.

"No, thanks. I was just leaving." Lucia stood up. It would be too easy to drift into the familiar bar pattern.

"I didn't mean to scare you away, little lady." The woman smiled a very winning smile at Lucia. "Your first night at the bar?"

"At this one. And my last time, I'm afraid," Lucia said as they walked toward the door.

"You from out of town?"

"No, just out of place."

The woman looked shocked. "Are you straight?" she asked as they left the bar.

Paddy overheard the question and answered it for Lucia. "Not on your bloody life, Emma. But you're chasing the wrong fox tonight."

Lucia waved good-bye and left the explanations in Paddy's capable hands. It felt early to be leaving, but the danger of mixing business and pleasure was entirely too great. "Reynolds would have been proud of me tonight," she thought. "Now if I can just figure out why I'm trying to prove my best suspect innocent."

Mazio's drive-up had a long line, but it moved quickly. She ordered two slices of Sicilian pizza with olives and mushrooms. When she got up to the red and green enamel window it was ready. She put the small cardboard boxes on the floor mat of the passenger side so the grease from them wouldn't soak into the upholstery. At least she didn't have to worry about them spilling on the way home.

The lights were on in her apartment and there was a note on the table from Cayetano. "Gone to visit mi familia. Back Dom. p.m. Please feed Gato." Lucia taped the note to the refrigerator so she wouldn't forget. She turned the oven on low and popped in the pizza. She opened the cupboard above the sink for a tall, handblown blue glass from Mexico. She congratulated herself once again for having had the wisdom to install an ice maker in the freezer. She filled the glass with ice and water, admiring how they looked in the glass. According to the old electric clock above the refrigerator, it was only nine o'clock. Not too late to call people. Like Amy.

Lucia plugged the phone in next to the sofa and tossed one of the small green throw pillows on the granite block she used for a coffee table. She brought over the slices of pizza and her water. Finally, she put her brief-case within reach. There was great satisfaction in the glance she gave her little nest. She snuggled down into the couch, slipped her shoes off and propped her feet up on the green pillow. Then she remembered napkins. "Yuck," she thought and grimaced at the necessity of getting up, but decided it beat getting grease on the sofa. She settled back down with a stack of thin beige napkins.

First she opened a box with a single pizza slice. The cheese had flowed over onto the bottom of the box. Lucia lifted the slice out and took a big bite of the tip. The phone rang.

"Lucia Ramos. May I help you?"

There was only heavy breathing on the other end.

"Sorry, you must have the wrong number." Lucia hung up.

The phone rang again immediately. It was the heavy breather again. Lucia put a pillow over the receiver and finished her pizza. By the time she wiped the grease off her fingers, the dial tone was back. She dialed Amy's number.

"Hi, Amy. This is Lucia. Nice to hear a real voice. I spent all afternoon talking to answering machines."

"I'm glad to hear your voice too, Lucia. Your suspect called late this afternoon and set up an appointment. I'm going to see Marita tomorrow at ten. Thank you for letting me do this."

Lucia smiled into the phone. "Well, you may have another one. I reached Rebecca Field. She is not anxious to talk to the police, but she will consider talking to a therapist. I told her you would call her. Her number's in the file."

"Great," Amy said. "What about the other client, Nya Kyle?"

"Just an answering machine message. But I need to talk to her first anyway."

"Wasn't she also involved in a sexual relationship with Dr. Freeman?" Amy's voice was very cool.

"Yes, but she teaches martial arts. That moves her up on the suspect list. Plus she's left town. I need to do the first interview, Amy." Lucia tried to keep the pleading out of her voice. Her growing desire to please Amy must not interfere in her case management. She could almost hear Lieutenant Reynolds growl, "Don't mix business and pleasure, Ramos. Keep your eye on the deer and your hands in your pockets."

"Of course, Lucia. But I would also like to talk to her if she's willing."

Lucia could feel herself relax. Amy was not going to make this into a problem.

"Are there any other interviews I could help you with? I've cleared my calendar for the whole weekend," Amy continued.

"There's a client named Sarah Carter. She's crushed out enough to bring her therapist presents. I don't think she's a likely suspect for murder as far as I know. Christian described her as a little lost soul."

"The perfect victim," commented Amy.

"My thought too. I'd appreciate it if you would interview her this weekend. It would be a great help."

"Sure, but I don't intend to work all weekend! How about a picnic tomorrow afternoon? Are you free?"

Lucia rearranged her mental schedule. The truth was that she really didn't have anything that had to be done after her visit to the college.

"I'd love to."

"Great. Meet me at home about eleven-thirty?"

"That would be good. What about food? Do you want me to pick up something since you'll be working?" Lucia remembered her own indecision in the grocery store. At least now she knew Amy wasn't a vegetarian.

"You've got work to do too. Why don't we just bring what we would normally have for lunch? I'll pack a cooler with drinks and you can just toss your lunch in. Dress for the country. I have a place in mind."

"Tomorrow then," Lucia said.

"Yes, about eleven-thirty. See you then." Lucia hung up and went to feed her neighbor's cat.

As she was drifting off to sleep that night, Lucia kept replaying her phone conversation with Amy. But in her fantasy she was much wittier. She flirted with great finesse. She was masterful, showing all her best qualities. Perhaps tomorrow, she thought sleepily as her mind slipped over the edge of reality into a dream world.

SATURDAY

Lucia turned off 24th into the old entrance to the college, since she preferred to park next to the chapel rather than the tennis courts. The light Saturday traffic on Commerce Street had left her about fifteen minutes early for her appointment with Sister Claire Blumburg, so she had decided to visit the chapel. There was no point in climbing the wide main steps. The doors were locked except on Sundays. Lucia entered the side door and went up the half flight to the wide sunny hallway that linked all the main buildings. She remembered the vocational retreat she had taken here when she was in high school. Where was that earnest teenager who so passionately wanted to serve God? She could no longer feel that passion. That earnest child had grown up and away from the purity of her ideal. But while her faith had crumbled under the pressure of the reality she came to see, her love remained for this glorious building that symbolized all the best of her old beliefs.

She remembered reverence. Her finger tips caressed the surface of the cool water fount as she entered the chapel. She paused, admiring the light that brought the stained glass to life. The air was cooled by a massive white marble altar that echoed the silhouette of the outside of the chapel. She walked slowly to a small pew, trying not to disturb the three elderly nuns who were scattered about the nave. Nave. Was that the right word? She no longer remembered. "Ten years of disuse can steal a lot of words," she thought.

Her watch said ten until nine. She would have to pay attention. Time had a way of being swallowed by the serenity and she was very tired from the convenience store shooting the night before. An unseen person began to play the organ. Bach. Lucia permitted her alertness to drain away. She sat. Unthinking. Only a tiny part of her mind on the time. The air vibrated with the organ. It seeped into her body. It was wholeness and unity. This beautiful chapel never failed her, unlike the church it represented. Here, she was always welcome as she was, whole. Slowly she rose and left. She would be late for her appointment, but only a little.

She could not hurry past the flying buttresses. They made her smile. She was still smiling at the door of Sister Claire Blumberg's office. Dean of Students, the door announced. Lucia rapped on it firmly. A plain blonde woman in her thirties opened the door. Her warm blue eyes assessed Lucia quite thoroughly.

"Please, come in, Officer Ramos. I'm Sister Claire." She ushered Lucia into a blue wing chair. The tiny office held two blue chairs, a coffee table, desk and desk chair.

"Thank you, Sister Claire. It was very kind of you to see me on a Saturday. I really appreciate it."

"How can I help you?"

"I understand that Dr. Freeman was under contract to do therapy here on Fridays," Lucia said.

"Yes," Sister Claire responded. "She saw only graduate students. It's funded by a grant."

"Is there any way of finding out the names of her clients?" Lucia held her breath. "Please," she thought, "let this be easy."

"Yes. All the appointments are made through my secretary since Dr. Freeman was not on campus. Of course, a student could contact her off campus and I wouldn't know it. At this time she had four regular clients. Why do you need to know their names? Are they under suspicion?"

"Let's just say we would like to know where all of her clients were between seven and ten Tuesday night. It eliminates certain possibilities when we know where people were."

Sister Claire took a deep breath. "Sister Jane Monda and I were together that evening. One of our elderly sisters had died Tuesday and we were at the Rosary. It was over about nine-thirty. We were both clients. I hope that is all you need to know about my therapy." She stopped abruptly. Her fingers played with her plain gold ring. "Married to God can't be as easy as I used to think it was," Lucia thought.

"Thank you for your forthrightness, Sister Claire." Lucia shook her head. "I didn't realize she was seeing anyone except students."

"She wasn't. We are both working on our Master of Social Work degree. One of the reasons our order maintains the college is to provide our sisters with the opportunity for advanced education. We are a teaching order and feel it is vital for our work."

"I really don't need to know anything else about your sessions at the present time. Probably never. But could you tell me who the other two clients were?"

"Three, actually. I saw Dr. Freeman on Thursday mornings at her office, not Fridays on campus."

Lucia threw up her hands. "You were the mystery client," she exclaimed. " 'S.C.B. contact Friday.' was all we had in her records. That's great. I had no idea how to reach S.C.B. There was no billing. No phone."

Sister Claire relaxed and smiled. "It was all part of the overall contract. I'm glad I solved one of your problems. I think I can solve one more. One of the three clients is blind. That would eliminate any suspicion on him, wouldn't it?"

"More than likely. Although suspicion seems too strong a word. At this point we're just eliminating possibilities. Could you give me the other two names?"

"Yes," Sister Claire said. "Although I trust you will treat this information as confidential."

"This is a murder investigation. I have to be honest and say that if there is some involvement in a crime, that will cause problems with confidentiality."

"Of course," said Sister Claire getting up. "I understand. Let me get the records." She left the door to the adjoining office open. Lucia was getting out her notebook when Sister Claire returned with an appointment calendar, two files and a student directory.

She sat again opening the files. "Mary Hohen is seeing, sorry, *was* seeing her. You can contact her in graduate student housing. She is a resident advisor. I believe she was referred by the dorm director because of depression. She doesn't have a car, however. I'm not sure how she could even get to Dr. Freeman's office. It's not on a bus line."

Noting Lucia's surprise, she continued. "I checked. It's sometimes difficult to schedule a convent car. I've had to miss some of my appointments. The other student is Derrick Milton. I don't know him as well as I know Mary. He was a spring semester transfer from City College of New York. He made the appointment himself; it wasn't a referral. The reason he listed is 'grief over mother's death.' That's all."

She handed Lucia the student directory. "I'd read you the phone numbers, but I'm dyslexic. I often invert digits."

Lucia flipped through the pages to Mary Hohen's name and copied the number in the notebook. She could not find Derrick Milton listed.

"Oh, spring transfer. Of course, he's not going to be in the directory. It came out in the fall. Here, it should be on his class registration form." Sister Claire handed Lucia his file.

"Do you have a file on every student?" Lucia asked.

"Yes, but only one file. Mr. Glasscock is our admissions and records director and we share files." She gestured toward the open door. "His office adjoins on the other side. We share secretarial help too."

"Doesn't that make information in the files less than confidential?" Lucia asked.

Sister Claire smiled. She reached into Mary's file and drew out a white card. On the card was written "Donnie $\Psi\cap$. "

"Donnie Donaldson is our dorm director. Ψ is for psychologist and upside down U is a sad mouth. I doubt if anyone but me could decipher it. The files are locked at all times. There are only three sets of keys: the dean's, the admissions director's and the president's. We do try to be careful."

During the explanation Lucia had been reading the file on her lap. "This student, Milton, is from New Jersey. Do you get many students from there?"

"No," Sister Claire responded. "We get quite a few from Long Island because we have a high school there. But New Jersey, no."

Lucia took down the address and phone and noted "Jersey—why San Antonio?" under it. "Do you mind if I call them from here? I'd like to talk to them as soon as possible."

Sister Claire smiled and gestured at the phone. "Be my guest." She retrieved Derrick Milton's file and went into the adjoining office to refile the folders. Lucia picked up the heavy black office phone and dialed Derrick Milton's number. A recording came on. "The number you have dialed is not in service." Lucia hung up and dialed Mary Hohen's number. The voice that answered was very young. Lucia identified herself and asked Mary if she was free for an interview. Mary agreed and suggested the lobby of the dorm.

"I'll be wearing a royal blue dress with a lavender scarf," Lucia said.

"On Saturday morning you'll be the only person in the lounge," Mary said. "See you in a minute."

Sister Claire had returned to the office and was standing by the door. "The lobby is just down the hallway."

"Providence Hall. Across from what used to be the Blue Lounge," Lucia said.

"Are you an alum?" Sister Claire smiled broadly.

"No, just took a few sociology classes. But I hung around here as a kid. I grew up over on Zarzamora."

"A neighbor, then." Sister Claire's smile didn't lessen.

"Sister Claire, I may need to talk to you again." The nun's smile disappeared. "About Dr. Freeman. Who her friends were. Who her colleagues were. We don't think her contact with the college is significant. Since her murder happened in her office, we are concentrating on people who saw her there." Sister Claire winced. "People who don't have alibis, Sister Claire. People who have cars." Lucia smiled at her. "Thank you again for all your help."

"Now, that's an alibi," Lucia thought as she left. "An entire church full of nuns as witnesses." The lounge was

111

only a few steps down the hall. Waiting for her was a stout young woman in jeans and a blue t-shirt. She did not look like the kind of person who is unhappy. Yet she definitely was. Gloom had settled on her like a suit of ill-fitting clothes.

"I'm Lucia Ramos from the Police Department. Thank you for meeting with me." Lucia smiled. Mary's smile in return seemed forced.

"I'm Mary Hohen. But you know that already, don't you? You want to talk about Dr. Freeman. I don't know if I can. I can't believe she's dead. Who would want to kill her? She was helping people. I don't know what I'll do now. I'm a mess. You can see that, can't you? I can see it in your face. I'm talking nervously. I need to be quiet now." Her speech stopped abruptly.

"Let's take a walk. I love the campus and maybe a walk will help you calm down. This really isn't going to be a terrible experience, okay?" Lucia started down the steps. "How about the pecan grove?"

"Sure," Mary replied. She seemed to be concentrating on not talking. She stared at her feet as they moved over the concrete steps and onto the asphalt drive. She didn't notice the blooms on the pear tree, a sole survivor of the freeze that had killed its companions years ago. But Lucia did and she carried one of the small blossoms with her to the pecan grove. They sat near the grotto. Mary continued to stare at her feet.

"Let's start with where you were Tuesday night." Lucia tried to catch Mary's eye.

"Studying," Mary said in a monotone.

"In your room or the library or..." Lucia asked.

"My room," Mary mumbled.

"Did anyone drop by?"

Mary looked up from her tennis shoes in shock. "My god. You think I killed her. You, I mean, oh my god. Don't you have to call a lawyer or something? I mean, on TV they always read them their rights before they arrest them. And nobody can swear where I was because I was alone. I'm dead meat. No way things could be worse than they were, only they are because now I'm pregnant and accused of murder. Oh, no. I just told a policeman I'm pregnant, only you're a woman. Are you going to arrest me? Shut up, Mary. You're just getting in deeper."

She stared wildly about as if contemplating flight before things got even worse.

Lucia spent most of Mary's speech trying hard not to smile. She concentrated on her own sensible pumps in blue leather with good arch supports. She turned one to check the heel wear. When Mary's talking halted, she looked at Mary as seriously as she was able.

"If you're going to confess, now's the time to do it, since I haven't read you your rights. But frankly, it would surprise me a lot, since you're not even a suspect. I probably won't even need to talk to you again. Unless, of course, you did commit a crime. And pregnancy isn't a crime. At least, not that I know of. Is that what Dr. Freeman was helping you deal with, the pregnancy?"

Mary nodded her head. "I don't know what I'm going to do. I was ready to kill myself. He wanted me to have an abortion. But I couldn't." Her speech slowed, became calmer. "I don't believe in abortion. It would be murder. But I'm not ready to be a mother. It would ruin everything. He won't marry me. I guess that's good. Dr. Freeman said it would probably end in divorce. I don't believe in that either. But I can't take care of a baby. I just don't know what to do." She began to weep. "And now my therapist is dead. I really liked her. She didn't think I was bad for being pregnant or stupid for not having an abortion and pretty soon everyone will know." Her sobs grew louder.

Lucia patted her gently on the shoulder. "A young woman who can't stand an abortion isn't a likely murderer," she thought.

"I know a solution that worked for another young woman. Would you like to hear about it?" The sobs lessened.

"Do policemen get involved in pregnancy? I thought you said it wasn't a crime." Mary wiped her tears with the back of her hand.

"Sometimes it's the result of a crime like rape or incest. Anyway, there's a couple in Cuero that run a home for difficult-to-adopt children. They often need summer help. Several girls I know have worked there during the last months of their pregnancy. It's good for everybody: the kids, Pete and Roz and the pregnant girls." Lucia pulled out a leather address book and her notebook and copied out an address. "Maybe you could even arrange field credit for the work."

"I don't know. It seems too easy. It isn't, you know. I'll have to give up the baby. I don't know if I can do that." Mary looked at Lucia, challenging her to disagree.

"You can't be sure what you'll do until the time comes. But I bet whatever you decide, you will work hard to make a good decision. That's all anybody can do. You can't go back and make mistakes not happen. You can only try to fix what went wrong the best you know how. I'm going to leave you alone to think about it. There are other people who can help. There's a woman named Donna at Birthright you could call...."

"I have," Mary interrupted. "She talked me into seeing Dr. Freeman. She said suicide would kill the baby just the same as abortion."

"Think about calling her again. She helped once. And if you run out of options, here's my card. Give me a call," Lucia said, hoping she had guessed right. "If this young woman is an emotional sponge, I may live to regret this offer," she thought. "And think about Dr. Freeman. We really do need help solving her murder. If something comes to mind that you think might help, please call me about that too." She put her card and paper with the address in Mary's hand and closed her hand over it. "Take care, Mary. I really believe you will work it out."

She got up, leaving behind Mary who was staring at her shoes again.

✧

Amy Traeger parked her yellow Saab under a huge oak. Jeff had talked about the tree when he rented her the office. "I put the parking under the oak on purpose," he said. "The oak has something in its roots that poisons other plants. Nothing will grow under one anyway." Amy thought about that comment every morning when she parked. "How like some families," she thought, collecting her papers off the passenger seat of the car. She locked the car door as she left. She always locked it, especially after Lucia's demonstration of hot wiring a car. It was amazing how quickly it could be done.

The office seemed a very empty place to talk to a murder suspect. All of the flowered upholstery showed on the empty overstuffed arm chairs in the reception

114

area. The office seemed very quiet without Connie's cheerful little sounds to fill it. Amy fixed a pot of coffee. Soon its perking took the edge off the silence.

Amy was pouring herself a cup of Barney's Best Coffee when she heard the forceful knock on the front door. She took a deep breath and went to answer it.

"I'm Amy Traeger." She extended her hand. Marita took it in a firm grip.

"Marita Peterson."

"It was a long drive into town, I understand. Thank you for coming."

"I don't have much choice, Dr. Traeger. I'm a murder suspect. I do what I'm told and hope I don't have to go to jail. So here I am."

"Okay. That's fair. Let me tell you how I operate in a police investigation." Amy felt her shoulders tighten. She took a deep breath and willed them to relax. They did. "I interview people that have been through a trauma. I try to use my training so that the trauma is not deepened more than necessary in the process of the investigation. Basically, however, I am acting as a police officer would and all the cautions of the Miranda warning still apply."

Marita shrugged. "So they cover the nightstick with a towel so it doesn't leave marks. So what?"

"So, nothing, I guess. Except I will keep confidential anything that does not apply to the investigation. But I do have to make a tape."

"Go ahead. What do you want to know? I told everything to the officer who came out to my house." Marita sank into the overstuffed chair near Amy's desk. Amy sat across from her in the leather desk chair. She turned on the tape recorder.

"How did you meet Dr. Freeman?"

"I ran my fingers down the list of therapists in the yellow pages. Called all the women. Asked them if they were lesbian. She was the first one who said she was. What would you have said?"

"I would have asked why you wanted to know. There can be many motivations behind a question like that— what would you have said then?"

"That I was tired of talking to people who thought it was sick to be queer. That I wanted to have a therapist who already knew what it was like. My last therapist was an old fart who couldn't get over that I was happy about being gay. I spent all my time talking about homosexuality and none of the time on me. I was tired of training therapists. So how about you, are you gay?"

Marita shifted forward in the chair with her hands on her knees.

"I truly believe it does not matter, Marita. A good therapist would focus on your needs and theirs wouldn't matter in therapy. But yes, I'm a lesbian." Amy willed her body to stay relaxed. She had a feeling Marita's next comment would be a zinger. It was.

"And the cop? She gay?"

"You'll have to ask her that." Amy made eye contact and held it.

"I thought so," Marita smiled. "She knew too much to be a het."

"Oh. Did Dr. Freeman admit to being a lesbian over the phone?"

"Yeah. So I went to her. If there had been a dyke shrink with the last name of Aardvark, I could have saved myself a whole lot of trouble," she snorted.

"And it was a lot of trouble?"

"Jesus, didn't the cop tell you anything?"

"Yes, but I would rather talk to you about it."

"I don't want to talk about it to you or anyone."

"Does it hurt that much?" Amy asked.

"Yes," Marita said, turning away from Amy.

"Can you tell me where it hurts? Do you feel it in your body?"

"If I did, it would be a miracle. I don't feel anything. I guess you could say that my body and me are no longer on speaking terms."

"Hmm," Amy murmured. "Really separated from your body."

"Yeah, after I stopped seeing Lizzie, I poured acid over my hand at work. I wanted to feel something, even pain."

Marita began to rub her left hand.

"Did it help?" Amy asked.

"No. The guy next to me grabbed the soda and dumped it all over. I hardly felt it. See," she said holding it out, "hardly any scars."

"Why did you stop seeing Dr. Freeman?"

"It was strange. My old apartment was being torn down so I had to find a new place. I was looking at this garage apartment I heard about. The dyke who lived in the house was just chatting about her lover and she asked me if I was seeing anyone. I told her I was sleeping with my therapist. She almost fainted. Then she went on and on about how unethical it was. I just walked off. I couldn't take it in. I just went dead inside. It was over." Marita's voice was very flat, with no emotion at all.

"What was over?" Amy asked very gently.

"Hope."

"How was hope over? I don't understand."

"I wanted to believe I could trust someone. I wanted it so bad I just ignored that it was wrong. I knew it was wrong. But I wanted it so much." Marita fell silent. She coughed a couple of times. Then she sat, staring at her hands.

"My father hurt me physically, but Lizzie just ripped it all open. All over again." She began to sob. "Shit," she said weeping, "I didn't want to do this. I hate crying. I keep doing it."

"Are you grieving?"

"Grieving?" Marita looked up, surprised out of her tears.

"For Dr. Freeman?" Amy asked.

"Lizzie? I hated her. Hated her. Do you hear me? I hated her." Marita was shouting. "She betrayed me just like my father. She's a shit. All she cared about was sex. She didn't care about me. She didn't care about anyone but herself. She didn't care about ethics or boundaries or what was right. She only cared about what she wanted, just like my father. I'm glad they're both dead. I want them out of my life." She stopped abruptly and looked at Amy. "Why should I believe you? You can tell that police-woman everything I say."

"Yes, I could. We both know that. You have been badly betrayed. You have no reason to trust any member of my profession. I apologize. That never should have happened. There is nothing that can make it up to you. I think, that for you, any trust involves a tremendous leap of faith, an act of will. That seems to be true of most incest survivors. I know it's often true of me."

117

Marita riveted her eyes on Amy. Neither spoke for a moment.

"I have my own agenda here," Amy finally said. "I do my healing by trying to help others heal. My father could lie about anything. He bragged that it made him the most published researcher at Northwestern. In my effort to distance myself from him, I try very hard to be trustworthy. But then, you have only my word on it." She realized she had tensed her hands and consciously relaxed them.

"Your word," spat out Marita. "What does that mean to me? Nothing. So you're an incest survivor. So what? Nothing. I'm beginning to think everyone is. So what? Everybody hurts."

"It has to stop. I am going to do my best to stop it," Amy said as gently as she was able.

"Who stopped my father? Who stopped Lizzie?"

"No one stopped your father. Someone did stop Lizzie. Was it you?" Amy struggled to keep her objectivity in the atmosphere of anger that surrounded Marita.

"No," she shouted. "No, no, no. I didn't do it. I wanted to. Oh god, I wanted to. But I couldn't ever do it. I couldn't do that to myself. She wasn't worth it." Her voice level dropped. "I wouldn't sink to that level."

"You think more of yourself than that," Amy offered tentatively.

"Forget the therapist shit. I got enough of that from Lizzie to last me a lifetime. Don't bullshit me. Don't use me. I've had it."

"Okay," Amy said. "What will work?"

"What do you mean 'what will work?' "Marita sounded confused. "What are you talking about?"

"A colleague of mine violated ethics and harmed you. I am taking responsibility for doing what I can to repair that harm, if you'll let me. I'd like to work with you if you think we can. If you are willing." Amy mentally crossed her fingers. She didn't feel like she had handled the conversation well. It was way too soon to ask for any commitment, but if Marita walked out, Amy suspected there would be no second chance to remedy Freeman's harmful behavior.

"I have no intention of every being vulnerable again. Ever." Marita shook her head. "I'm not going to let you hypnotize me."

"Okay. That seems reasonable." Amy smiled in relief. "Given that limitation, are you willing to give it a try?"

"Just like that. You want me to trust you, to go along with you." Marita shook her head again.

"No, I really want you to let me go along with you. If you say that there is nothing I can do, I'll accept that. What I cannot accept is Dr. Freeman's behavior determining what help is available to you. It just isn't right."

"Why is this so important to you?" Marita asked suspiciously.

"My profession is important to me. I want to respect what I do and the people I do it with. It's important to my self-respect." Amy felt her voice becoming strident and pulled back. "It's part of my dues in making this a decent world to live in. I want to help repair the damage done by the abusers. I don't know," she laughed at her own intensity. "It makes me happy, Marita. I guess that's what it really comes down to, it makes me happy."

"So how much is it likely to cost?" Marita looked Amy in the eyes.

"Let's leave it at no charge until you feel we're finished with the damage Dr. Freeman did. Then it's back to standard fee. You be the judge of when that happens." Amy put out her hand. "Shake on it?"

"It's a deal." They shook hands. "I sure hope this isn't another mind trip. I can't take it." Marita smiled wryly. "Okay. Let's do it."

"All right. What do you want to talk about? What will help?"

"Why did she die? Somehow, I feel cheated. That's really weird." Marita rubbed her eyebrows. "Who would kill her? Do you know?"

Amy shook her head no. "Officer Ramos has shared a lot of the details of her investigation, but there doesn't seem anything definitive."

"Am I the prime suspect, or can't you talk about that?" Marita stared at Amy intently.

"I don't think you are. You seem to have a good alibi. And by the way, I'm willing to share anything I know except confidential client information. But I think the case details really don't have a lot to do with your pain."

"I don't know about pain, but it sure might do something about my fear. I'm scared shitless that I'm going to end up in jail." A shy nervous smile appeared on Marita's face transforming it. She looked both young and vulnerable.

"The only person who will go to jail is the person who killed Dr. Freeman. I'm fairly sure of that."

"Fairly. Fairly. Nothing much in my life has gone fairly. Why should it change now?"

"Because you're ready to make it change. That's when it changes. And it doesn't become perfect overnight...or ever."

Marita did not respond. She sat with a blank look on her face staring at Amy. In Amy's mind that was the moment when therapy really began.

They talked for another half hour about Marita's fears. Often the blank look would return to Marita's face signaling Amy that important material was being touched. She let Marita control the direction of the discussion. She waited until Marita said "That's it. I don't want to talk about it anymore. It's too hard without the hypnosis."

"When would you like to come back?" Amy said.

"You're sure this is free?" Marita replied.

"I'm sure," Amy laughed, "But let's not meet on weekends. I try to keep them free for recreation."

"Like this one," Marita challenged.

"I'm leaving this office and going to a picnic as soon as we're done. I like my playtime too much to give it up. How about Wednesday at 4 p.m.? I'm free then." Amy held her pen poised above the calendar on her desk.

"Sure. Why not?" Marita shrugged. She got up and left the office abruptly. Amy thought she saw tears in Marita's eyes as she left. Amy sat in her chair a moment. She ran through a relaxation exercise. When she was very calm, very centered, she visualized Marita as a small child in Amy's arms. Amy then visualized a great protective spirit. She imagined placing Marita into the arms of the spirit. "Be safe," she said, then led herself back to the everyday environment of her office.

She took the phone numbers of Rebecca Field and Sarah Carter out of the thick file. There was work to be done.

✧

Lucia drove to the People's Cornucopia Food Bank on her way back to her office. Three men and a woman were sitting on the sidewalk next to the battered wooden door of the Food Bank. The boarded-up windows gave the place an abandoned look. Layers of posters had been glued to the boards, then torn off or washed off by the rain. Bits of old information in faded colors made a tattered collage of the plywood sheets.

The four people waiting for food resembled the windows. Their eyes looked boarded-up and gave a vacant appearance to their bodies. The faded tatters of clothing were ill-matched and ill-fitting. They seemed as discarded as the long-abandoned posters above their heads.

Lucia knocked on the door, ignoring the sullen dislike that seemed to emanate from the sitting people.

"Go away. Come back at noon. We open at noon," a voice shouted from inside.

"Police," Lucia shouted back. "I need to talk to one of your employees." All of the people on the sidewalk managed to get to their feet and seek another place to wait. Obviously the police were not viewed as friends and protectors by this group.

The bolt was thrown on the door. A fierce-looking Chicano in his mid-forties opened the door. His blue short-sleeve shirt and Levis were old, but clean. A sharp crease had been ironed into his jeans. His black straight hair was neatly combed back without a part. He scowled at Lucia. "Come in," he said. Lucia did.

"I'm looking for Sarah Carter," she said.

"She's not here."

"Do you know where she is?"

"No," he answered. "You got a badge?"

"Sure," Lucia said, flipping open her wallet to the ID. "Officer Lucia Ramos, homicide."

"Sarah being questioned by homicide? Why?" His voice was accusatory.

"Her therapist was killed. We're interviewing all her clients. No big deal. We just want to find out if she knows anything that might help."

He shrugged. "She not here."

"I left a message for her yesterday."

He shrugged again. "I know nothing, Officer." He said with a heavy artificial Mexican accent. Lucia winced.

"Can I leave another message?"

"Sure." He gestured toward a three-foot square blackboard attached to the wall below the phone. It was blank. A short stick of chalk hung suspended from a long string. An eraser was suspended by a long string from the other side of the message board.

"How often is the board cleaned?"

"Every night at closing," he smiled.

"Sarah lives here?" Lucia asked.

"Yeah."

"Could I see her room?"

"You got a search warrant, Officer?" He smiled again.

"I just want to leave her a note, under her door."

"Yeah. Well, go all the way to the back." He pointed down a dark corridor lined with mostly empty shelves. "Light's on the last post on your right. There's only one stairs back there. One door at the top. Used to be an office. That's Sarah's room."

Lucia followed his directions easily. She wrote a brief note asking Sarah to call Amy and giving both home and office numbers for Amy, as well as Lucia's own. On her way out, she stopped to thank the man who had let her in. "I really respect what you are doing here," she said.

"Bandaids." He spat the word out as if it was foul tasting. "Things just get worse. We don't make them better. Frijoles like you live off gringos by oppressing your brothers. I don't want or need your respect, Officer." He turned his back and walked away.

"When will Sarah work again?" she called to his back.

"Friday. She works eight to six every Friday," he answered without turning around. Lucia didn't ask if Sarah was in when she left the first message. Lucia didn't want to know.

Lucia let herself out the door. Half a dozen people were sitting on the sidewalk. The odor of alcohol was unmistakable. This time, all looked of Mexican heritage. All looked like discards. "What am I doing while my brothers and sisters starve?" Lucia asked herself. "Am I a frijole, brown on the outside and white inside?"

"No," she decided. "My work is hard, but it isn't wrong. I keep people from killing each other. That's worth doing. But still..." She shook the accusation out of her head and refocused on the case.

The drive to the office gave her time to assemble a mental list of her next activities. In short order she called Nya Kyle (still out), David Freeman (still out) and the phone company. The number she had written down for Derrick Milton had the last two digits inverted. Tom Van Lander's phone was unlisted on a list that required a supervisor's okay to release. Lucia gave the weekend liaison her badge number and extension number. Within five minutes, she had a return phone call from the supervisor who gave her Van Lander's home phone. Tom Van Lander was very abrupt on the phone, but agreed to meet with her on Sunday morning at his home in Quarry Heights. He would leave word at the gate so security would be expecting her. The address was 7 Marble Path.

The next call was to Derrick Milton. There was no answer. Lucia input what little data she had added that morning, condensing as she went. She decided she would wait until Monday to write the official closing to the convenience store shooting. There was no hurry. She headed home.

After feeding Cayetano's cat, Lucia changed quickly into her jeans and a turquoise t-shirt with a silver tiger. Then, she put on her turquoise running shoes and tossed her dirty clothes into the wicker basket in the corner of her bedroom before she dashed to her car. As she was putting her key in the car door, she remembered her briefcase and the copy of the additions to the file she had made for Amy. She ran back in the house and got the briefcase. She had started the car when she remembered her lunch. Back in the house again, she took a box of cold fried chicken out of the refrigerator. There were two pieces left. "Perfect," she thought and tossed it in a paper bag with an apple and several napkins. She got all the way to Amy's house without anymore forgotten items coming to mind.

Amy was almost ready when Lucia arrived. Her apartment was the bottom floor of a huge old house that had been adapted for apartment use by the owners, a gay male couple who lived upstairs. It had an air of eclectic elegance. Comfortable arm chairs sat behind a freeform

123

glass table with a solid piece of tree trunk for a base. The rust color of the velvet couch matched the rust in the oriental rug in front of it. A cherry bookcase covered all of one wall, surrounding a door, a window and several paintings. Lucia asked if she could use the phone. Amy mumbled an affirmative while she rummaged through a cherry chest for a picnic blanket. Lucia dialed Derrick Milton's number. This time it was answered on the first ring. Lucia identified herself and asked Derrick when it would be convenient to meet.

"I have time free this afternoon or tomorrow morning. I'm in a study session for an exam tomorrow afternoon that I'd rather not miss."

"Let me check something," Lucia said, then put her palm over the receiver. "Could you interview one of the college students tomorrow morning? I've got an appointment that could take all morning with the lawyer Van Lander."

"I could do it at nine. I have an appointment with Rebecca Field at ten-thirty. By the way, the only place she'll see me is at Freeman's office. Is that okay?"

"Sure. The yellow tape is down so forensics won't mind and the lease runs to the end of the month so it will be available." Lucia removed her hand from the receiver and continued her conversation with Derrick. "I won't be able to make either of those times, but my colleague, Dr. Amy Traeger, is free tomorrow morning at nine if that would be okay."

"Yes," Derrick replied.

"I'll do it at his place. I'd rather not go to my office again on the weekend," Amy whispered.

"Good," Lucia said. "Dr. Traeger will be at your home at nine o'clock tomorrow morning. Thank you."

Derrick said good-bye and hung up. She called David Freeman's home phone and once again there was no answer.

"Just one more call," Lucia said dialing Nya Kyle's number. This message had been changed. Lucia identified herself and Nya picked up the call from the answering machine.

"I'm home, Officer. But I have appointments all day today. Could we talk tomorrow?"

Lucia agreed to Sunday afternoon. She hung up with a big grin on her face. "I'm done. Time to play. Let's get out of here before the phone rings."

As if on cue, the phone began to ring. Instinctively, Lucia reached for it. But before she could get it, Amy took her hand and dragged her away.

"It will wait. Let's go." She picked up her picnic basket with her free hand. "You get the blanket." Lucia did so. "My car," Amy said. "I'm driving, since I know the way."

"Fine with me," Lucia replied, not at all sad to be a passenger in Amy's yellow Saab. She stopped at the Sentra to get lunch and her briefcase. She took Freeman's flute tapes out of the briefcase, then put it in the trunk with the lunches. "Mind if we play these?"

Amy answered by popping one of the cassettes in the tape deck. She rolled down all the windows and headed for Interstate 10. Both women were quiet. Enjoying the freedom from both her job and her personal responsibilities, Lucia closed her eyes and leaned back into the headrest. The flute music flowed out into the neighborhoods they passed.

As Amy went up the Woodlawn entrance to I-10, she closed the windows and turned on the air conditioning. "No shade on the Interstate," she commented.

"What?"

"I said there's no shade on the Interstate. It makes it hotter."

"What?" Lucia asked, not quite catching Amy's words over the music.

Amy turned down the volume on the flute solo. "It's lovely, but hard to talk over."

"What kind of woman is obsessed with sex and yet plays such beautiful music? I just can't get a handle on the victim at all. I go from despising her to respecting her in seconds. It's too complex. I know the answer to her murder is in her personality, but where? She changes every time I think I finally understand her. I talked to two clients this morning she really seemed to have helped." Lucia rested her head on the back of the seat. The Saab was much more comfortable than her Sentra. She tried to form an image of Freeman, but kept returning to the cold dead face on the office floor.

"Even bad therapists help some clients. That doesn't make her a good therapist." Lucia could detect an injured note in Amy's voice. "She certainly damaged Marita Peterson."

"Did anything turn up in the interview?"

"A lot of pain. As for helpful facts, not many. She knew Freeman was a lesbian before she met her. Apparently Freeman was willing to disclose that information over the phone. Peterson wanted to know if I was a lesbian and if you were."

"What did you tell her?" Lucia tried to keep the alarm out of her voice. "After all, Freddie knows," she thought. "I'm hardly in the closet on this case."

"I said I was and she'd have to ask you herself."

"Thanks," Lucia said.

"The thanks are a little premature. Marita took my answer as a 'yes' for both of us."

"Oh, well!" Lucia shrugged. "It probably won't matter."

"Hope it doesn't. Anyway, Freeman damaged Marita badly enough that Marita deliberately poured acid on her own hand at work. That would seem to indicate that Marita's anger was somewhat directed inward. She realizes that the sexualization of the therapeutic relationship was a recapitulation of the original incestuous relationship. I believe she brings a great deal of self-guilt to her response. She did admit to hating Dr. Freeman, but said she wasn't worth killing. Marita seems really afraid of being charged with the murder. But she seems genuinely willing to try to work out the damage Freeman did."

"She didn't talk about leaving Freeman a note, did she?" Lucia asked.

"No. But we really didn't get that kind of specific. I didn't want to play the heavy too much."

"Anything else?"

"Well," Amy hesitated, "it probably doesn't have any bearing, but Freeman used hypnosis with Marita too."

"Too?"

"Yes, she's using hypnosis on the tape we listened to, the session with the multiple personality."

"Rebecca Field."

"Yes."

126

"Do you think that's important, Amy?"

"Probably not. I use it myself sometimes. But there are a lot of questions about its appropriateness in dealing with incest memories. I use it primarily for relaxation for clients. To reduce anxiety. But Marita implied that Freeman was doing a lot of therapeutic work primarily through hypnosis."

"How does hypnosis work?"

"Well, it's very simple and terribly complex. The simple part is how it works. The complex is why. I'm not sure I've read any literature that explains it to my satisfaction."

"Bumblebees," Lucia commented idly.

"Excuse me?" Amy said.

"Bumblebees. I read somewhere that no one can figure out why they fly. They shouldn't. Too heavy."

"Perhaps. Fortunately the 'how' is pretty simple. When people focus on something like a repetitive voice and let themselves relax, they become highly suggestible. At the most profound stage of hypnosis, an EEG will show the patient's brain waves in an alpha state. But even before reaching the deeper levels, the patient will be more open to suggestion. There are techniques that can be used in therapy that..." Amy let her voice soften and then stop. Lucia's eyes were closed. She was sound asleep.

Amy hummed with the flute tape. The music provided a pattern for the dance the traffic seemed to weave to. Darting in and out between the lumbering trucks, the yellow Saab made excellent time to the Tapatia exit north of Boerne. The forty minute drive had seemed short. The tight turn of the exit shifted Lucia enough to wake her up.

"Where are we?" she said groggily.

"North of Boerne. Almost there," Amy answered.

"Sorry I'm so tired. I was called out on a homicide last night. Ice house robbery. About midnight, this kid pulled a gun on a clerk. The clerk pulled a gun too. A real Old West shoot out." Lucia's voice was heavy with disgust. "The kid was on something. He shot at the clerk and missed. The clerk nailed him. Clear cut self-defense. The kid was twelve. Twelve years old and executed for attempted armed robbery. It's a hell of a life, sometimes."

The rest of the drive passed in silence. The shoulder of the road became very narrow after they passed the entrance to Tapatillo. Amy ignored the small "Dead End" sign. When the road led to a locked gate, she stopped the car and opened the gate.

"You have a key?" Lucia asked.

"No. There's a split link on the other side of the gate. People see the lock and leave the gate alone. There are no cattle in here anyway. The gate is to keep the hunters out," Amy said driving passed the metal stock gate.

Lucia hopped out of the car on the other side to close the gate. From the back it was easy to see how to attach the split link. It was even polished to a different color by its years of use as the hidden lock. Lucia leaned over the gate. The padlock on the other side was rusty from disuse. The lack of weeds in the road indicated it was used much more often than the lock. "If you look really hard at the evidence, you should be able to see the solution," she thought. "But that's always easier to say after you see the solution." Lucia climbed back into the car.

"You seem fascinated by the lock."

"Yeah. It's so simple once you know it."

Amy shifted into first and took off down the dirt road, then drove through a field of knee-high grass. She parked next to a grove of live oak on a stream bank. "Let's unpack."

They took the blanket out first and spread it under the oaks. Amy brought her picnic basket and Lucia her paper sack. Lucia opened the box of chicken and took out a drumstick. As she took a bite, she noticed Amy smiling.

"What's so funny?" She asked with her mouth full.

"That's cold fast-food chicken. I can't believe you eat that stuff. It's okay hot, but cold? That implies choice, not just grabbing food in a hurry."

"I'm hooked," Lucia said and told Amy about the summer she had discovered the delights of cold Church's chicken. She was a sophomore at San Antonio College and desperate for money. Her friend Teresa called her about a rumored opening at a recreation center. The rec leader was sick. They needed someone right away. Lucia interviewed. She got fingerprinted. She filled out all the applications and she got the job. She borrowed twenty dollars from her aunt for the material to make the uniform. Then the day before she started she figured out the bus route. It was a killer.

"I got up at a quarter to five, dressed and stirred up eggs and salsa. I'd fold them inside a tortilla and run for the bus. I would have skipped breakfast except I would have died. Those kids ran me ragged. I had a thirty minute bus trip to downtown, then a thirty minute wait for the transfer, then an hour ride, then another twenty minute walk to the rec center. Well, there was a Church's stand about two blocks from the center. I didn't have the energy to pack a lunch or walk farther for a burger or a taco. So everyday I ate the chicken. By the end of that summer I loved it." She took another large bite.

"I can't imagine a schedule like that, five hours a day, to and from work. I would have hated it." Amy opened her basket and took out a peanut butter and jelly sandwich. The jelly was so thick that it oozed out the edges with her bites.

"No, it was okay. The worst part was that I never had time to see Yolanda, but I needed the money for school and the kids were great. We won city tourneys in chess and shuffleboard. My girls' softball team should have won the under-twelve division, but we were up against a team of third graders. The strike zone on a third grader is practically nonexistent. We walked every player." Lucia finished her drumstick and tossed it back in the box.

"What's a strike zone? I've often wondered," Amy asked, cleaning a bit of jelly off her cheek with her finger. She licked the jelly off her finger tip, teasing Lucia a bit. "Actually, that's a lie, I never wondered 'til now."

Lucia laughed. She looked around for a fallen oak branch of the right length. She stripped off the twigs, then she took up a batter's stance. "See, between the knees and the shoulder. If a pitch doesn't go over the base in this zone it's a ball, not a strike. Come on, I'll show you."

She pulled Amy to her feet and handed her the stick. "Now, bend your knees a little and get your weight off your heels." Lucia grabbed the sack her box of chicken had come in and wadded it up into a ball shape. "Okay. Batter up." She wound up in an exaggerated pitch and tossed the "ball." Amy swung way too high.

"Too many piñatas and not enough softball in your childhood. I can tell from your swing." She moved up behind Amy and put her arms around Amy so they were both holding the bat.

"You're supposed to swing level, like this." She demonstrated her advice. Amy let go of the stick and turned in Lucia's arms. Lucia caught her breath. They embraced. Amy brushed her lips across Lucia's cheek. Then across Lucia's lips. Lucia felt the oak stick fall as she freed her hands to caress Amy's back.

Lucia could feel fingers slipping through her hair. Amy kissed her eyelids, her ears. Then very gently, Amy drew her lips across Lucia's. Lucia stopped breathing. She parted her lips slightly, almost involuntarily. Amy nibbled at Lucia's lips, then traced them with the tip of her tongue. Lucia opened her lips wider.

Amy cupped Lucia's head in her hands and searched Lucia's mouth with her tongue. A fire started in Lucia's center and quickly spread to every part of her body. She sucked on Amy's tongue. She pulled her body close. Then, when she sensed a slight pulling back she opened her arms. Amy ended the kiss slowly, almost in the exact reverse order in which it began. It gave Lucia a sense of being treasured.

"Let's take a walk," Amy said. Lucia nodded agreement. At that moment, Lucia would have agreed to almost anything Amy suggested.

They walked under the branches of a huge live oak, the crisp leaves crunching under their tennis shoes. There was no path to follow on the other side of the tree, but Amy struck off to the right at a brisk clip as though she knew where she was going. Lucia followed her through the mesquite scrub and bunching grasses. Occasionally she would brush her finger tips against the lacy mesquite leaves, being careful to avoid the thorns on the twigs.

The stream came back into view. It was more narrow here with grassy banks instead of rock. Lucia could see a short ledge of limestone ahead.

"It's the spring," Amy said. "There by the ledge. You can see it's a gentle hill beyond." She ran, almost skipping to the spring which fed the stream. "Here, come see it." She pointed to the ledge next to her. Lucia came closer.

Embedded in the limestone was a shell. "It's been here for millions and millions of years. Isn't it beautiful?" Amy said, pressing her palm over it.

"It's exquisite," Lucia whispered. Amy took Lucia's hand and pressed her palm over the shell. Lucia could feel the shell's ridges cool against her hot palm. The contrast with Amy's warm hand was intriguing. Neither woman moved for many long moments.

"This is my favorite place to meditate," Amy said, sitting with her back to the ledge. Lucia followed her example. "It's so restful just to sit here with my eyes closed and listen to the day."

Lucia closed her eyes and listened. There was a light breeze rustling distant leaves. A mockingbird ran through an entire repertoire of songs. She began to let go of some of the tension she usually felt.

Amy's voice was low and nonintrusive, almost a monotone as she said, "The air is so rich and full here. I love to fill my entire lungs with it." Lucia heard her taking deep breaths. It seemed a good idea, so Lucia, too, filled her lungs with the spring air and slowly exhaled. It was very relaxing.

"It makes me very aware of my body. Especially of the parts I need to relax. I start with my feet." Lucia listened to Amy's calm voice as she went through the inventory. She found it easy to follow Amy's lead and let her body sink into relaxation. She had to agree when Amy said "I feel very safe, very relaxed here."

It took too much effort to nod, but Lucia silently agreed with her. It felt very safe. "Sometimes," Amy said in the same reassuring tone, "I use this time to stretch my imagination. I might imagine that a cloud comes down and carries me to a desert oasis." As Amy's gentle voice described what might be at the oasis, Lucia formed an image of the oasis in her mind. She let herself flow into the scene she was imagining.

Vaguely, she heard Amy's voice point out a shell in the sand near the water. Lucia picked up the shell and waded into the warm water of the oasis. She relaxed totally as the water lapped gently around her. Far in the distance she could hear Amy's voice saying that the message of the shell would stay with her. That whenever she wished to relax she could touch the shell and focus her intention to relax. "It will always be there to help you. You will remember everything that has happened. I will count backwards from ten. When I reach one you will open your eyes feeling refreshed and alert." When Amy reached "one," Lucia opened her eyes amazed.

"You hypnotized me!" She exclaimed. "That's what it's like. Amazing."

"I hope you don't mind my being less than direct. Frankly, I'm not sure I'm good enough to hypnotize you when you were aware what I was doing. It requires both trust and cooperation. I manipulated you a bit." There was a strong note of concern in Amy's voice. "I hope you don't mind."

Lucia laughed out loud. "You did exactly what I wanted. I feel wonderful. Is it always like that?"

"No, I gave you suggestions to feel good. They wear off if they are not reinforced," Amy said looking relieved.

"How often do they need to be reinforced?" Lucia reached in her back pocket for her notebook and pen. As she opened it, Amy laughed.

"I don't believe it. Don't you go anywhere without that notebook?" she said.

"Nope. I even have a plastic one for the shower. Care to see?" She leered at Amy and winked suggestively.

"Wouldn't miss it for the world," Amy replied.

"Great. May I suggest this evening?"

"Delighted," Amy answered.

"Now, back to hypnotism. Tell me about the reinforcement."

"It depends. If you're doing one of those silly parlor tricks, like telling people to act like a chicken, you really don't need any. It's short-term behavior and doesn't trigger any defense responses. But long-term behavior changes would take pretty frequent reinforcement. I can't say, exactly once a week for losing weight or three times a week for quitting smoking. It just doesn't work like that. It depends on how stable the behavior is that you are trying to alter and what that behavior is doing for the person. It's much easier to reinforce existing behavior." Amy thought for a moment pressing her finger against her pursed lips. "You already knew how to relax and feel good. So that was easy. But the more stress you're under, the more reinforcement it takes to maintain relaxation. This is all pretty vague, isn't it?"

Despite the poised pen, Lucia was not writing. "Yes," Lucia said. "Let me get specific. Can you hypnotize someone to commit murder?"

"Sure. You would just suggest that a situation exists in which the murderous action would be reasonable and necessary." Amy looked puzzled. "Do you think the murderer was hypnotized?"

"No, I'm just curious. I wonder, though, could you hypnotize someone to fall in love with you?"

"It depends on how you define the behavior, but yes, you could suggest to someone that they found you sexually attractive, that they trust you, that they want to please you. Most people would call the resulting behavior 'love.' "

Lucia began writing furiously. "Do you think Dr. Freeman could have used hypnotism to seduce her patients?"

"It wouldn't be ethical, but I doubt if that would have stopped her, given what we know about her ethics. She probably wouldn't need to use hypnosis, though. Most clients are very susceptible to seduction. Usually they are pretty desperate for the therapist's approval. I can jazz this up with proper therapeutic terminology, but it comes down to being very similar to the incest situations we dealt with in Juvenile. How can they say no? They can't." She shook her head sadly. "No, hypnotism wouldn't be necessary at all."

Lucia sighed. "I can understand the kids, Amy, but grown-ups know better. Why don't they just walk out when their shrink makes a pass at them? I mean, they're both consenting adults, aren't they? I don't get it, not really."

Amy stood up and pulled Lucia to her feet. "I'm not going to give you a graduate seminar in professionals abusing trust situations and the dynamics thereof. What I'm going to do is loan you a book titled *Sex in the Forbidden Zone* when we get back to my place. Then you are going to fix me a sumptuous meal in trade for the free consultations. And if we keep talking about work, you are going to have to wash the dishes too." She linked her arm through Lucia's and set an ambling pace back toward the car.

The rest of the afternoon passed mostly with Lucia napping on the picnic blanket. When she would drift out of sleep for a moment, she watched Amy reading or looking at small rocks for fossils. Once she woke up to find a wild daisy had been placed next to her hand. She smiled and fell back into a light sleep. The sun dropped in the sky enough to shift the shade of a large oak onto the blanket. Lucia woke with a slight chill. Amy was nowhere to be seen. Lucia picked up the blanket to shake the twigs and dirt off it. She was folding it as Amy skipped back into the clearing.

"You'll never guess what I found. It's this wonderful fossil. See, it was some kind of tube worm or something. Here look." She shoved an inch square rock into Lucia's hand. "It makes a 'W'. I wonder if any of the others like it make letters. Maybe I could collect a whole alphabet. Wouldn't that be amazing?"

Lucia nodded her head wordlessly. For a moment, she wondered if she was still asleep and this was a dream. This changeable, fluid person seemed so different from the earnest professional she had come to know at work. She wasn't sure how to respond so she just smiled. Amy smiled back. She reached for the rock and hugged Lucia. Then Amy handed Lucia a sprig of aromatic leaves she had plucked near the stream.

"Mmm," Lucia murmured, sniffing it. "Mentha piperita. Yerba buena. Good for stomach cramps."

"A botanist as well as a police officer?"

"Leftover information from my first lover. She was working on her Ph.D. in botany when she got sick and died."

"I'm so sorry. It must have been such a shock." She caressed Lucia's dark hair.

"It was. I sort of flipped out for a while. She got a virus in the lining around her heart. She died in two days. My friends made me move back to San Antonio to get away from the memories." Lucia's voice quavered as she quickly changed the subject. "How about you? How did you lose your first lover?"

"For a baby. She wanted a family. She decided that meant a typical home. She dumped me oh-so-gently for a gay guy who wanted the same thing. She was willing to keep our relationship on the side, but I had to move out of the house we bought together. I didn't want to live that way so I left."

"Life's a bitch," Lucia commented.

"Sometimes, but not today. Today is wonderful, but it's getting cold. Lucia," she said, "time to shop for dinner."

✧

Lucia found Amy's kitchen easy to work in. The wide natural wood counters were clear of clutter. If Amy was an appliance addict, she had hidden every evidence of her vice. Not even an electric can opener sat on the counter, only blue French canning jars in every imaginable size. Lucia admired the interesting shapes of beans and grains and pastas not quite hidden by the deep blue glass. Amy noticed her admiration.

"My Aunt Meg calls it my 'Milk of Magnesia Collection,' " she said with a slight smile.

"I like it," Lucia said.

"Not too monochrome for your tastes?" Amy quizzed.

"I have broad tastes. Where's your can opener?" Lucia asked, removing the cans from the paper shopping bag.

"Second drawer to the right of the sink."

"Saucepans?"

"Small ones to the right of the stove, large on the left."

Lucia took a small saucepan and emptied a can of tomato sauce into it. She mixed in a small can of chopped green chilies and a teaspoon of beef bouillon powder. Next she shook in a bit of oregano and stirred. She carefully broke four eggs into the pan and gently spooned sauce over the eggs. She covered the enamelware pot with its lid.

"Can these pans go in the oven?" she asked.

"Sure."

"Great. Where's the metal foil?"

Amy pointed across the room. "Drawer next to the refrigerator."

Lucia wrapped the flour tortillas in foil and left them on the counter. She slid the pan into the oven and set the temperature at 300°. Then she popped the cork on the bottle of champagne.

"What exactly are we celebrating?" Amy asked as she brought wine glasses in from the glassware cabinet in the dining room.

"Sulfites. They give me a headache. The cheapest decent wine without them is champagne. So that's my wine of choice. Although I do like the bubbles. I guess that's why I drink beer too." She filled both glasses and lifted hers up. "A toast." Amy raised her glass. "To an evening without headaches." Amy smiled her agreement and gently grazed the edge of Lucia's glass with her own.

"Oh, no," Lucia moaned.

"What is it?" ask Amy.

"I forgot the garlic salt. It's too late. You can't stir once the eggs are in. You are much too distracting."

"We'll salt them as we eat them. Simple enough."

"How come I get all light-headed around you now? We worked together for a year and I never did stupid things like this."

"Courtship behavior. Like peacocks spreading their feathers," explained Amy.

"Am I courting you?" Lucia lifted her left eyebrow.

"No, I'm courting you. My last lover couldn't cook worth anything, so I thought I'd try that talent out first."

"I think I just flunked. I can cut cheese and open cans of olives but really cooking, when the heat's on, I melt."

"I've never objected to women melting."

"Oh, Patience..." Lucia sighed dramatically.

"Oh, Sarah..." Amy responded giggling. "Perhaps chopping wood is more your style."

"Too much work. Just get those little ceramic logs with gas jets in them."

"You Philistine. How can you be romantic in front of gas logs?" Amy retorted.

"Come in the living room. I'll show you." She tugged Amy away from the kitchen. Then she returned to turn the oven down to warm and turned the timer off. By the time she got to the living room Amy had settled at one end of the couch. Lucia sat next to her. She brushed a light kiss on Amy's temple on her way down.

"No cook or lumberjack potential. I guess I'd better stay a cop."

"Actually, I like your attitude towards food. I've had such a love/hate relationship with it all my life that it's refreshing to be around someone who seems to pack less emotional baggage into it."

"My familia. That's where it all comes from, right? They didn't have big hang-ups on food. When you were hungry, you ate. And you ate what was there. But the women talked about meals the way the men talked politics. There was a banquet after a wedding in Monterrey at the Grand Hotel Ancira. I can tell you every single dish that was on the table and it happened years before I was born. Food and families. That was women's work. It hit them hard when they realized I wasn't going to have a family like that."

"You, too?"

"No. I think I always kind of knew. I was comfortable around men, but I knew they didn't do anything for me sexually. I liked dancing with them, but not kissing them. I decided I should be a nun. That lasted two whole days. Then I got involved with another student my freshmen year at San Antonio College. All my questions were answered. I was queer."

Amy took her hand. "Do I detect a little bitterness?"

"Sometimes. It's not an easy life. I look at my sisters and my cousins. They have nothing to hide. They can hold hands with a sweetheart while they walk down the street. It makes me sad that I can't." She raised Amy's hand to her lips and kissed her finger tips and they were quiet for a few moments.

Then Lucia asked the question that was always part of the conversation in the Southwest. "How did you get from Illinois to Texas? The weather?"

"No. Cold doesn't bother me. I did it to irritate my father. A civics teacher I loved had gone to Rice University in Houston." Lucia nodded her recognition of the prestigious school. Amy continued, "When I said I wanted to go there too, he had a fit. I was destined to go to Northwestern where he could 'keep an eye on me.' It wasn't his eye that bothered me. I wasn't about to spend four more years being raped by that man."

"I'm sorry," Lucia said, putting her arm around Amy's shoulder as if to protect her. She never knew quite what to say when Amy talked about her own incest.

"So am I. His rage over the possibility of my leaving was very frightening. I read this article about violence

137

that said most murders are committed by family members. Then I really got scared. I wasn't sure if he was going to kill me or I was going to kill him. Either way was terrible." Amy stared at her champagne glass with total concentration.

"How did you get away?" Lucia asked gently.

"Aunt Meg, his sister. We talked about it a few years ago, after I confronted the family about the incest. He raped her too when she was a child. She was worried about me. She found out that the assistant provost of Northwestern was a Rice graduate. Actually, she wrote Rice and asked if they knew of any of their graduates on the faculty of Northwestern. His being pretty high up in the hierarchy was just luck." Amy snuggled into the crook of Lucia's arm.

"Then Aunt Meg threw a cocktail party for a few of the faculty, including my father and the assistant provost. She maneuvered the two of them into a conversation. Then she mentioned that I wanted to go to Rice. The assistant provost was very enthusiastic about the idea. My father didn't dare disagree. I got early admission. And I never went back to Illinois until the confrontation a few years ago."

"Your Aunt Meg is a wonderful person. I wish I could meet her," Lucia said.

"You may. She comes to see me for Fiesta."

"Next week. I had almost lost track of the date with this case. Reynolds told me yesterday that I was running out of time."

"Shhh," Amy said putting her finger to Lucia's lips. "No more about work."

Lucia bit softly on Amy's finger tip. Amy put her hand up, fingers open. Lucia nibbled each finger in turn. Amy began to trace every line of the tiger on Lucia's t-shirt. She drew the shirt up over Lucia's shoulders and dropped it on the floor.

"You are very lovely," Amy said.

"Thank you," Lucia murmured as Amy placed Lucia's hand on her breast. Lucia took long gentle strokes to caress all of Amy's ample breasts. Then she reached behind and slowly undid the zipper on Amy's blouse. She slipped the blouse off over Amy's arms. Then she leaned forward and put her head on Amy's breasts.

Lucia reached down and unfastened Amy's jeans. She knelt on the rug and pulled the jeans off. Then she pulled Amy off the couch.

Lucia put both of her hands around Amy's breast. It's slight coolness yielded to the warmth of her hands.

"Your breasts are wonderful. It makes my mouth water for the taste of them," Lucia said. Very slowly she lowered her head until her mouth grazed Amy's nipple.

Lucia blew and watched as it tightened. Then she ran her tongue across its surface. Amy let out a tiny moan. Encouraged, Lucia pulled Amy's nipple into her mouth.

"Yes," Amy said hoarsely. "I love sucking." She pressed Lucia's head closer to her breast. Lucia caught Amy's nipple between her teeth.

"More, please," Amy said, then moaned her pleasure as Lucia complied. Without stopping, Lucia reached for Amy's other nipple. She ran her finger tips across it until it too was tight. She quickened the rhythm of her sucking to match the increased tempo of Amy's breathing.

Each breath of Amy's whispered through Lucia's hair. Lucia lay prone along the length of Amy's body so she could feel her every movement. Amy's legs circled her back and clasped her tightly. Lucia was a little surprised at their strength. "Perhaps I've discovered a sport she truly enjoys," Lucia thought wickedly. She rested her weight on one elbow to free her hand again, stroking Amy's shoulder and side, down past her hips. She paused to caress the inside of Amy's knee as Amy's fingers dug into Lucia's back. Then, ever so slowly, Lucia drew her finger tips up Amy's thigh, just barely grazing the soft brown nest of hair hiding her labia.

"You're driving me wild, woman. Touch me. Please, touch me," Amy cried out.

Lucia shifted her mouth to the other breast and stroked Amy's round belly and ample thighs. "Mmm," she murmured in contentment, feeling Amy's hands on her breasts, Amy's finger tips on her nipples. Her own breathing was becoming rapid.

Lucia dipped her finger tips in the moisture that was flowing copiously around Amy's labia. Slick and moist, her fingers caressed Amy's clit. Then Lucia rubbed her fingers on either side of the hardened button until she could feel Amy's climax approach. She began to breath

139

with Amy, feeling the surges of Amy's passion in her own warm wet center. Lucia's stroking became harder and faster.

In one shuddering moment Amy came. Lucia cupped her hand on Amy's damp triangle of curly hair. Then, Amy pulled Lucia on top of her and hummed a tuneless note. After a few minutes, she tugged Lucia's jeans off and pulled her into a kneeling position. Then Amy slipped her body underneath Lucia until her mouth was directly below Lucia's cunt.

"Time for dessert now," Amy whispered. Lucia could feel Amy blowing up at her clit and she gasped. The breeze of Amy's breath swiftly rekindled Lucia's passion. She struggled to maintain her balance as Amy's tongue darted in and out of her vagina.

Amy licked Lucia's clit with a wet rough tongue. Harder. Faster. Lucia flung her arms up. She began to whimper. Amy took her clit gently between her teeth and sucked, then harder. Lucia screamed. Amy sucked faster. Lucia could not find the breath to scream anymore. Amy's mouth pulled insistently on Lucia's clit. Lucia tried to sink, then she rose up on her knees. Amy's mouth followed her. Then the waves of passion broke around Lucia and she fell to the floor gasping.

"Yes, oh yes," Lucia murmured. "Oh yes."

SUNDAY

Lucia pulled her Sentra up to the side of the security booth. "Please open the gate. I have an appointment with Mr. Van Lander at 7 Marble Path."

"You are Officer Lucia Ramos?" the blue-uniformed security man asked. There was a note of military rigidity in his voice.

"Yes."

"Please go immediately to Mr. Van Lander's home. Do not sightsee. He will buzz me when you arrive so we will know the elapsed time."

"Afraid I'm going to case the houses for a burglary?" Lucia said lightly.

"As a matter of fact, yes. It wouldn't be the first time officers of the law were involved in theft." His blue eyes hardened.

"Right," Lucia responded. Privately she wondered if he was one of the failed police trainees. That would certainly explain his attitude. The thought of a poorly trained security man with a semi-automatic weapon on his hip and a power trip on his brain did not add to her sense of comfort at all. She wondered if getting lost in a residential neighborhood would strike him as meriting the death penalty. She did not intend to find out.

Fortunately, the route to Van Lander's house proved simple. Lucia noticed that it bordered on the greenbelt at the edge of the development. For a moment, she summoned visions of land mines under the bushes. How far would the homeowners go to hold back what they must imagine to be hordes of robbers, rapists and kidnappers? Surely they could not be ignorant of the fact that they were most likely to be victimized by their neighbors, friends and family. Yet all of these were welcomed inside the walls. "Well, it takes all kinds," Lucia thought.

Van Lander opened the door promptly at her ring. He was a sallow-faced man with a receding hairline and narrow hazel eyes distorted by thick lenses set into grey metal frames. His grey knit shirt had a small animal insignia on the left. Lucia noted that he was about her size in both height and weight.

"Make it fast," he said. "I normally get hundreds of dollars an hour for my time." He blocked the door and made it clear that there would be no invitation to enter.

"I'm Officer Lucia Ramos...."

"Yes, of course. Get on with it."

"You have the right to remain silent..."

"I waive my rights under the Miranda decision. Get on with it, Officer." His lips curled back in the left side of his face in an impatient sneer. It did not improve his looks. He said nothing when Lucia started the tape.

"Were you a patient of Dr. Elizabeth Freeman's?"

"Yes, and on the evening of her death I was on the phone from six to nine having a serious altercation with my ex-wife about child support. She will not substantiate this. She will, and this is her phrasing, perjure herself to God's face if it would help me burn in the electric chair. Therefore, I have no alibi. Nor do I have a motive."

"Did you know anything about her outside of therapy?"

"I had my secretary check her credentials before I initiated therapy. She was licensed. She had one complaint lodged by a client, topic confidential. It was discharged without prejudice. She was one of the few therapists that my ex-wife had not seen. These facts were sufficient basis for a decision. I didn't care to know anything else. Is that all?"

"No. I have a few more questions." Lucia found her temptation to draw out the interview at war with her desire not to spend any additional time in Van Lander's company. "Did you know any of her colleagues, clients, friends or family?"

"No, why should I?"

"Did Dr. Freeman ever offer you alcoholic beverages before, during or after therapy?"

"No."

"Did your relationship with Dr. Freeman have a sexual element?"

"Were we lovers? You've got to be kidding. I could retire on what I would have won in damages. Was she screwing clients?"

"It's just a routine question in a murder investigation."

"Yeah, right. Do you think I'm stupid, Officer?" Lucia refrained from answering his question. Instead she asked for the name and phone number of his ex-wife. He gave it to her readily. She gave him her card and asked him to call if he thought of anything that might assist the investigation.

Lucia assessed the interview as a zero and returned to her car. She had no doubt that the ex-wife would deny the phone call. Van Lander could be telling the absolute truth or total lies. It was impossible to tell. Fortunately the phone company would be able to confirm or disprove a local call of that length made from either his or his ex-wife's phone. The new metered phone service had really improved her ability to check out this type of call.

Lucia wondered why Van Lander was in therapy. While he did not seem a happy man, neither did he seem the type to look for answers inside himself. Nor did he seem the type to suffer betrayal lightly. If Freeman had…"No," Lucia thought, "Freddie said she was afraid of Van Lander." Her thoughts were interrupted by the radio. "Shooting in progress…." The address was very close. Off duty was a meaningless term when you leave your radio on. She stopped the car long enough to affix the mobile flasher unit. She flipped on the flasher and the siren and smirked a bit as she sped past the guard box.

◇

Amy knocked on the door of the duplex. It opened immediately. The young man who stood beside it was quite good looking. His straight dark hair was neatly trimmed and freshly combed. He stood just under six feet. The short sleeves of his white, button-down shirt revealed tanned muscular arms. He extended his hand.

"I'm Derrick Milton. Please come in. You must be Dr. Traeger."

"Yes." Amy said. "Thank you for seeing me. I'm working with Officer Ramos who is investigating the death of Dr. Freeman."

He escorted her into a very neat efficiency apartment. The worn linoleum floor was spotless and shiny. Even the ancient casement windows were free of any trace of dirt. Derrick gestured toward one of the two chairs at the formica table. Amy put the small tape recorder on the table and turned it on.

"You are my first house guest. I haven't had much time or energy for making friends." He smiled somewhat apologetically.

"Would you be willing to tell me why you were seeing Dr. Freeman?" Amy asked.

"Sure. My mother died recently and I've had a very hard time dealing with it. We were close. She was all the family I had. Her death from cancer was very painful and drawn out. I have a great deal of unresolved anger about it and..." He stopped suddenly. "And I guess I wanted some help. It was just luck that it was available free."

"How well did you know Dr. Freeman?" Amy's voice was gently insistent.

"Not very well. I had only been going for a couple of months. I'm afraid I wasn't very cooperative."

A fairly long silence followed that statement. Then Derrick said, "I have trouble trusting people."

There was another silence before he continued, "My parents' divorce was very bitter. I came to believe that my mother was the only person I could count on. We were very close."

His voice began to tremble slightly on the last sentence.

"She was like a good friend as well as a mother?" Amy asked.

"She was my only real friend. And they just let her die because she was poor. Nobody cared except Evelyn. She was the discharge planner at the hospital. She tried

144

to help, but there was no money for anything. My mother didn't have to die. She kept telling them about the pain in her stomach, but they just told her it was in her mind. By the time they bothered to do x-rays, it was too late. The cancer was everywhere. It just ate her alive. She didn't have to die. She didn't have to be poor. If that bitch hadn't convinced my father..." He stopped and looked down at his clenched fists. "No," he whispered, then fell silent.

"The anger doesn't go away," Amy said.

"No," he whispered.

There was a long silent pause.

"Did Dr. Freeman ever offer you something to 'help' with the anger, perhaps a drink?" Derrick looked stunned.

"No. No. How could you..." He paused and visibly collected himself. "How could you think such a thing? That would be totally unethical. I've had enough sociology to know that professionals don't do that sort of thing." His earlier vulnerability disappeared.

"I do not mean to impugn your therapist. I'm simply trying to understand what happened." Amy tried to catch the eye of the now pale and shaking young man across the table from her.

Derrick sat silently staring at his hands. Then he said, "I've been remiss. I'm unused to visitors. Would you like coffee or something else to drink?" His voice was very polite.

"No, thank you, Derrick."

There was a very long pause.

"Well, if there's nothing else you need, I've got a test day after tomorrow in family systems."

"I do have a few other questions. They shouldn't take long," Amy said. "Did you know anything about Dr. Freeman's personal life? Did she ever mention friends or family to you?"

"She said she was from Maryland. That's where she got her degree. I don't remember anything else. Oh, and she said she had just lost her mother too. She seemed to think our mothers were alike. Their deaths sure weren't. Hers died in her sleep. A heart attack. I don't remember anything else."

"Dr. Freeman didn't happen to mention any names, did she?"

"No. I don't really remember."

"Did you know any of her other clients?"

"There was a nun who had an appointment before mine but we didn't speak other than to say good afternoon so I don't know her name. Sorry."

"Where were you Tuesday evening?" Amy asked.

"St. Mary's library working on my paper for family systems. They have a lot of journals we don't carry. Why?" His forehead creased with worry lines.

"It's traditional in a murder investigation to find out where everybody was when the murder occurred. It doesn't mean anything in particular about you. Did anyone see you at the library?"

"Sure. But I didn't see anyone I knew, so I don't know if anyone would remember me."

Amy got up. She reached over the table and put her hand over Derrick's fist. "Thank you," she said. "I appreciate your help. And I'm sorry I interrupted your studies. If you remember anything later on that Dr. Freeman mentioned, please call me." She turned off the tape recorder and slipped it into her briefcase. As she turned she noticed a bike hung on the wall behind the door.

Derrick noticed her glance. "My wheels. I can't afford a car. My sport too. I do marathons. I'm pretty good."

Amy slid into her therapist-with-adolescent-male mode. "How fast do you go in a marathon? You must have to pace yourself pretty slowly to last."

"No, I can do a hundred and twenty-five miles in a little over four hours if the course is flat. The problem with time is the traffic lights. I have to get out to the country to really open up. And hills. There aren't many decent hills in town. A few over by the zoo. And Inspiration Hill, of course."

"It sounds like you're pretty good."

"I've won a couple of big races. But that was back in New Jersey. I haven't had much time here. I want to get really good grades so I can get an assistantship when I go for my Ph.D." He seemed to open up to praise.

"I'm sure you'll do well. You're very determined. You probably work very hard to get what you want." Amy watched as his face closed up again and wondered what she had said wrong.

"Yeah, right. Well, good-bye." He hurried her out the door. Amy pondered her errors in the interview during the half-hour drive to Dr. Freeman's office. The combination of police investigator and therapist were not a good fit. Pushing direct questions at people tended to shut them down emotionally. Indirect guidance could take months to achieve simple information. "Not a good fit, at all," she thought to herself as she parked her car next to a blue Volvo. Her brow furrowed. Dr. Freeman's blue Volvo had been impounded. A chill shivered through Amy's body. But never in any reading had she heard of ghost cars. Perhaps Rebecca Field was emulating her therapist in her choice of vehicles.

The door to the office complex was unlocked. So was the door to office D. Amy entered cautiously. Standing in front of a poster, staring at it, was a woman in her early thirties. She was wearing very fashionable and very tight jeans and a halter top which barely covered her generous breasts. Her red hair was hanging loose and shiny. She could have been posing for the cover of a fashion magazine.

"Ms. Field?" Amy asked.

"Yes." She turned languidly. "And you are Dr. Traeger?"

"Yes. Shall I sit at the desk?"

"It would seem appropriate. You are the therapist." She licked her lips to give them a shine.

Amy sat and took out the tape recorder. "I'll need to record our conversation."

"I'm used to that," Rebecca said. "Dr. Freeman always taped our sessions."

"There are some questions that I must ask you since I am helping the police investigate Dr. Freeman's death," Amy said.

"Murder," Rebecca corrected.

"Yes, murder," Amy agreed. "Because of that, I need to tell you that nothing you say to me is going to be confidential. If you say anything that might relate to the investigation, I will share that information with the police."

"I'm used to that, the first therapist I consulted wrote up everything for a journal article. She changed my name, but that was all. Dr. Freeman was planning an

147

article too. But at least she told me about it. Decent of her, don't you think?" She adjusted one side of the halter so it was off her shoulder.

"I suppose. Did it make you feel exposed, to be written up that way?"

"Quite. What did you wish to ask me?"

"How long had you been consulting with Dr. Freeman?"

"Six months or so. And I don't recall where I was on the night of her death. I'm sure that is one of your questions. We might as well be done with it early."

"Yes, it was one of the questions. Does it bother you?"

"Of course," Rebecca said. "Just get on with it."

"Did you ever have a drink with Dr. Freeman, an alcoholic drink?"

"Yes."

"During therapy?"

"Yes."

"Did your relationship with Dr. Freeman extend beyond the normal client-therapist pattern?"

"What exactly do you mean?" Rebecca ran her fingers through her hair to fluff it.

"Was there a sexual element?"

"Yes."

"How did you feel about that?"

"It kept her happy. That and the opportunity to write an article on the hot new topic of Multiple Personality Disorder kept her quite attentive to my case."

"You seem very cynical about Dr. Freeman's motivation," Amy said, "yet you still remained her client. Are you willing to tell me why?"

"She was good to me," Rebecca said, pulling her halter strap back onto her shoulder. "I never found any therapist who was perfect, or any person for that matter. She was less dogmatic than most." Rebecca got up and walked over to the shelves. Her finger tips touched lightly over the surface of the Katchina with a black feather headdress. "I felt safe here. Truly stupid of me. I've been through the therapy mill long enough to know that sex with a patient is a totally forbidden relationship. That no ethical therapist would dream of doing it."

"But..." Amy said.

"But she helped me much more than the half dozen ethical therapists I saw before her. Perhaps because the situation was so familiar, so similar to incest."

Amy realized that she was the object of intense scrutiny from Rebecca. She suppressed a sudden desire to scratch her nose. Any movement might be misconstrued, she thought.

"And…" Amy said.

"Good. Very good. You didn't flinch at the word. You didn't leap on it either. Elizabeth was also unflappable. All the others were either leapers or flinchers." Rebecca's smile held no real humor.

"Do you want me to acknowledge personality shifts, Rebecca? Or would you prefer to continue the discussion without a break?" Amy asked, hoping that the crisis had passed. She scratched the bridge of her nose.

"Ignore them. We're all one happy family. We have very little boundary amnesia anymore, so if you talk to one of us, you talk to all of us. And we all listen to each other. Rather like a committee. Elizabeth always wanted to talk to the chairman, but she tolerated our anarchy." Rebecca picked up the wooden image of the Indian spirit and carried it to the end table.

"She was always put here when we did hypnosis. She is the guardian spirit. She went with me and protected me. Actually, she protected us. We are not comfortable with the plural pronouns. They are too new."

Rebecca gazed directly into Amy's eyes as if trying to read her soul.

"That was her gift to us," Rebecca said. "And our gift back was sex. She gave us ourselves in plural pronouns and we gave her herself in sex. A fair exchange."

"But not without cost," Amy said.

"There has been no experience with exchanges in which there is no cost," Rebecca replied.

"And Freeman certainly didn't try to change that pattern," Amy thought.

"Have you thought about what you are going to do now?"

"A decision has not yet been made. Some of the children are not able to deal with it yet. There is a lot of grief," Rebecca said.

"And anger?"

"Yes."

"I would like to offer my help if you decide you want help."

"We don't know." Rebecca's eyes became unfocused as if she were in a trance. Several minutes passed in silence. "We are not ready to make a decision. Shut up, ol' stuffy brain, I want to talk." The visual change in Rebecca was dramatic. The cool manner disappeared. The person speaking was now a fidgety child. "She always hogs things. She doesn't think any of us better talk or we'll get into trouble. 'We, we, we,' just like a little pig. The Princess always gets to talk. I want to talk too. Do you think one of us killed her?" Her voice got small and scared sounding. She tugged at the bottom of the halter top.

"Do you?" Amy asked.

"The boys are rough. Maybe if one of them got mad. I don't remember." She curled into a ball on the couch.

"Sometimes," Amy said, "when it's very scary, I don't remember things. Or sometimes, it's very confusing. Do you get confused or scared too?"

"Yes, yes, yes. Go away. Leave me alone." The figure on the couch began to rock. She rocked for a long time, saying nothing. After almost twenty minutes she sat up and straightened her halter. "We would like to talk again, some other day. We are very, very tired now." She got up and left the office.

✧

The last thing Lucia expected Nya Kyle to be was exactly what she was. The person holding the door open was tiny and black. The photo on the flyer had accurately portrayed her Caucasian features, but had not conveyed the deep milk chocolate tone to her skin. The combination was breathtaking. A lavender bandana was tied around her natural Afro hair. Lucia looked down at her face, which was inscrutable. Nya was about four-foot ten. She was dressed in what Lucia thought of as a karate suit. Nya bowed deeply in the Japanese manner. Lucia ducked her head in response.

"You are Officer Ramos, I presume," Nya gave a wide graceful gesture. "Please enter my humble school."

"Thank you," Lucia replied. "I hope my being early isn't a problem."

"No. It's fine. Would you care for tea?"

"Yes, thank you." Lucia followed her to a mat set in the center of the huge room. A pottery teapot with a bamboo handle sat warming on a hibachi. Nya sank into a graceful cross-legged position. Mentally cursing her own skirt and heels, Lucia attempted to do likewise. She took out her tape recorder and placed it next to her. She started to speak, but before she could get a word out, Nya cut in.

"Yes, you may tape this," Nya said as she reached over and turned on Lucia's recorder.

"You are here to talk about the death of Dr. Elizabeth Freeman, my therapist and lover. First, you will warn me that anything I say can and will be held against me. You will then advise me to speak only in the presence of my lawyer and notify me that a lawyer will be provided if I am unable to afford one. But I have nothing to hide." She gestured widely with both arms. "My life is as free of secrets as this room is free of furniture."

"Yet you kept your relationship with Freddie a secret from Dr. Freeman," Lucia commented.

"She did not ask. I would have answered truthfully if she had asked."

"But you wouldn't volunteer the information."

"No," Nya said sprinkling leaves into the pot of hot water.

Lucia thought for a few moments. This interview had the feel of formal competition and she was not sure what rules Nya might impose on it.

"What questions should I ask you to obtain the information most useful to my investigation of this murder?" she asked.

Nya bowed her head in acknowledgment.

"First, did I commit the crime? No. Second, do I know who did commit the crime? No. Third, do I know who might have had reason to commit the crime? Yes."

As she paused for breath, Lucia asked "Who are they and what are their reasons?"

"Freddie Christian, out of jealousy. She is not as blasé as she would have people believe. Marita Peterson, out of anger..."

"You knew about Dr. Freeman's other clients?" Lucia could not quite keep the surprise out of her voice.

151

"Lizbeth trusted me. She often asked my opinion on matters." Nya's voice was impassive.

"And you had told her nothing that would disturb you if she told someone else?"

"I have no secrets."

"Please continue your list. I find it very helpful."

"Rebecca Field, who has one very violent personality. Dr. Oliver Whitney, whose role on the licensing board was very useful to Lizbeth and who may have grown to resent being used. David Freeman, a very greedy man who may have believed he would profit by her death. Arturo Flores, who lost his job at Sidney Lanier Elementary School because Lizbeth reported him for child molestation. He may still be in prison. One hopes so."

"Any others you can think of?" Lucia asked, making a mental note to call in for the whereabouts of Arturo Flores.

Nya poured the tea in small handleless cups that matched the pottery teapot. "No."

"No ex-husbands?"

"They are both dead."

"Natural death?"

"Heart attack and cancer. She was attracted to older men."

"And women?"

"For stable relationships, yes, I suppose."

"If you had been put in a position where you had to choose between Dr. Freeman and Freddie Christian, which one would you choose?"

"Freddie. She was the more considerate lover."

"And richer," Lucia commented. "This place looks very expensive to keep up. With Dr. Freeman dead, Freddie might turn to you for consolation...."

"I have plenty of money of my own, Officer. I don't need to kill someone to pay the rent." There were small body signals that Nya Kyle was losing her temper. Lucia decided to push a bit harder.

"Where were you on Tuesday evening?"

"Driving to Fort Worth for a martial arts competition. I am qualified to compete in tai chi, karate and akido."

"Or you could have driven up later. You have no witnesses."

"And you have no evidence or you would have followed me to Fort Worth and arrested me. I believe I will take advantage of my excellent advice to myself when this conversation began. I do not choose to speak with you any longer unless my lawyer is present. Call Juanita Morales to set up the interview."

"I know her number," Lucia admitted with chagrin at losing control of the interview. Nya swiftly rose and showed Lucia to the door.

Lucia checked the time. Despite sandwiching a shooting in between them, the two interviews had gone so quickly and so badly that she was not yet late for her lunch appointment with Amy. But she could be by the time she got to Cafe Toro.

She called in to the station on her radio. The desk sergeant checked his computer. Arturo Flores was safely locked up. The record showed he had pleaded guilty to a reduced charge. Next, Lucia asked him to check on Sonia Gardener, the perpetrator in that morning's shooting.

"Nice collar. You beat the uniforms to the murder scene. San Antonio Program is sending over one of their young lawyers. Should be here soon. Great way to spend a weekend, Ramos. You weren't even on duty."

"Oh, but I was. I had an interview in the neighborhood when the call came in." She signed off and remembered to turn off her radio. Enough was enough.

Lucia pulled off Zarzamora into the parking lot of Cafe Toro and smiled as she saw Amy's car. She sat for a moment remembering the evening before. "Perhaps introducing Amy to the best hamburger in San Antonio will make her forget that I scorched the huevos rancheros," Lucia thought. She let her mind wander to intimate moments of the previous night. Then she shook the thoughts out of her head and reminded herself to keep to business as she joined Amy in a much repaired orange booth.

"Sorry I'm late. I made the mistake of leaving my police radio on. There was a shooting near Van Lander's house and I was the first one on the scene. A woman killed her husband. She was still screaming at him and pulling the trigger when I got there. The gun was empty by then, but she was in shock. He beat her up pretty badly, but the charge will be first degree murder. It always is. And

153

they usually end up with a life term." Lucia looked disgusted.

"Wasn't it self-defense?" Amy asked.

"No," Lucia shook her head. "You know and I know it was self-defense, but legally it's premeditated murder because she ran to another room for the gun. The prosecution will say that if she was in fear of her life she should have run away, not for a gun."

"There is no justice in it. Anywhere. How can you be a part of it?" There was deep anger in Amy's voice.

"Hey, I didn't make the system. And I'm doing what I can to help change it, like you with Dr. Freeman, okay?" Lucia kept her voice very controlled. Amy's comments about killing her father echoed in Lucia's mind.

Amy sighed a deep sigh. "Wrong target. Sorry. I have a better handle on anger when I'm in my professional mode. I still don't have the knack for handling it personally."

"It's okay. I lose it sometimes too. Then I think I'll go be a travel agent or something."

"With your luck, you'd end up like Stoner MacTavish and find dead bodies strewn all over your landscape."

"Well, while we're on the topic of dealing with dead bodies—what was the Milton kid like?"

"Fairly straight, as you might expect. He was a little taller than average. Had dark brown hair, trimmed above his ears. He was wearing jeans and a white oxford style shirt. He looked very middle-class. But," Amy wrinkled her forehead, then rubbed it, "this is always the hard part." she continued. Lucia nodded. "I always feel like I shouldn't reveal my impressions of a client to the police."

"He's not a client, Amy," Lucia reminded her.

"I know," said Amy. "But confidentiality is a hard habit to break."

"It is certainly harder to keep your mind on work when you let business and pleasure mix," Lucia thought, but said nothing.

"Derrick bites his fingernails. That's not unusual. He had dark circles under his eyes and he looked down a lot. I think Dr. Freeman's death has him a lot more upset than he's willing to admit, even to himself. But that's pretty typical. He kept his hands clenched into fists the whole time we talked. And he kept crossing and uncrossing his legs at the ankle. There is a lot of emotion bottled up in Derrick. But he would not let anything out while we talked. He seems to work it off by bicycling. He races in marathons."

"Real tight, huh? Seems like almost everybody we've talked to about this case is like that. Even the bigwigs like Whitney have something to hide. What's your guess on Milton? What did he seem to be hiding? A murder?" Lucia settled into the vinyl upholstery.

Amy's answer was delayed by the arrival of a dark-eyed young woman with the water and the flatware. Lucia smiled at her.

"Could I have an extra napkin, please?" Lucia asked. "The burgers here are awfully juicy."

"No entiendo." The young woman smiled with a shrug.

"Una mas serviete, por favor," Lucia repeated in Spanish.

"Sí." She returned quickly with several of the paper napkins.

"Gracias," Lucia said and turned her attention back to Amy.

"Derrick probably wanted to murder his mother, but he's years away from realizing it. She was a very close-binding mother. She kept him isolated from the rest of society. He said she was his 'only real friend.' How sad. He had apparently begun to transfer some of his feelings of protectiveness toward his mother onto Dr. Freeman because when I asked him about being offered alcohol during therapy, he became unglued. Then he closed down and that pretty much ended the interview."

"Did you ask him about having sex with Freeman?" Lucia was madly taking notes.

"No."

"Do you think I should talk to him?"

Amy shrugged. "There is more in him than we talked about, but he didn't seem like the murderous type. Just the opposite. Super controlled. I don't know. I guess not." She gave Lucia the tape marked "Milton."

"By the way," Amy said, "Sarah Carter called this morning about eight. I made an appointment with her for three-thirty in my office. I didn't really want to leave it for later. This is the last one, isn't it?"

"I promise, Amy. No more."

"Is there any chance we're going to find out who killed Freeman or is it as hopeless as I think it is?"

"It doesn't look real good. I'm sorry you spent so much time on a pointless hunt." Lucia's heart started beating faster as Amy reached out and took her hand.

"It wasn't pointless, Lucia. I got what I wanted, a chance to help undo some of the harm that Freeman did to her clients," she said.

"Well, I may have messed that up for you on my last interview. I pushed hard at Nya Kyle and now she won't talk without a lawyer. And guess who her lawyer is? The same lawyer as Freddie's."

"You can't win them all, Lucia."

"Well, I'm batting zero in this inning. How did you do with Rebecca Field?"

The arrival of the meal cut the conversation short. Amy picked up a pickle slice. She ate the edges off the slice, then the soft center. Lucia suppressed the desire to kiss the finger tips Amy was licking. She picked up her burger instead. Unfortunately, the burgers were not as Lucia remembered them. After a couple of bites, both women left them on their plates next to the cold greasy french fries.

"Not like it was. This is terrible food. I apologize," said Lucia.

"Probably the cook's day off."

"The tea tastes enough like dishwater that I'd believe they let the dishwasher take over. I hate to pay for garbage like this, but if I don't, they'll take it out of the waitress's salary." Lucia took her wallet out of her briefcase. "At least let me pay for it."

"Sure. I'll chalk it up as an abortive dinner. But let me get the tip. What about Rebecca Field? Do you want to hear about that interview? There isn't much."

"Nya implied that Freeman thought one of the personalities was violent. Did Rebecca talk about that?"

"Rebecca's afraid of that too. She said that the boys are rough, which could mean anything. She seemed very scared and not very organized. I think that there is a good possibility that she'll come back for treatment. She's never experienced a relationship where the other person didn't make demands on her. Freeman was

156

straightforward in what she wanted. That was apparently a step up from her other therapists."

"What's her alibi?" Lucia asked.

"She couldn't remember where she was."

"What about the Milton kid?"

"He was in the library studying. He didn't see anyone he knew."

"Wouldn't have helped anyway. Nobody watches carefully enough to swear he never left. Oh, well, nobody else has an alibi, why should Rebecca Field?" Lucia picked up the bill. "I have to go handle this morning's homicide. Is there any chance we could talk tonight?"

Amy met and held her eyes. "Yes." Lucia felt warmth rush through her body. "After all, you owe me several more dinners, but I think I'd like to make you dinner tonight. And I want to talk, then eat, then play. I'm going to lose weight if we keep burning dinner."

Lucia smiled, "You're on."

"I certainly am," Amy replied, leaving a ten dollar tip. She noticed Lucia's glance. "I can afford it and she needs it. Who else is going to tip for this food? See you later." She left Lucia at the cash register.

✧

Lucia spent the rest of the afternoon on that morning's domestic homicide. It was obvious that the lawyer from the San Antonio Program was very inexperienced at criminal defense. Finally Lucia went out for a walk and made a call while she was out. A couple of hours later, an ACLU attorney showed up to talk to the accused. Lucia smiled at the attorney on her way out. Sometimes justice could be helped along with a gentle nudge.

When she got to her house, Cayetano was waiting.

"Thanks for feeding Gato," he said "Your Tía Luz called. She tried all night to call you and was worried when she couldn't get you, so she called us to see if you were okay. You better call her before she has a stroke. She feels like she has to look after you. Me? I figure you have a new girlfriend, maybe that pretty blond who was here last week for dinner."

"You're a worse gossip than Tía Luz. Don't you tell her I'm seeing someone. She'll have us married in June. She hasn't given up matchmaking. My being gay just makes it more of a challenge. She doesn't know many

157

single lesbian Chicana doctors. But I do," she laughed as she opened the door.

"You're kidding. She's a Chicana lesbian doctor?"

"Well, two out of three isn't bad." Lucia flung her briefcase on the couch. "Go help your wife take care of your baby. I need time to think before I call Tía Luz. Go away, mocoso."

Cayetano left smiling. Lucia turned the water in the tub on hot. She poured in lavender scented bath oil. While the tub was filling she put a Kay Gardener tape in the cassette player. Then she stripped off her clothes and tossed them in the wicker basket. She stuck her foot in the tub and decided to add some cold water. The water was almost too hot, but Lucia sank into it gratefully. She closed her eyes. Yesterday's memories flowed into her mind. She could almost feel herself in the desert oasis. She took a deep cleansing breath and floated in the warm water. The flute solo surrounded her, seeping into her body. For a few blessed minutes, all the tension of the day washed away.

Then, reluctantly Lucia rose out of the cooling tub. She quickly shampooed and rinsed her hair. Then she toweled off. "I've been wearing too much blue," she thought. "White tonight." She took out the embroidered blouse she had brought in Reynosa and the matching white drawstring pants.

"Oh Tía Luz, Tía Luz," she sighed. "Time for me to face the music." She sat on the couch and dialed her aunt's number.

"Rosa? This is Lucía. Is Tía Luz there?" she asked.

"Oh, Lucía, she's outside bringing in the laundry. I don't know why she won't use the dryer we bought her. It's so much easier." The light voice on the other end of the line raised its volume. "Mama, it's Lucía. I'll get the drying. You come to the phone." Rosa came back to the receiver. "Are you coming to Jimmie's Confirmation next Sunday? He's so excited."

"Sure, if nothing comes up. You know how the job is," Lucia replied.

"Well, be there or be square, cuz. Here's Mama."

A soft liquid voice flowed from the phone. "Lucita, where have you been? I was trying to reach you all day

158

yesterday. I thought perhaps I should call the police." Tía Luz gave a brief hearty chuckle at her own Joke.

"I'm on a case, Tía," Lucia replied.

"All night, too?"

"Well, no."

"Aha!" There were miles of discovery in her tone.

"I was on a date, Tía," Lucia admitted.

"Is she nice? Where did you meet her? What does she look like? What does she do? How long have you been seeing her?"

"Down, Tía. Relax. She's very nice, very good looking. Kind of like a younger, heavier Candice Bergen. I met her through work. She's helping me on my case. We've had one date, so don't send out the wedding announcements yet," she said.

"Don't make fun of your tía or she won't give you empanadas at Christmas. You sound so good, honey. There is joy in your voice like you had before Yolanda died. We missed your happiness and want it back for you. Is that so terrible?" Tía Luz voice sounded falsely mournful.

"You are an unrepentant matchmaker, that's what you are, dearest aunt."

"True. But I make the best fajitas in south Texas, so you forgive me. And I'm making them tonight. So come to dinner and tell me about your new sweetheart."

"I'd love to, but I..." Lucia paused for more impact, "have a date with her tonight."

"Good, good. Can she cook?"

"I'll find out tonight, Tía."

"Okay. We'll miss you. Jerry's coming over and Felicia's oldest two. But you have to come over soon and tell all to your tía."

"I will, I will. Love you all. Bye." Lucia waited for all of Tía Luz's gentle endearments, then hung up. She took a deep breath. That had been easier then she had feared. Only a little intrusive. Not the steam roller Tía Luz could sometimes be. But Lucia would forgive her Tía Luz anything out of gratitude for the nurturing that had filled in when tuberculosis killed Lucia's mother. Tía Luz had held the terrified five-year-old in her ample arms and announced that she was "taking this niña and her familia" back to her home in San Antonio. And she had been Lucia's mother ever since.

Even Lucia's father had acquiesced to Lucia's strong-willed aunt. He had accompanied his two sons and his daughter to the large house on Zarzamora. Lucia smiled at the memory of the huge family dinners and the ease on her father's face as he watched his children become absorbed into Luz's open heart.

Relaxed and refreshed, she went to her desk. It was time to work on the list she started when the case opened. All of the names were filled in next to the initials, as were both deceased husbands' names. She added the words "no alibi" next to Van Lander, Kyle and Milton. She put Flores' name on the list. She paused there. Did Flores have brothers, father, cousins, sons who might want revenge? But she had the same problem with that theory that she had with Marita as a suspect. Why the time lag? It would imply a degree of premeditation. That would apply to Freeman's brother in New York, also. If he flew to San Antonio to murder his sister, where was the motive? Her money? That seemed an unlikely motive for a successful attorney.

Nya had added new information, but it did not seem useful. Or was it the split link that opened the case up, but she didn't recognize it because she was looking at it wrong? Lucia decided that another talk with Freddie might clarify something. She made a quick call to Freddie confirming their appointment for Monday afternoon. Then she rummaged through her papers for Freeman's brother's phone number. She tried the phone again. David Freeman was still out.

Lucia sighed. She replaced all the papers in her briefcase and snapped it closed. "Time for a real break from work before Monday's madness begins it all again," she thought.

She stopped for flowers at the grocery store. A sweet bunch with a tea rose and baby's breath caught her eye. "Red for passion," she thought, smiling broadly at the checker. Memories of last night's passion sped her along. She fudged more than a trifle on the speed limit. Sunday evening traffic was light and she was at Amy's house with no clear memory of how she got there. Not that it mattered. Amy responded immediately to her knock. She was wearing a white peasant dress from Mexico.

"They say a couple grows to be alike, but I thought it took more than one night," Amy laughed, giving Lucia a warm hug and pulling her through the door.

"Extrasensory perception, no doubt," Lucia said softly in Amy's ear. Then she kissed the ear.

"None of that. Talk, eat, play. In that order. Like civilized folks," Amy said, plunging her face into the flowers in Lucia's hand. "I consider flowers especially civilized. Thank you, Officer Ramos."

"No more burned dinners, I promise on my honor as an officer of the law, Dr. Traeger." Lucia saluted her.

"Excellent. I feel totally safe in your hands, Officer Ramos."

They wandered into the living room arm in arm. There was a bowl of popcorn on the table. Lucia sat on the couch and popped a handful in her mouth.

"I thought you might like popcorn to go with the video," Amy said.

"Video?" Lucia asked.

"*Sybil,*" Amy replied. "I thought it might help. It's old-fashioned, but gives a decent idea of what Multiple Personality Disorder is about."

"Thanks, but I'll pass. I've seen it several times on the late show. I'd rather spend tonight with work far away. How about it? Is that okay with you?"

Amy grinned. "Great. Let's start with some liquid refreshment. Soda, fruit juices, something alcoholic?"

"Liquor would put me right to sleep. How about one of those juice seltzers?"

"Berry, tropical or citrus?"

"Decisions, decisions. Which is your favorite?"

"Berry."

"Sold," Lucia said to Amy's already departing back. Amy was back in an instant with two glasses of wine-colored bubbly water. She sat next to Lucia and put the glasses on either side of the popcorn.

"So, no video. I guess I'll just have to entertain you myself."

Lucia leaned back into the sofa and closed her eyes. There was a low music coming from the CD player. An

161

instrumental on synthesizer. She found it interesting, but not intrusive. She felt Amy stroke her hair.

"How about stories from our childhoods? What is your very favorite memory from when you were a kid?" Amy asked.

"You first. Then I'll know how honest to be." Lucia almost purred under Amy's gentle stroking.

"That's easy. It's the day I realized that I would be leaving home for good. It was in late spring. I was walking past the late blossoms on my way to the library on the university campus. It was my sanctuary. A professor's kid was always welcome, if you were well-behaved. I was, after all, a senior about to leave home. Graduation was very soon. I could leave. I could soon walk out forever," Amy continued.

"I'll never forget that walk. It was as if I walked out of my skin. Our front door was heavy and wooden, with leaded glass on one side of it so we could look out to see who had rung the bell. The door was always locked. We kept it locked because my parents believed all sorts of terrible people were outside. I remember laughing to myself as I left it secretly ajar. If terrible people walked in, maybe they would enjoy meeting my father. They had a lot in common after all.

"My mother wasn't at home. I never would have endangered her. If she had been, I would have locked the door. I rather hoped, however, that a murderer would wander in and set me free.

"But I was, for that moment, free. My father was asleep on my semen-soaked bed. I was walking away from the house, practicing what I would soon do forever. Walking away. I was beyond feelings. I noted facts.

"I remember noticing that a neighbor's car needed a wash. There was something of secret evil implied in a Cadillac that needed a wash. Were the owners on the road to financial ruin? What else could account for such slovenliness? And the roses at the next house are imprinted on my memory. They were correctly pruned. Anyone could tell that at a glance. And they were all divested of dead blossoms. Not a hint of brown anywhere. I could tell you every detail of every house I passed. I was going to be free. On that day I became sure of it in my heart."

Lucia breathed a great sigh and opened her eyes. "Oh," she said, not knowing what else to say.

"What's your favorite memory, Lucia?"

"Nothing like yours. I can't imagine the kind of life you must have lived. I'm very glad you got out of there." She nuzzled her head into Amy's caressing finger tips.

"Me, too. But I really want to know about your favorite time."

Lucia scrunched her face up remembering.

"I don't know," she said, "Maybe midnight mass on Christmas Eve. The whole family would stay up real late wrapping presents, then everybody would pile into the car and go to church. One year, the poinsettias on the south side of the church were especially gorgeous. It was a warm year and they were twenty feet tall and in full bloom. Someone had rigged floodlights on them.

"Then we would walk into the church. It was crammed full of friends of mine and their families. Everybody knew everybody. Even families that had been feuding for years would talk and laugh before midnight mass. Then the carols would begin. 'Noche de Paz' was my favorite. 'Silent Night.' It sounds better in Spanish, you know. 'Night of Peace.' It was. It truly was." Amy was quietly enraptured by Lucia's delight. She watched every happy gesture Lucia made in her enthusiasm. Lucia spread her fingers wide and made a broad arch in front of her.

"And the candles. The altar boys would light every candle. The altar was on fire. It was glorious. The singing. The lights. The incense. I still love it. I go every year. I love it." Suddenly Lucia became aware that she had been swept away by the memories. She was a little embarrassed.

"That's marvelous, Lucia. I'd forgotten how wonderful it can be. We were Episcopalian, so there was a little less ritual, but it was wonderful. I could see it all again when you described it. Isn't it hard, being lesbian, with your family so traditional?"

"I was so afraid they would find out about Yolanda and me. We moved to Austin to be safe. And for Yolanda's degree. U.T. had a good botany program. It was much easier to be in the closet only on weekends. Even then, we were terrified that some niece would walk in on us when we were making love. It was very hard," Lucia said.

"After Yolanda died I was a mess," she continued. "My friends Barbara and Evie saved my life. I would get home from work, but the house was so empty. I would drive over to their place...I don't know how I did it. I guess, I was on automatic pilot. Evie would answer the door. She put her arms around me and I would start crying. We would sit on the couch with me in the middle. Then Barbara would put an afghan over me just like an abuelita tucking in a niña. Evie would work on her thesis with all these journal articles and her notebooks and reams of computer paper from the research. But when she wasn't busy with both hands, she would pat my knee and say all those comforting things that get said to crying kids.

"They were like family. They are my family as much as Papa or Tía Luz. Finally, Barbara said to me 'Your tía called. She's very worried. You need to tell her what's going on.' So I told my tía what was going on. Why I had lost thirty pounds in a month. Do you know what she said? She said, 'You tell Evie to feed you chocolate ice cream and flour tortillas. You'll eat that. If you don't, I'll come get you and bring you home where you belong. You're going to make yourself sick and your querida would not have wanted that.'

"She said it so naturally, 'your querida.' That was all. I had been so afraid for nothing. I asked Tía Luz about it later. They had already figured everything out. She was so worried they would lose me. That I would drift away from family or get sick and die to follow my novia.

"I think the only reason I had the courage to come out to them was that I was dead inside. Nothing mattered. I couldn't possibly hurt any more than I already did. She had left me, why not mi familia también?"

Amy kissed away Lucia's tears. More took their place. Lucia wiped them away.

"I hate to cry. Let's eat instead," she said.

They talked about holidays all through dinner. The mushroom soup was rich and hearty. Lucia had noticed that it had been cooked in a crockpot. Amy was apparently not going to risk another burned dinner. Lucia accepted a small second helping. It was nice to eat soup that never lived in a metal can.

"This soup's delicious. What's in it?" Lucia asked.

"A lot of mushrooms. Half a pound of both shitake and oyster. A pound of regular mushrooms and a quarter of a cup of rehydrated tree ears. Couple of onions, couple of stalks of celery, six cloves garlic. Everything is chopped, then sauteed in olive oil. Cover with water. It's a quick soup," Amy replied, dipping a chunk of sourdough bread in the broth.

Lucia smiled to herself. It was much easier to get Amy to talk about food than herself. She decided to let the conversation stay on food. "There's no meat at all in it?"

"No meat," Amy answered. "I think I'd like to be a vegetarian when I grow up," she said pensively. "It seems the right thing to do. We don't need animal protein if we understand how to combine the vegetable proteins. It is so terribly wasteful of food to use it to make animal protein when people are starving. I go weeks with no meat, then I have a craving for it. There go all my ideals in a single steak dinner," she sighed.

"I think it's better to be comfortable with how you eat. After all, you eat very little meat if you only eat it every now and then. I'm not nearly that noble," Lucia said.

"You have a terrible diet full of junk food," Amy reproached her.

"So, come cook for me always and I'll be pure. I don't have time to cook healthy meals. But I adore eating them and it would make my tía so happy."

"Who?" Amy asked.

"My tía, my aunt. She raised me when my mother died and she's always trying to marry me off. Even now that she knows I'm gay. Only now she's looking for a good woman instead of a good man."

"They're easier to find."

"How would you know, sweetie? Ever go looking? Did you lead a closet straight life that you're going to spring on me when we're old and gray?"

"Never. On my honor. How about you?"

"I kissed my share of boys when I was younger, but I liked playing softball with them better. No, what I enjoyed was kissing girls."

"And you do it so well," Amy bantered.

Lucia felt herself flush. The memory of last night's lust surfaced on her skin, her lips, her breasts. There was an aching in her vagina, a desire to be touched. Her fingers trembled as she reached across the table to stroke Amy's cheek. The silence lasted a long time. Amy got up and ran her hands over Lucia's back until Lucia relaxed into them.

Amy's hands reached under Lucia's arms to cup her breasts. Only one thin layer of cloth was between Amy and the velvet softness of Lucia's breasts. She slowly lifted off the blouse. Lucia turned in the chair and kissed Amy, long and gentle. Amy gradually pulled Lucia out of the chair. Then she slowly led her into the large bathroom and loosened the cord of Lucia's pants, letting them fall to the floor. Then she caught the bottom of her own dress and broke the kiss to lift it over her head.

"Time for the shower you promised," she said, turning on the faucets.

Lucia adjusted the water temperature to almost body warmth and stepped into the shower stall. Through the clear plastic curtain, she could see a wavy image of Amy. Lucia breathed faster. Amy's creamy white skin was punctuated by a triangle of golden brown curls just below her belly. Lucia remembered the ripe warmth hidden there and ached to hold it again. As Lucia watched, Amy opened a drawer and took out a plastic tube of shower gel. Smiling, she drew back the curtain and joined Lucia in the shower.

"To think I once wondered why the boys had such a huge shower installed. Now it seems just the right size."

"Oops. I forgot my plastic covered notebook. I'll be right back." Lucia made a small gesture of leaving.

"Fat chance I'll let you out of my nefarious clutches now that I have you where I want you." Amy put her arms around Lucia as if to restrain her. "Now I will give you the shower of your life." She turned Lucia around and placed her so that the main stream of water pounded on Lucia's pelvis. Then she spread some of the shower gel on Lucia's back and began to caress her slowly.

"Don't I get to wash you?" Lucia asked.

"Later."

Despite the warmth of the water, Lucia shivered with anticipation. Amy's finger tips inserted themselves

166

along the crease in Lucia's firm ass. "Oh," Lucia murmured, startled and excited by the gentle intrusion. "Where will those finger tips end up?" She wondered to herself. She soon found out as Amy gently tapped on her asshole with a sticky, soapy finger. "Oh," Lucia exclaimed, tightening her ass.

"Does this seem unpleasant?" Amy asked solicitously.

"No, I was just startled. I've never experienced anything quite like it, but yes, I am enjoying..." Lucia gasped as Amy inserted her finger a tiny way up.

"Still enjoying?" Amy asked.

"More so," Lucia was barely able to mumble. She leaned forward to give herself more support with her arms on the shower wall. The water now hit her breasts and her ass was even more exposed. Amy rubbed her soapy fingers in and out as Lucia began to moan. Then Amy slipped her other arm around Lucia, rinsed off the soap, caressing Lucia's nipples under the warm water and then ran her hand down Lucia's belly to her clitoris.

"Spread your legs a little," Amy whispered in her ear. Lucia moaned and complied. Amy cupped her palm over Lucia's clitoris and entered her warm wet vagina. Lucia's knees weakened with sexual passion. She contracted and relaxed to the pulse of Amy's stroking entries and exits.

"I can't bear it, " she whispered hoarsely. "My knees are going to give out. I can't come standing up. I can't..." A shuddering screaming came from deep in her belly as she climaxed. Amy released her as she slipped to the floor of the shower, still gasping for air. For a few moments, she continued to breath in deep shuddering sighs as Amy stroked her head.

"Jesus y María," Lucia muttered, turning around. She stood up and took the tube of gel. She outlined Amy's nipples. Then she held Amy's face in her hands and kissed her deeply as her own breasts, lubricated by the gel, slid smoothly over Amy's. Amy sucked hard on Lucia's tongue. Lucia lowered her hands to pinch Amy's nipples into hardness. She pulled Amy deeper into the shower's spray. When most of the soap was rinsed off, she moved to Amy's breast, pulling it with both hands into her hungry mouth.

"Yes," Amy cried. "Harder," she said pressing Lucia's head into her breast. Lucia sucked the nipple deep within her mouth, then released it to sink her teeth into the aureole and flick the nipple back and forth with her tongue. She could hear Amy making small screaming sounds with each flick.

"Bite me. Please. I can't bear it. Please bite me."

Lucia obliged gently. Then she knelt, placing her mouth over Amy's cunt, delighting in the warm-sea taste of her. She put her arms around Amy's thighs and pulled them into her breasts. Lucia tried to lick Amy's sea into her mouth. She licked her waves rushing and retreating. Then she nibbled on Amy's clit, tasting the passion that flowed from it. It crested. And crested again. Then, abruptly, Amy's knees gave out.

They sat, cuddled in each others arms in the warm spray until their fingers began to wrinkle.

"Time to dry off," Lucia said, running her fingers through Amy's wet hair.

"I don't see you leaping out," Amy teased.

"It might be cold out there."

"But it will be dry, little mermaid."

"Thank you for the shower of my life," Lucia said.

"The pleasure was mine," Amy said standing up. She held out her hand to Lucia. "Come. Let's towel off."

When they were dry and dressed, they went back into the dining room to clean up. Amy washed the pottery bowls and the silver spoons while Lucia dried.

" 'Talk, eat, play.' Well, we did all that. What do we do now, Officer Ramos?"

"Work, I guess."

"I don't suppose you'll count washing dishes as work and we'll just move back to the beginning of the list?" Amy teased with a wry grin on her face.

Lucia sighed. "I hate to spoil the evening, but I'm running short on time. There are so few detectives and so many murders that the case will go inactive."

"It's fine, Lucia. I don't mind working, even if I made my own dinner. In fact, the deal is off. I'll do real pro bono work, no compensation needed."

"Is this a comment on my cooking?"

Amy rubbed her thumb across the creases between Lucia's eyebrows. "No. I just want these lines to go away. I don't mind working, really."

"Thanks, Amy," Lucia said, opening her briefcase. "So, how did it go with Sarah Carter?"

"You can judge for yourself. I want you to hear this tape," Amy said dropping a cassette into the tape player. "I'll start it at the important part."

Lucia listened as Amy asked, "Can you tell me why you sought therapeutic help?"

The voice that responded was so low Lucia turned up the volume to hear the reply clearly. "I felt lost. I was just drifting. I would wash up against something, then the current would just carry me away. I guess I was looking for stability, for a reason for living." There was a questioning tone in the last sentence.

Then Amy's voice, strong and reassuring, asked "Did Dr. Freeman help you change that?"

Sarah's voice grew stronger and was almost excited. "Yes. I began to understand the universe better. Dr. Freeman taught me a lot of very important things."

"Could you share some of them with me?"

"I don't know. I don't think she would like that," Sarah whispered

"I'm hoping this information may help find her killer."

"Death is only a transition anyway. It really doesn't matter. It sets the decision back a few years, but I'll wait for her." The note of resignation in Sarah's voice was real and sad.

"The decision?" Amy prompted in a soft, unobtrusive voice.

"That's not to be discussed except by the chosen," Sarah said reluctantly.

"And the chosen. You are..." Again Amy's prompting was very quiet.

"Chosen. Yes. So is Dr. Freeman. Liz. It doesn't seem right to call her such a formal name when our lives were so intimately intertwined. Even before we were born."

"In past lives?"

Lucia pushed the hold button on the tape player. She shook her head vigorously, sending her black curls flying. Then she rubbed her eyes.

"Oh, no," she said, "is this headed where I think it is or is she just crazy?"

Amy smiled. "We don't say crazy. It's not professional. But no. She seemed sad, lost, needy. Not crazy. I'm afraid it's my best judgment that the idea of 'the chosen' came from Dr. Freeman, not the client."

"And she used this line to seduce her client?"

Amy leaned back in the heavy wooden chair and exhaled a very soft "Yes."

"Damn," said Lucia. "Another suspect. I'll listen to the tape on the way home. Tell me about her."

She watched Amy reach into the bright, floral carpet-bag and take out a stenographer's notebook. The symbols were neat and precise and totally incomprehensible to Lucia.

"Sarah is thirty-one. Divorced from a six month marriage in her early twenties. No children…" Amy read on, remembering the shy young woman's tentative entrance into the office. She had smiled. She never stopped smiling. Her soft green eyes did not smile. They moved around the room several times before Sarah spoke. They focused on the watercolor of dandelion puffs that hung behind Amy. They rarely left the picture.

Sarah's voice was hesitant with long pauses. "I feel terrible, like I'm betraying her trust. But I want you to understand how important she is." She hung her head so her face was completely hidden by her long brown hair. "I wish she were here to tell me what to do. I don't want to mess up again…."

Amy shifted her attention back to the present.

"Lucia, she's very passive, very dependant. I would be surprised if she could risk experiencing anger. And I believe it took a lot of anger to swing that bottle at Dr. Freeman's head. Believe me, there's no aggression in this child." Lucia could hear the sympathy in Amy's voice.

"How about an alibi?"

"She was at a poetry reading at the Zapata Center that night. She doesn't have a car. I suppose she could have gotten a ride or called a cab, but I just can't believe she would be cold-blooded enough to show up at a poetry reading within two hours of killing her lover. I don't think she could do it."

"You're probably right. But who did? I can't believe there isn't an answer somewhere. There was no real planning. The killer must have made a mistake somewhere. Marita is my best suspect, but it doesn't seem logical for her to wait all those months and then kill Freeman." Lucia ran her hand through her short black hair.

"People have done stranger things. Pain can fester if it isn't dealt with. Then something minor happens and it explodes. It isn't necessarily the triggering event that causes the outburst of anger, but the underlying pain and fear."

"So Marita could have gone to her office to clear up the bill or something like that and just blown up when Freeman said the wrong thing."

Amy nodded. "But the same scenario could fit anyone except someone incapable of an angry outburst and I really think that Sarah is incapable."

"Well, unfortunately, it could fit Marita," Lucia said. "She smashed up a bunch of bottles at a party at Christian's. So we know she's given to angry outbursts."

"Did she hurt anyone?" Amy asked

"No. Just the bottles."

"Is there anyone else on the list of suspects who has a problem with anger?"

"The Andrews guy, I forget his first name. But he has an alibi."

"Well, who else has an alibi? Maybe we can eliminate suspects that way."

"I've already done that. Only Andrews and the nuns have ironclad alibis. The rest have some holes in their time that evening or no alibi at all. Marita has a pretty good alibi, Freddie has none at all. And Rebecca Field doesn't remember. Do you think there's any way for her to find out? Maybe one of the other personalities would remember."

"I'll call and ask her. Do you have her number handy?"

"My briefcase is in the car." Lucia went out to get it. When she returned, Amy's cat was lying in front of Amy, demanding attention. Amy smiled and shrugged.

"I know I shouldn't let him on the table, but we're alone most of the time, so no one sees us being naughty." She rubbed him behind his ears and he responded with a tremendous purr. "He is a fine watch cat. Except he doesn't like other males. If a man comes in, even the boys from upstairs, he hisses continually. Sometimes I have to shut him in the bedroom. Isn't that right, Tiger?" The cat did not deign to answer.

Lucia handed Amy the sheet with Rebecca's phone number on it and took over petting the cat. He was lost in rumbling ecstasy that caused his black fur to quiver. Only the green irises in his white eyes broke the solid black.

"He likes you," Amy said as she re-entered the kitchen. "But he's easy, just like his owner." Relief was written all over Amy's face. "Rebecca remembered where she was. There was a co-op meeting on Tuesday night from six-thirty to nine-thirty. Lots of people saw her. She was at a table of officers all evening without leaving. It wasn't her." Amy smiled. "I'm really glad. She is much calmer and less fragmented since all of her realized they couldn't have done it. And she is willing to see me, but only if she pays. Then, she says, she'll know the cost up front. I'm so happy, Lucia. This is exactly what I hoped for. Thank you, thank you, sweet woman, for this." She hugged Lucia, then sat down.

"You know, Amy. You're a lot of different people yourself. I'm only beginning to realize how different you can be from time to time. Sometimes I feel like I've known you forever and sometimes it feels like I've just met you." Lucia didn't try to hide the wonderment in her voice.

"True. I've got some of the symptoms of Multiple Personality Disorder, but to a very light degree. It's a continuum, of course, like most human behavior. I have mood shifts, but not true personality shifts. There is a core that is always present, not just observing. No amnesia. Just fickle and fluid. It keeps me interesting." She joined Lucia in stroking the cat to hide her nervousness.

"It's okay. It's just that I've worked with you for years and never noticed. And I'm supposed to be a detective."

"I keep a pretty strong hold on my therapist hat when I'm in a work relationship, but..."

"It's not work anymore," Lucia finished.

"No, it's not." Amy smiled a big contented smile.

"See, here we go again. I'm trying to talk about work and you distract me. No wonder I burned dinner last night." Lucia smiled back at her.

"Okay, okay, slave driver. There's no reasoning with a task-oriented woman, so back to work. Who else can you eliminate?"

"Both students. No car and no bus service. Way too far away to walk. Mrs. Martinez and her family, as well as Carl Jarvis and his family. No motive. Same for Van Lander and Garcia. She never leaves her house anyway." Lucia looked at her list as she spoke.

"And that leaves..."

"Marita, despite her alibi. Freddie, no alibi and strong motive. Also Nya Kyle and Oliver Whitney. No, he's got a strong alibi. I just don't like him. David Freeman is a total unknown. Plus persons unknown. I just found out today that she played a part in nailing a child molester who's in the pen.

"Gillette didn't mention it when he told me about Freeman working for the schools," Lucia continued. "Maybe it wasn't in her file, but it proves there's a whole lot of Freeman's life we just don't know about. The murderer could have had a motive unrelated to her practice or her love life. She could have been involved in a financial deal that made enemies. Hell, she could have been a drug dealer for all we know." Lucia sighed. "A sure sign of failure of imagination. When the police find a dead-end case, we always say it was drug related." She got out of her chair and strode back and forth across the dining room.

"You could kill anybody you wanted and leave a bag of cocaine next to the body. End of investigation. Or we grab some ex-con we don't like and if he wasn't sitting in church with a hundred nuns when it happened, the jury will find him guilty. It stinks, it really stinks." She restrained her impulse to kick something...after all, it wasn't her house. "Time is running out and I'm getting nowhere. Forget it. No more work tonight. I'm tired and this case just frustrates me." She sat back down at the table. Amy got up and went to a bookcase in the living room.

"Before we quit entirely, here's the book about abusive therapists that I promised you." Amy stood behind Lucia and massaged her knotted neck. "So what would you like to talk about instead?"

173

"How did you ever find that picnic spot? Somehow I can't imagine you ignoring 'No Trespassing' signs in a survey of the possible luncheon sites in central Texas."

"No, you're right. It's not likely. Actually the land is owned by a friend of mine, a nurse," Amy replied.

"A friend, huh?"

"A hopelessly heterosexual friend, and more's the pity. She would make a great lesbian if she didn't have this unnatural attraction for the opposite sex. The land was an inheritance from a distant relative. She said it was badly overgrazed when she got it. She puts her horses on it in the spring for a couple of months so she can declare it agricultural use, but mostly it's just for the wildlife and her friends and family." Amy stroked Lucia's hair making her feel like purring. "Liberty is a very nice woman. A trifle eccentric, but delightful. You'll enjoy her."

"With a name like Liberty? I will?" Lucia asked. "How can you be so sure?"

"She charms everybody. I met her at a workshop on death and dying. She lives in Fowlerton, on the river. She has about ten acres of hay and six horses she feeds it to, three of which are ridable. The others are mistreated horses she's adopted. 'They just stand around, knee-deep in hay and make manure.' That is a quote. She stays with me when she has business in San Antonio, so you'll probably meet her."

Their conversation moved lightly around their daily lives until Lucia noticed how late it had become. As she left, Amy pressed a sea shell into her hand.

"To remember the oasis better," she said, kissing Lucia lightly. Lucia held it all the way home, despite the awkwardness it caused while she shifted gears. Touching it helped her remember to relax, to breathe deeply.

She had no trouble sleeping as soon as she was in bed. She dreamed of the little house she had rented with Yolanda in Austin. It looked like a basic tract house. Two bedrooms painted white, a living room/dining room painted white, a kitchen with wallpaper that had tiny yellow flowers on it. But it had a tree. None of the other houses had a tree. The tree was a middle-aged elm—not huge, but big enough to cast a lot of shade—none of which reached the house because the tree was in the middle of the backyard.

She dreamed of the picnics and barbecues and sitting outside reading in the spring. Then Lucia dreamed of making love in the late afternoon when the heat inside the house reached its peak and the sweat would bead up all over their bodies and then Yolanda would lie on top of Lucia. It was so wet they didn't stick, they lubricated and rolled easily over each others' bodies. The free-moving weight of Yolanda would press against Lucia's clit and they would roll over and up and down locked in this great sweaty bear hug and the heat was the same inside and outside their bodies. They would breathe in the hot wet air and it would add to their own hot wet selves and the passion seemed to be in the very air itself—inescapable and at times almost suffocating, but deep in a new way, very deep in every cell of Lucia's body.

She would stretch and push into Yolanda's sex with her knee or thigh and feel her movements roll through. Yolanda's slippery hands moved over Lucia's back and her fingernails lightly scratched and Lucia was surrounded and centered inside of her passion. When the convulsions shook Yolanda's body, arching and pushing, Lucia would feel the slippery heat everywhere, all through her, in her lungs as much as her pelvis. Yolanda's strong sweaty fingers would grasp Lucia's ass and pull her into her groin and surge and surge against her hard wet warmth. She could not tell if the surges were emanating from her pelvis or Yolanda's so much did they move together as one wet mass of passion and rock in the wet heat until they were exhausted.

The warm comfort of Yolanda's body slipped away as Lucia reached out in her sleep and was surprised to find only emptiness. A surge of grief shook Lucia as her drowsiness cleared. She tried to choke back a sob, but gave into deep, wracking cries as she grasped her pillow fiercely. The pain gradually subsided. Lucia stared unfocused as emptiness took over her mind. Startled at how easily this no-longer-familiar pattern fell back into place, she forced herself out of bed rather than lose herself to the numbness. She turned on the lights and rummaged in her closet until she found the needlework she had started for Tía Luz's birthday present. Sitting on the couch she began to work at the word "paz" in the dicho with blue thread. As always, the concentrated repetition of movement soothed her.

"I wonder what made that dream come back?" Lucia wondered. "It's been at least two years since the last time." She finished the part of the pattern to be worked in blue and knotted the thread. "Amy," she thought. "I haven't felt this way since Yolanda loved me. Now there's Amy. And my heart cries for Yolanda. No one can ever take her place." Lucia firmly stuffed the needlework back in its canvas storage bag and went to bed.

She closed her eyes, ignoring both the gentle tears that were wetting her cheeks and the nagging thought that Yolanda's place was empty. It was time to sleep.

MONDAY

"Okay, Ramos. Let's start with the basics. How much money does she have and who gets it when she dies?"

"I don't know," Lucia was embarrassed to admit.

"Exactly who was she sleeping with and who was mad about it?" Reynolds pointed the brown, gooey, chewed end of the cigar at Lucia as he asked.

"One, her lover Christian who could be mad about the others. Two, Kyle the tai chi teacher and client who believes you don't get mad, you get even. Three, another client, Field, who's a multiple personality with a lot of different opinions. Four, another client, Carter, who is very nonviolent, a real victim type."

"So, the worm sometimes turns," Reynolds muttered.

"Then there were two more she was no longer sleeping with that may have motives. Peterson, who filed a complaint against Freeman when she found out Freeman was sleeping with another client, Field. And Whitney, the therapist, who was supervising Freeman during licensing. That affair was ended by Freeman over a year ago. He seems pretty attached still."

Reynolds narrowed his brow so his eyebrows looked like two furry caterpillars becoming one. "Who doesn't have an alibi?"

"Hardly anyone has a good one. Christian and Kyle have none at all. But that would suggest premeditation on Christian's part since she had no reason to be in Freeman's office. And I don't think this was premeditated," Lucia said.

"So maybe she stopped by for a grocery list and they got into a fight." Reynolds paused and chewed his cigar. "It's there in your notes somewhere, Ramos. That file is too thick to have completely missed the murderer. Somewhere is a detail that doesn't fit. A lie. Find it or we lose. Cowley's going back to street patrol. They need him. You don't, do you?"

Lucia shook her head. "Not really."

"Two days, Ramos. We can't waste any more time than that. The trail's cold. What we got here is a murderer who probably never killed anyone before and probably won't kill anyone again. So he gets away. Bad luck for us. Good luck for him. Don't get an ulcer over it. There are plenty of killers out there we will get."

"Yeah, thanks, Lieutenant Reynolds. I hope I have *her* by Wednesday."

He did not acknowledge the last comment. Lucia left the office grimly. It would be luck, nothing more, if she caught the killer in the next two days. Once the case was on the back burner, it was almost never solved. Already all the trails were cold. None seemed more likely than others. Even a mediocre public defender from the San Antonio Program could get Marita off with the evidence as meager as it was. If it didn't convince Lucia, how could it convince twelve "good men and true?"

Lucia decided to give another try to shaking some more information out of her prime suspect before she saw Freddie at 2:30. But first, she put the finishing touches on her report of the ice house shooting, then pulled up the file on yesterday's killing of the abusive husband. Charges had been dropped. A patrolperson had found neighbors who had previously summoned police when the husband caught up with the wife as she tried to flee the house. Lucia skimmed the eight month old domestic violence report. The wife spent two weeks in the hospital and the husband spent six weeks in a treatment program. Running away had not been an

178

option. "Thank heavens," she muttered. At least that poor woman wouldn't have to go to jail.

Her call to Cowley caught him just before he left the station.

"Thanks for the help. You're great to work with. Sorry we didn't have a collar. Did you get a chance to talk to Helen Garcia?"

"Yeah. It was a bust. Two Mormon missionaries spent Tuesday evening with her. She seems to enjoy company. Too bad she can't go out and make friends. She's a real nice lady. Makes great bisquichitos. Do you want me to follow up on the gay angle?"

"No. The doctor was very closeted. I don't think bars or churches are going to give us a decent lead. I'll be off the case myself on Wednesday. I hope I can work with you again, Cowley. You're the best," Lucia said regretfully.

"And don't you forget it. Good luck, Ramos." He hung up.

Lucia checked her list. One person left to contact, David Freeman. She tried his home phone again. There was still no answer. At least his lack of an answering machine had saved the department some money. It was still too early to appear on Marita's doorstep. Lucia took out her mileage record and began the arduous job of filling out the mileage reimbursement request form. As usual she had forgotten to log at least a third of her trips. Once again she was grateful for her Sentra's good mileage. The rates were set for the bigwigs with gas-guzzlers, so she wouldn't be out of pocket too much.

Next she called the phone company to check Van Lander's story. A call had been made from his wife's phone at six o'clock Tuesday evening. It lasted two hours and twelve minutes. Van Lander appeared to be off the hook. There was a call waiting for Lucia as she hung up.

A voice she did not recognize said, "Officer Ramos? One moment please for Juanita Morales."

A new voice came on the line. "This is Juanita Morales, attorney at law. I am representing Nya Kyle. She has requested that I forward to you the class list with phone numbers for her women's self-defense class which met at 5 p.m. on Tuesday, April 6. The class did not finish until 6 p.m. I am also to give you a copy of the computerized registration form from the Marriott in Fort Worth. It will show her check in at 9:57 p.m., a time sufficiently early to have made murder in the interim extremely unlikely. Should you need to speak to Ms. Kyle further, I will arrange a meeting. Please do not contact her directly. As per my advice, she will speak of these matters only with an attorney present. Do you have any questions?"

"No," Lucia answered.

"Good-bye." The line went dead. Lucia shrugged. She wouldn't be getting anymore information from that direction. She rummaged through her briefcase for the tapes of Marita's two interviews and Freddie's interview. She also pulled Nya's.

As she listened to the tapes she made notes of questions. At least this time she had more information going into the interview. Listening to the tapes again, she caught things she had missed before. Like Marita referring to Freddie talking to her publisher. If she had caught that the first time, she would have been more prepared for Freddie being a woman. Lucia checked her watch. It was time to go.

Finding Marita's the second time was much easier. The dogs followed the car up the last part of the driveway, jumping and barking. Marita was standing in front of her trailer. This time her t-shirt announced WIMINFEST, but otherwise her appearance seemed little changed.

"Good morning, Office Ramos. You're up and about early." She seemed less tense than during the first interview. Had Amy set her mind at ease? Or did she decide she was getting away with murder? There was no way to know. Lucia joined her under the awning.

"Coffee, Officer?" Marita asked.

"No thanks. Just some questions," Lucia replied. "I'd like to know more about the Fourth of July party you attended at Dr. Freeman's house."

"Like I said, I don't remember much. I was pretty drunk. I was terrified to meet her lover Freddie. I mean Lizzie made it pretty clear that Freddie was going to have a heart attack any day and then we could be together. It felt really weird being at a party when you were the other woman and Freddie looked as healthy as a horse. I relied a little heavily on bottled courage. It's all a blur after that."

"There seemed to be an argument with a bartender?"

"Yeah. Lizzie told me about it later. I was pretty ashamed of myself, acting like that in front of Freddie and all their friends." Marita looked quite uncomfortable at the memory.

"But you have no memory of what happened?" Lucia asked.

"No, I was thinking about AA, but since I broke up with Lizzie I haven't been drinking much. No fights, no blackouts. A six-pack lasts me a week or more. So I decided it was the woman not the booze giving me problems."

Lucia checked her notes. "Did Dr. Freeman ever discuss her relationship with her lover?"

"Yeah. Freddie was too sick for sex. Or so Lizzie said. I have my doubts now."

"Other than that, did they get along or were there fights?"

Marita shook her head no.

"Was Freddie ever violent as far as you know?"

Marita looked stunned. "Battering? No, I don't think so. I would have seen bruises if there were any since Lizzie didn't like to have sex with her clothes on."

"Did you know any of her other clients besides Rebecca Field?"

"No, who's she?" Marita looked genuinely bemused.

Lucia decided to drop it. Rebecca had an alibi. It didn't matter how Marita met her or what name Rebecca was using. "How about Dr. Freeman's family?" drew another negative. So did a question about other lovers. Obviously Lizzie hadn't gossiped as much to Marita as she had to Nya or Freddie. Lucia decided to get to the important questions.

"Can you think how your cigarettes might have gotten into the ashtray of Dr. Freeman's car any time after March 27?" Lucia knew the date of the last car wash from the expired coupon in the car.

"No. I haven't seen her in a long time and I was never in her car."

"You're sure?"

"Well, if I have been, it's AA time for sure because that would be a major blackout." Marita stared accusingly at the pack in her hands. "Are you sure they're mine?"

"No. Same brand though. Are you willing to have a blood test to prove they're not? It's purely voluntary. You're under no obligation to do this. And if it turns up that your blood type matches saliva from the cigarettes, it would be evidence that can be used against you."

Marita took in a ragged breath. She looked ready to cry. "Yeah. I'll do it."

"And while we're talking about the contents of Dr. Freeman's car, could you explain how this came to be in her car?" Lucia handed Marita a copy of the note that had been found.

Marita froze. She just stared at the note in Lucia's hand. "Can you explain it?" Lucia waited for a reply. "Is it confession time?" she thought, holding her breath. Marita still said nothing. "Do you recognize the handwriting?"

"I wrote that. Or notes like that. Maybe a dozen. But I haven't written one in over a year. I swear to you. I didn't kill her. I don't know how that note got in her car. I would put them under her windshield or under her office door. I never put them in her car. She always kept the windows rolled up. Besides, sometimes it was such a mess in her car I don't think she would have seen a note." Marita's voice was flat and hopeless sounding.

"How did you know what the inside of her car looked like?" Lucia asked.

"I'd look in the window. I was curious. I wanted to know everything about her. Now I'm going to jail for it. It was a set-up, the shrink and all. And I fell for it. Damn. When am I going to learn? Trust people and get smashed. What a stupid fool I've been." She seemed to be talking to herself and she didn't sound like a murderer to Lucia.

"You're not going to jail, Marita," Lucia said. Marita stared at the piece of paper and said nothing. "You said you don't know how the note got in the car. I believe you. Maybe someone is trying to frame you. Maybe Dr. Freeman put it there herself. It could even be still there from a year ago. Cleaning up didn't seem one of Dr. Freeman's strong points." With each word Marita seemed to come more alive. "If you've been set up, it's not by me or by Dr. Traegar. My sole interest is in catching the real murderer. Not in framing an innocent person who has suffered enough already. If you want to bad mouth the whole human race, be my guest. But not on my account. I have betrayed no trust. And you should have better evidence than I've heard today before you accuse Dr. Traegar of it."

"You're lovers, aren't you?" Marita asked.

"It's none of your damn business," Lucia flared. "This is what mixing business and pleasure gets me into," she thought.

Marita laughed. "Cool down, Officer Ramos. I think I love you. You're not going to arrest me. I'm sure I love you. I'm free. My father's dead. Lizzie's dead. I didn't have to kill either of them and I'm free." She burst into sobs. "I'm free. And I'm alone. Is that the only way to be safe? To be alone?"

"I sure hope not," Lucia said. "But I think this is something you need to talk to Dr. Traegar about, not me." She gently disengaged the copy of the note from Marita's fingers.

"Just the facts, ma'am. Like on *Dragnet*. Just the facts." Marita wiped her eyes. Lucia could not tell if she was crying or laughing. She seemed hysterical.

"Is there someone I could call to be with you? Maybe a friend from the bar? I can patch it through radio dispatch," Lucia offered.

"No, I'll be fine. Really. I'll be fine. Fine."

Lucia thought maybe she was right. She gave Marita her card again and left. "Well," she thought as she drove back down the hill, "if she's a murderer, she sure has me fooled." She pulled out her map. The square miles covered by San Antonio were immense since the last annexation. City planners had learned their lesson since Castle Hills and Alamo Heights had gone their independent and wealthy way, taking millions in tax revenues with them. Now the city limits extended almost to Boerne. San Antonio was becoming almost all of Bexar County. No longer was a circle drawn with the cathedral at the center. And no way were there enough public servants to begin to serve the outlying areas.

Lucia shrugged. Lunch in Helotes would be a reasonable side trip. If she was lucky she could find a place with ham and grits. She wasn't. But the hamburger was at least edible if unremarkable. "Not worth a detour," she thought, "but sitting at a table instead of in the car is." It got old, eating in the car. She felt fortified for her next encounter with Freddie.

She was unprepared for her reception. The woman at the door was not Freddie. She introduced herself as Margaret Dexter, a cardiac care nurse. She sternly lectured Lucia on the danger of stress for the patient while she led Lucia to Freddie's bedroom. She seemed reluctant to leave the room, but Freddie ordered her out in a voice that brooked no nonsense.

"You didn't tell me you were ill," Lucia accused.

"Didn't want to risk you not coming out. I want to know what's going on. Who did it, Ramos? I want to know before I die." Freddie did not look ready to die, despite the medical equipment lined up beside her bed. She looked quite good in her cream silk negligee.

"So do I, Ms. Christian. So do I."

"No suspects yet?"

"Oh, I've got suspects. More than enough of those," Lucia said.

"Including me."

"Yes, including you. I have some questions I'd like to ask you if you feel able.

"Well, I can't run away this time. My doctor says if I did more crying it would do me good. It just isn't the way I was raised."

"Okay. Let's start. Do you think there is any possibility that this murder was aimed at harming you? You are not an easy person to get access to. Could someone have struck out at you through your lover?"

"Oh god. I never thought about that." Freddie looked stunned. "I don't know. I can't imagine who could hate me that much. Certainly no one comes to mind."

"No jilted lovers?"

"No. All of them are still friends."

"What about former spouses or lovers of your lovers?"

"I had never gotten involved with a woman who was still in a relationship until I met Lizzie. It's certainly not my usual style."

"Why did you change your pattern with Dr. Freeman?"

"She led me to believe that hers was a marriage in name only. That she and her husband had not been

184

sexual in years because of his ill health. I now have reason to believe that she was less than honest with me." She stroked the cream silk sheets with her finger tips. "It's what she told Nya about me. I presume she used the same line with others. In some ways Lizzie was not... imaginative."

"What can you tell me about her husbands?" Lucia was madly taking notes in case any of the medical equipment interfered with the tape recording.

"They were both psychology professors and they were both married when she met them. The first one was her advisor on her doctoral studies, Howard Drinel. He was very helpful to her on her dissertation. She was thirty-five when she married. He was fifty."

"Do you know if she was a virgin before she married?"

"She was not." Freddie looked extremely uncomfortable.

"Was she promiscuous?"

"I don't see what possible reason you could have...."

Determined not to lose control of this interview as she had the first one, Lucia leapt in. "Do you want to help find her murderer?" Freddie nodded as a small child might. "Then don't withhold information." She thought better of shaking her finger at Freddie.

"It is such a shameful thing. Not to be spoken of."

"It was incest, wasn't it?"

"Yes, how did you know?" Freddie looked dumb-founded. Her hands shook as she reached for a glass of water.

"I worked juvenile division for a long time. You don't get used to incest, but you begin to have a certain talent for seeing the symptoms. I've never worked with adults, but compulsive sexual behavior is certainly a clue with kids." Lucia tried to rest her hand while she talked. At the moment she envied Amy's shorthand. "Who was the perpetrator, her father?"

"Yes, and her brother David. How she could speak to that excrement I'll never know. He was so jealous of her, even years later. He did everything he could to break us up. I detest the man thoroughly."

"Do you think he might have killed her? Out of jealousy or perhaps for money?"

"Why *now,* if he was jealous?" Freddie dismissed the idea with a wave of her elegant fingers. Lucia noticed that she kept her nails short. "And the money theory is totally ludicrous. Lizzie would never give that scoundrel a cent. Not a cent."

"Who did she leave her money to?" Lucia asked.

"It's really quite absurd. She left it all to me. The kind of grandiose gesture she sometimes made that I found quite endearing. She was afraid that I would think she only loved my money. I didn't, of course. Her husbands left her quite comfortable, though not rich. Quite absurd." Freddie's eyes were red-rimmed and brimming with tears. "I don't want her money. I'll just give it away. I'm tired of profiting by the death of people I love. Maybe I'll take up serious smoking again instead of just having three or four a week." She managed to look both pitiful and quite proud of herself.

"You smoke?" Lucia asked keeping the excitement out of her voice.

"A bit. Because of my heart I've cut way back, but I'd have a few, especially when I was a passenger and Lizzie was driving. She was not a good driver. Took curves too fast and then heavy braking. That sort of thing."

"What brand?"

"Camel Lights."

"Bingo," Lucia thought. "That takes care of Marita's cigarettes." She took the copy of the note out of her briefcase and showed it to Freddie. "Have you ever seen this before?"

"No. Should I have?"

Lucia decided to try a new tack. "Do you think Nya Kyle is capable of violence?"

"Young woman, don't you know it's impolite to barge around a conversation like that?" Freddie looked quite miffed.

"I'm sorry, but I'm really not here for polite conversation. I don't intend to be rude, but I do intend to find out what I need to know. Nya had good reason to anticipate that you would turn to her if Lizzie was out of the way."

"And vice versa," Freddie commented.

"You are a very wealthy woman...." Lucia continued.

Freddie began to guffaw. "I can see you haven't run a background check on Nya—or rather on Nancy Kolder. She is one of the wealthier young women in the U.S. The white blood in the Kolder family ran thin—no heirs. It was a question of giving it to non-family or ignoring racism. Family won over racism. Her grandfather, who was president of a black college, became the sole heir of the Kolder salt fortune. Upstate New York. About 70 percent of the table salt used in the U.S. comes from the Kolder mines."

Freddie wiped the tears of laughter off her cheek with a lace-trimmed handkerchief. "When her grandfather died, two-thirds of the money went into trust for the grandchildren to avoid estate taxes. In fifteen months, when she hits forty, Nya will inherit one twelfth of 2.8 billion dollars. A tidy sum for almost anyone. No, it's definitely not my money Nya is after, Officer Ramos. One of the things I've helped her with is the foundation she is setting up to get rid of the excess money so it doesn't all go to the government."

"Morales," Lucia murmured.

"Yes, Juanita is a veritable genius at tax accounting. I have never regretted sending that young woman to Harvard, although in those days it took a considerable endowment to assure consideration of a Mexican-American woman. I had watched her grow up in Freer. Had the judges been unprejudiced she would have won the state debate championship her freshman year in high school. As it was, it took until her senior year. She was a National Merit Scholar, of course." Freddie sat propped up in bed with a smug look on her face.

"This is all very interesting, but I would like to get back to Nya or Nancy."

"Nya. She hates Nancy."

"Since money is not the issue, could jealousy have been a problem?" In truth, Lucia had not minded the diversion about Morales since it had allowed her to rest her cramping fingers.

"Nya doesn't believe in possessions. Either people or objects. I think she is trying to achieve nirvana or something like it. She and Lizzie would have long boring discussions about Eastern religions. Either of them was more interesting on the topic alone. Together they were the dreadfully dull of the true believer. No, I doubt that Nya feels jealousy, much less that she would kill for it. As flattering as it would be to this old lady, I would rule jealousy out."

"What about rage?" Lucia asked.

"Even less likely. Nya prides herself on controlling emotions. Besides, she wouldn't need a bottle to kill someone. She had her hands." Freddie demonstrated a very smooth chopping movement with her right hand. "She is very good at martial arts. She will never be raped again."

"She was raped?"

"As a child. A Sunday school teacher. It went on for a year. I believe it warped her view of both men and God, but it is really none of my business."

The nurse came back into the room and shooed Lucia out. "No more questions today, Officer. We don't want another cardiac incident, especially this far from a hospital." Freddie shrugged with resignation at her loss of audience. After she closed the door to Freddie's bedroom, the nurse said, "It isn't terribly dangerous, just a bit of angina, but if I don't exaggerate, she pays no attention to me at all."

Lucia was back at her desk before she realized that she hadn't asked about Sarah Carter. She had an excellent alibi, but there were other possibilities; perhaps someone close to Sarah was trying to protect her. For that matter, perhaps someone close to Nya or Rebecca or even Marita was the murderer, but it was very unlikely. Tilt your rifle into the sky and fire. You might hit a deer flying by. Lucia mentally shrugged. The case was grinding to an agonizing halt.

She typed in the new information, once again cursing her lack of proficiency at the keyboard. She gave David Freeman one more futile call while she waited for the printer to finish the new pages. She ran a second copy for Amy. She checked her watch. Amy could still be at the office.

Connie answered the phone on the first ring. "You just missed her. Her last client canceled, so she went home early. Do you want her home phone?"

"Thanks, I have it." Lucia admitted. She wondered if Amy had mentioned the change in relationship to Connie.

Connie had certainly never offered Amy's home phone before. Or was Connie trying to confirm some guesses? Lucia could feel a blush rise as she hung up. Delivering the report was just an excuse to see Amy before their date on Wednesday. The case was all but closed. The crime would go unpunished unless David Freeman had new information. Given that he had not seen his sister in years, it seemed unlikely to Lucia that he would add anything substantial.

Lucia decided that she would not stay at Amy's, even if invited. This was her last evening on the Freeman case. She wanted to put all her energy into reviewing the piles of data she had amassed. Lucia put copies of all the interview tapes in her briefcase. She shrugged and called David Freeman again. This time the phone was answered. A woman who identified herself as Mrs. Freeman took a message. Her husband would return the call as soon as he came home, which might be late.

Lucia enjoyed the drive through downtown. The deserted streets were easy to negotiate. It took only a few minutes to get to McCullough Street instead of the usual twenty minutes. Lucia parked on the street and took the now thick report in to Amy.

It was not easy for Lucia to turn down Amy's offer of dinner. Her body ached to spend another evening in Amy's arms. The sweet honey of Amy's kisses didn't strengthen her resolve, but she held firm. The case deserved one last evening of concentrated work, she kept telling herself as she drove away, so distracted she almost hit a cyclist when she missed a stop sign near Amy's. The adrenalin rush from the near-miss cleared her head and she arrived home without incident.

The best suspect was Freddie, Lucia decided. She had no alibi. She was taking martial arts training and she knew of Lizzie's affairs. The first task Lucia set for herself was to review all the material that related to Freddie. She listened to both interview tapes. Freddie had reacted badly to the comment about her sexual prowess and Lucia had not followed up. She should have. Was Freddie weakening as a lover? Lucia rearranged the facts into a new pattern of possibilities. Was Nya about to win Lizzie?

What if Lizzie was tired of Freddie? With a relationship with another wealthy woman already in place, perhaps

Lizzie was preparing to leave Freddie as she had left her husbands. Then Lucia remembered. Lizzie had cheated on her husbands, but not left them. But would Freddie count on that pattern or would she worry that Lizzie would leave and take Nya with her. Freddie was used to having what she wanted. Losing two lovers at once might be sufficient aggravation to motivate murder.

Lucia reread every bit of the file looking for support for this new theory. It seemed weak. It was almost dark when the phone rang. It was David Freeman, with a very abrupt greeting.

"Thank you for calling me back Mr. Freeman. As I mentioned in my message, it's about your sister Elizabeth." Lucia didn't know quite how to break her news.

"What's wrong? Has something happened to her?" His voice sounded only mildly interested.

"I'm sorry. This is not the kind of message to get by phone, but your sister is dead."

"An accident?" The question seemed almost casual.

"No. She's been murdered." Lucia felt awkward with the abruptness of the conversation, but couldn't think how to change it.

"Murdered? How?" David Freeman's voice seemed much more interested.

"In her office. She was killed by a blow to the head."

"One of her crazy clients."

"We don't know yet. We are still investigating." Lucia tried not to think about how soon the investigating would stop.

"I would have expected her to be shot by an outraged wife. Or husband, given her current taste in lovers."

"You knew about her homosexuality?" Lucia asked.

"She tried to use me to cover up one of her filthy little liaisons. She's a slut. She always has been. Even as a child." Venom dripped from his words.

"Well, jealousy has found its way on to the list of motives we are examining. Would it be all right if I asked some background questions?"

"As an officer of the court I'm happy to comply as long as none of the questions would lead to self-incrimination." His voice was very cold.

Lucia knew that the statute of limitations on his incestuous abuse had passed many years ago. She wondered what self-incriminating information David Freeman might have in the back of his mind. "Certainly. How long has it been since you've seen your sister?"

"Years. Perhaps four or five years."

"Where were you between 5 and 10 p.m. last Tuesday?"

"On an airplane somewhere between Chicago and Honolulu. Is that when she died?"

"Yes."

"That was almost a week ago. Why wasn't I contacted earlier?" Irritation sharpened his words.

"We were unable to get your address and phone until Friday. By then you were out of town." Lucia knew she sounded defensive.

"I've been out of town since Tuesday. In Honolulu with my wife."

"I'm sorry it took so long to inform you."

"It really doesn't matter. Elizabeth meant very little to me."

"Could you tell me anything about her financial affairs?" Lucia asked with some trepidation.

"I haven't talked to her about money in years. The last time was a phone call about her stepson's trust."

"Her stepson?"

"Yes. Welter's son. When Welter died he left half the estate in trust for his son from his first marriage. Elizabeth was trustee. She had some legal questions about the trust." For the first time in the conversation, his voice showed some interest.

"Can you tell me what those questions were?" Lucia was writing and thinking furiously.

"I'm not in the habit of talking about my clients but...well, Elizabeth is my sister, not a client. She never paid me, so there's no question of confidentiality. She had lost touch with the boy. She wanted to know how far she had to go to find him. I said that several ads in his last known place of residence would be sufficient, but that the trust would have to be maintained more or less indefinitely. Then she wanted to know if she could be reimbursed by the trust for her duties as trustee."

"And could she?"

"Certainly. A trustee fee of 5 to 10 percent of the annual proceeds would be considered reasonable in most cases. It could be challenged if it wasn't written into the trust, but the court would probably uphold it." His voice seemed oddly triumphant.

"Do you know if Dr. Freeman ever made contact with her stepson?" Lucia drew the questions back to the case.

"I have no idea."

"What is the stepson's name?"

"Welter, of course," he retorted curtly.

"And his first name?" Lucia began to see a pattern she had missed in the overwhelming amount of information in the case.

"I really don't remember. It's been years since I heard it, if I ever did."

"How old would the stepson be?" Lucia pressed for any details.

"He was a child when Elizabeth married his father. That was more than ten years ago. He's probably in his early twenties."

Lucia pounded her fist on the desk in aggravation at her own obtuseness. "Do you know if there were any other stepchildren?" she asked, not wanting to miss any other important facts.

"Not as far as I know. I presume the stepson is a suspect?"

"At this point, we haven't really identified suspects. We're interested in all Dr. Freeman's contacts. Can you tell me where Dr. Freeman lost track of her stepson?" Lucia tried to keep the eagerness out of her voice.

"Cape May, New Jersey."

"Thank you very much, Mr. Freeman. I appreciate your help. May I call you again if I need further information?" Lucia rushed to the end of the interview.

"Certainly. Whatever I can do to help. Good evening."

"Why did he move from New Jersey?" Lucia said to herself. "I wrote that in my notes. Why did he move from New Jersey? Then I just dropped it. Damn."

Lucia looked up Derrick Milton's phone number. There were suddenly a lot of questions she wanted to ask this young man. "But," Lucia thought, "how could Freeman forget a name like Derrick? Surely she'd remember her own stepson's name. I've got to be on the wrong track." At the twelfth ring, she gave up. "Maybe Amy will remember something else from her interview," Lucia thought dialing Amy's number. The line was busy.

✧

The last light of sunset was hidden behind a bank of storm clouds. Amy closed the heavy white drapes in the living room and bedroom and returned to her desk. The stack of journals still tantalized her. As a child she had hunted through every creek bed for a nugget of gold. She went back to the psychology journals with the same optimism. Most of the articles she had just read had the lacy beauty of a cobweb beside the stream bed. Intricate and impermanent. Rarely did anything merit note-taking.

But Amy had taken out her legal pad and her pen just in case. Already half the stack of journals was finished and not a word was written on Amy's pad. She could not quite place the sound that had pulled her out of her fascination with "Ego development in late adolescence." "Perhaps the boys are coming home early tonight," she thought and went back to her article.

Tiger hissed in the bedroom. Amy stood up quickly. Then paused. "If it's an intruder, I may need help" she thought, reaching for the phone. She got the number nine dialed before it was torn out of her hand. Her eyes followed the arm up to a face she recognized.

"Derrick," she whispered just before he clamped his hand over her mouth. The set of his face was both awkward and unyielding.

✧

Lucia read over her notes on Amy's interview of Derrick Milton for the third time. There was so little. She dialed Amy again.

"Come on, Amy," she thought. "Hang up the phone. I need to talk to you. How long can a therapist stay on a call? Hours." Lucia answered herself. She went through her notes a fourth time. "Forget the ordinary stuff," she told herself. "What's unusual?" She almost heard Reynolds's voice saying "Find the horizontals."

New Jersey was a horizontal. Freeman followed her lover to San Antonio. "But what about Derrick?" she thought. The small college on the west side didn't have a national reputation. How did Derrick choose it? If he was Freeman's stepson, why didn't she recognize him?

193

Surely she wouldn't have tried to do therapy with her own stepson? Cross that thought out. With Freeman all bets were off when it came to professional issues.

"Stop it," Lucia told herself. "You're running around in circles. Try Amy's phone again." The line was still busy. Lucia dialed the operator and asked for an intercept. The operator double checked the authorization code. Then he tried the intercept.

"Sorry, Officer, the phone's off the hook. There's no conversation. All I can hear are background noises, kind of like a cat screaming and hissing." The operator rang off.

"Tiger must have knocked the phone off the hook," Lucia thought. She went back to the Derrick Milton interview. He lived in a slum. That fits a grad student. He wears white shirts with button-down collars. That fits East Coast. Very neat. Maybe that fit, but most men she knew in their early twenties were not neat.

"If the bitch hadn't convinced my father...." Was Freeman the bitch? The focus for the anger in Derrick? The anger he himself acknowledged? Did the topic of drinking with Freeman upset him because he had picked up a vodka bottle and swung it at his stepmother's head? The anger was there. Had he discovered the money that might have saved his mother's life, the inheritance that Dr. Freeman was trying to withhold? His mother was the key. Had Freeman set off an explosion? "The details," Lucia thought. "Keep your mind on the details. What doesn't fit?"

The bicycle. A college student who lives in the slums does not bring a very expensive bike with him. "It's his hobby. He's a marathon cyclist," her mind retorted. "Shit." All the pieces fell into place for Lucia. And the picture she saw was a glimpse of a rider on a blue racing cycle less than a block from Amy's apartment, the cyclist she almost hit.

Lucia picked up her phone. "Dispatch, I need a patrol car at 2417 Kings Highway. Now. This is Officer Lucia Ramos. Badge 5034. I'll meet them there. Possible homicide in progress."

"How can I say that?" Lucia thought. Her mind was already at Amy's apartment. None of the images passing through her mind were good. Amy's body lying on the carpet the way Lucia had seen Dr. Freeman's body. "No," Lucia thought, "I'm overreacting because I've mixed up my personal and professional lives. I'm going to get there and it will just be an embarrassing moment. No killer. Just an angry cat. A cat that hisses at men. Shit." Lucia pulled her briefcase to the top of her desk. She opened it and took out her service revolver. It felt heavy and uncomfortable in her hand. She checked the clip. It was full. She had never fired at a person. She put the gun back into the briefcase and ran for her car.

Lucia grabbed her mobile flasher unit and put it on the car roof. She flipped on the magnetic hold, but not the siren switch. She needed a silent approach to catch Derrick. "Why didn't I ask Freddie about stepchildren?" she thought. "Then Amy would be safe. Damn Freddie for being so distracting."

Her maroon Sentra swung left on Woodlawn. She accelerated to over sixty between the too frequent stop lights. A marked squad car fell in behind her as she made a squealing right turn onto McCullough. San Pedro was closer, but had two extra stops. Her mind calculated the odds with cold logic. At least fifteen minutes had elapsed since her first call to Amy. Murder took only seconds. Less if the murderer had a gun. A slow-moving white pickup pulled into the center lane just in time to trap Lucia. She pounded the steering wheel with frustration. The squad car flipped on its siren.

"That's blown it," Lucia thought. "Now he knows we're coming." The white truck turned left into St. Anthony's school. She didn't bother to pull out and accelerate. They were at the Kings Highway turn. She took a deep breath. There was another marked squad car parked in front of Amy's apartment. Lucia realized that she had not turned on her car's police radio. She pulled to a screeching stop on the opposite side of the street and grabbed her service revolver out of the briefcase. The squad car behind her followed suit. Its single occupant leapt out to join her sprint for the already kicked down front door. Lucia was slowed by her unaccustomed gun.

She could not see anything through the curtained windows. The first thing she saw in the living room was Amy. Lucia's heart felt like it was bursting. Amy was sitting on the floor near the couch holding Derrick, who was sobbing against her breast. His arms were hand-cuffed behind him. The officer was standing next to him holding Amy's tape recorder.

"Has he been Mirandized?" Lucia asked.

"Yep," was the officer's reply. "And he still sang like a little canary. This one is going to stick. Mr. Paul Derrick Milton-Welter the Third is going to jail with all the other scumbags," he continued sarcastically.

"Named for his father, I'll bet," Lucia thought. "He probably used his middle name after his parents' divorce. If Milton is his mother's maiden name, it all makes perfect sense. Freeman wouldn't have recognized the name he's using now. If only I had asked for birth certificates...." She shook the absurd thought out of her mind and walked toward the couch.

Amy held the sobbing boy closer. "He isn't really a murderer, Lucia. He came here to kill me and couldn't. I think it was almost an accident that he killed Freeman."

Lucia tossed her keys to the patrolman behind her. "Lock the car and bring in my briefcase, please." She put her revolver on safety and lay it on the coffee table. "Are you okay?" she said to Amy. Amy, close to tears, nodded.

Derrick stiffened in her arms and stood up. "I think I need a lawyer," he said sounding very young and very scared.

Amy stood up next to him. She put her arm around his shoulder. "There's a good criminal lawyer I know, Dan O'Hare. He's represented some children who are my clients and they really like him. If he doesn't work out, maybe he can recommend someone who will. Do you want me to call him?"

Derrick nodded wordlessly, then said, "I don't have any money."

"Yes, you do," Lucia said. "Your father left you a trust fund. Half his estate is yours." Derrick received the news open-mouthed and stunned. Whatever his motive for the murder, it wasn't money.

"My mom didn't need to die. The money would have saved her," Derrick blurted out.

"Quiet, boy," the arresting patrolman chided. "Once you ask for a lawyer, you shouldn't say anything else." He grinned knowing that they already had enough evidence without further disclosure. Amy looked at Lucia pleading for help for Derrick. Lucia shrugged. It was out of her hands at this point.

"Why don't you take him in and book him? I'll finish up here," Lucia said.

"Sure," the patrolman replied. "You gonna bring the doc down for her statement?"

"Yeah, I'll bring the tape too, if you'd like. Forensics will get the rest." He nodded his agreement and prodded Derrick out to his squad car. The other officer asked Lucia if she needed his help. With her negative response, he too left.

"It's over," Lucia said taking Amy's recorder and pressing the rewind button.

"Thank god. I was terrified." Lucia turned on her own tape recorder. "He came in a bedroom window. I thought he was going to strangle me. Then he couldn't do it. He just fell apart. He started talking about his parents and their divorce. He was still talking when the officer kicked the front door in. The officer read him his rights and Derrick didn't stop talking. It was like a dam breaking. I don't think he could stop." Amy began to shiver. "I think I'm a little shocky myself."

"Come over to the sofa. You'll feel better sitting down. I want to hear the tape." Lucia arranged the recorders so that hers would tape as the other one was playing. She turned on Amy's recorder and led Amy to the sofa.

First was the voice of the patrolman completing the Miranda warning. Then Derrick's voice waiving his rights. Lucia shook her head. There was no way a lawyer would get him out of this confession.

The next part of the tape was clearly audible. "She told me Mom had chosen to come into that particular life and die that particular death. She said I should let go of my anger. She just kept talking about how Mom really wanted to die like that. I just wanted her to shut up. I didn't want her to die. I remembered all the pain. Cancer hurts a lot in the colon. The doctors kept telling her the pain was unresolved anger over the divorce. They didn't even check until it was too late. It was her fault that Mom died. If she hadn't taken my father away, it never would have happened.

197

"She wouldn't stop. I kept saying to stop, 'You don't know my mother, just shut up.' But she wouldn't. She said I wanted sex with my mother. How could she say shit like that? Then she said I hated my mother.

"I had to stop her. She had no right to say all those terrible things. I wanted to talk about how angry I was with her, but she wouldn't shut up. I couldn't get her to stop. I just wanted her to stop. I hit her with the bottle to make her stop. I didn't mean to kill her. In the movies they do it all the time and nobody ever dies. She wasn't supposed to die."

The next few moments on the tape were filled with Derrick sobbing. As his sobbing lessened, Amy asked, "Why me, Derrick?"

"You knew. I could see it in your eyes. You asked me about the bottle. I knew then that you knew. You even asked about anger. And I could tell you didn't believe me when I said I was in the library. Then you saw my bike. I didn't realize until later what your questions were about. You were trying to figure out if I could make it to her office on my bike. I kept expecting someone to come and arrest me. Then I thought maybe you hadn't talked to the police yet. I decided I had to kill you and get the tape back. So this afternoon I followed you home from your office. But I wanted to wait until dark. I thought it would be safer. But then I couldn't do it. I didn't want to hurt you. I didn't want to hurt anyone. It's all a mess, I'm sorry. I'm so sorry." He began sobbing. Then Lucia heard her own entry. She turned off Amy's tape recorder.

"Are you okay?" she asked Amy.

"Better. At least I'm sure I'll live. There for a bit it was touch and go. I never saw it, Lucia. All those things he thought I saw, I didn't. I didn't see any of it. I missed that incredible guilt, all that suppressed anger. My god, he had only seen her a couple of times. Where did it come from? I can't imagine how it could have developed that quickly."

"He was Freeman's stepson."

"What?" Amy screamed. "He's what? When did you find that out?"

"David Freeman mentioned that Lizzie was administering a trust fund for her stepson in New Jersey. Derrick is from New Jersey and about the right age. I tried to call him, but there wasn't an answer. So I tried to call you. The operator could hear Tiger hissing. That's when I got worried and called for help. It would have been very embarrassing if you had been having tea with your landlords."

"Tea with the boys," Amy began to giggle. She didn't seem able to stop. Lucia realized that she was hysterical and drew Amy into her arms.

"It's okay now. It's over, Amy. You're all right. He's in jail. You're safe, sweetheart." She held Amy tighter as Amy sobbed.

Finally Amy could talk again. "He could have killed me. I couldn't stop him. I was helpless. Just like when I was a child. I was helpless."

Lucia gently tilted Amy's head up and looked her in the eyes. "First, there is no perfect defense against murder. Second, there are things you can do to strengthen yourself against attack. Will you let me go through your apartment and make suggestions? I'll start with the front door. Get a metal door."

Amy started to giggle again, but this time without hysteria. "Then how can you kick it in the next time I need you?"

"There's a wonderful new invention called a key."

"Some women will go to any lengths to get a key to my apartment."

"Any length at all, Amy. Any length at all." Lucia stood and pulled Amy to her feet. "Forensics will be here soon. Would you like to take your purse when you go to the station?" Amy nodded and went into the bedroom while Lucia put Amy's tape recorder in an evidence bag and tagged it. A huge man stepped through the shattered door. "Nice work, Ramos. I didn't think you had it in you. By the way, thanks for lunch."

"Thanks for the quick work on the Volvo, Shapiro."

"Sure. What do you want from here?" He gestured around the apartment.

"Prints on the back window. Evidence of forced entry. Should be a blue bike somewhere nearby. Prints off it and bring it in," Lucia instructed.

"A bike? Really?"

"Evidence that he didn't need a car or cab to get to Freeman's office."

"You mean this call is about the Freeman case? I thought it was dead."

Lucia patted the evidence bag. "We got a confession after an attempted murder. Patrolman Stone took the suspect in. I'm taking the intended victim in for a statement."

"You want a complete vacuum to match with the dirt on his shoes? That kind of thing?"

"No. We got him cold on this one." Lucia turned toward Amy as she re-entered the room. "Besides, the attempted murder will probably be plea-bargained away for a more serious murder conviction." Amy nodded. So did the friendly giant from forensics.

After the statement at the station, Amy waited while Lucia finished up the essentials. While she was waiting, she listened to the tape of her interview with Derrick. Her fingers trembled as she turned on the tape. Then she played it again. Nowhere did she find clues that she had missed. Without any information except the conversation, she could not have known that Derrick had murdered Dr. Freeman. That knowledge comforted her. Then she called her landlords, who could not believe what had happened while they were out happily watching a movie.

"We should have rented a video, honey. Then we could have saved you," Harry said. "We'll nail some plywood over the door. We thought you had been robbed until Joe saw your car was there. We were just frantic. I'm so glad you called. Where are you going to sleep, darling? You can't sleep in the apartment, it would be simply gruesome."

"I'm going to the Hilton Del Rio. I deserve a little luxury tonight," Amy replied.

"You take care of yourself, you hear. We love you." He hung up just as Lucia returned to her desk.

"Ready to go?" Lucia asked.

"Not home. At least, not to sleep. I'll pick up some clothes and go to a hotel. I don't think I'll feel safe until I've made some changes," Amy said as they left.

"How about a cup of coffee and a talk?" Lucia asked. Amy agreed. They ended up at Jim's on North St. Mary's Street. The orange booths and dark formica tables did little to improve the mediocre coffee.

"Derrick will go to prison, won't he?" Amy asked, putting a spoonful of vanilla ice cream in her coffee.

"Probably. That confession is pretty clear. It was witnessed and taped. There's not much anybody can do to keep him out of prison," Lucia replied. "If he hadn't changed his name to his mother's maiden name, we would have nailed him on Friday."

"I feel so sorry for him. It's almost like Freeman was goading him. Whatever could she have been thinking of?"

"I doubt if she knew she was talking to her stepson." Lucia speared a bite of sausage.

"Even so, to fling out the possibility of an oedipal factor in their relationship is unbelievable. Perhaps she had been drinking. It was such a terrible thing for a therapist to do."

"She died for it."

"And that poor confused boy has ruined his life. For what? Oh Lucia, it's all so futile. How do you bear it? The utter futility of these deaths? Where is the meaning in it? There is none. None." Amy mashed her ice cream with her spoon until it was soupy.

"I guess I hope some kid reads the newspaper and sees that a guy hit someone over the head with a bottle and he goes to prison when that person died. Maybe that kid stops the impulse to pick up a bottle and swing it sometime in his life. Maybe what I do stops another futile death. That hope keeps me going."

"All of us, it's the hope.... Take me to the hotel, please, Lucia. I'm very tired."

"Would you like to stay with me tonight? I'd feel safer if I were nearby...." Lucia felt suddenly very tentative.

"Thanks for the offer, but I need some solitude to collect myself." Amy smiled shyly.

Amy hooked her arm through Lucia's as they walked together into the night.

Amy's gold card produced a room instantly at the Hilton Del Rio. The sparkling lights of the city grew smaller as the elevator took them swiftly to the top floor.

"No ground floor windows for stranglers to enter by," Lucia said.

"Right, Officer Ramos. You're very perceptive," Amy replied as she slipped the key card into the slot. "Could you come in for a bit?"

"I was hoping to be asked. There's something about almost getting murdered that's a little unnerving." Lucia strode into the rooms of the suite and began checking closets and under the bed. She even checked the spacious bathroom thoroughly.

"That's exactly what I needed. Thanks, Lucia." Amy stood in the center of the living room with her overnight case. She strongly resembled a mislaid child in an airport. "Did this ever happen to you? I mean, almost getting killed?" Her voice wavered as if the information was just beginning to hit her endocrine system.

Lucia took the overnight case from her and set it in the bedroom on the luggage rack. When she came back, Amy had not moved. Lucia almost expected to see her stick her thumb in her mouth. She looked so lost and forlorn. She led Amy to the couch and pulled her down beside her.

"No. I got slugged by an outraged father who couldn't believe I would say such things about him and his kid. Almost broke my jaw. We added assault on a police officer to the incest charge. Then it all got dropped when the DA decided it would be hard to prosecute. An eighteen-month-old does not make a credible witness."

Amy began to shake. "I'm sorry," Lucia said. "I guess incest is the last thing you need to hear about tonight."

"I was so scared," Amy sobbed. "It brought back all the old terror. I was totally helpless." Lucia cuddled her tightly. Then she pulled Amy onto her lap.

"It's okay, Amy. It's over now," she murmured.

"No, no, no," Amy whispered, her voice out of control. "No."

"It's all right, niña, I'm right here. You're safe now." Lucia rocked the weeping woman in her arms. "Feel my arms; they'll keep you safe." Lucia repeated all her reassurances until Amy relaxed. "Are you ready for bed, now? I think it would be good if you could sleep, honey."

"Okay," Amy said. Her voice sounded very young and very worn out as she stood.

"How about if I sleep on the couch between you and the door?" Lucia added.

"Would you really?" Quiet tears rolled down Amy's face. "It seems a lot to ask."

"You didn't ask; I offered. Go to bed, m'jita. You'll be safe." Amy nodded and closed the bedroom door behind her.

Lucia picked up the phone. "I'd like a five-thirty wake-up call in Room 2810," she said. She hung up and whispered to the closed door, "Tomorrow's going to be a long day. Sleep safely, Amy."

Photo by Tee Corinne

After a couple of grim decades in Texas, Mary Morell settled permanently in New Mexico. She and Anne Grey Frost, her partner in both business and pleasure, are immeshed in their feminist bookstore, Full Circle Books. The store uses all the skills Mary learned as an English teacher, a counselor and a manager of travel agencies. For relaxation she picks up pretty rocks which she has agreed not to bring in the house. She also writes novels, poems, plays, political diatribes and occasional recipes. Her partner helps in the writing, but their two dogs, four cats and two horses do not.

About the Spinsters Book Company Lesbian Fiction Contest

The purpose of this contest is to encourage well-crafted, novel-length fiction that focuses on the lives of lesbians. Our goal is to increase the body of literature about lesbians: not only about our histories and daily lives, but also new visions and ways of writing about our worlds. We want to publish and promote fiction that treats that our lives with the complexity and honesty they deserve. Too often, novels written about lesbians have fallen into the category of "escape" fiction, with sex and romance being the only required ingredients. We see our contest as a means to balance the record: quality fiction with lesbians appearing as main characters.

Manuscripts are evaluated by a panel of readers, with the best five going to a finals judge. The judging process is done "blind," with the identity of the author concealed throughout the entire process, so that it is the writing itself and not the celebrity or status of the writer that is judged. The finals judge changes each year, the selection reflecting the diversity of writers we seek to publish. The judge is always an accomplished and published writer, and her name is announced at the end of each contest. The judge of the 1990 Lesbian Fiction Contest was Joanna Russ, author of *On Strike Against God* and *The Female Man,* who chose *Final Session* because it has "a fascinating group of characters and...much to reflect on and feel strengthened by."

Submissions to the contest are accepted yearly between January 1 and February 28 and the winner is announced in the summer. The winner will be given a contract to publish her novel with Spinsters and $2000 in prize money (which is in addition to any royalties she earns on the book). The book is published the following spring. Contact Spinsters Book Company, P.O. Box 410687, San Francisco, CA 94141 for more information and guidelines.

▨ spinsters book company

Spinsters Book Company was founded in 1978 to produce vital books for diverse women's communities. In 1986 we merged with Aunt Lute Books to become Spinsters/Aunt Lute. In 1990, the Aunt Lute Foundation became an independent non-profit publishing program.

Spinsters is committed to publishing works outside the scope of mainstream commercial publishers: books that not only name crucial issues in women's lives, but more importantly encourage change and growth; books that help to make the best in our lives more possible. We sponsor an annual Lesbian Fiction Contest for the best lesbian novel each year. And we are particularly interested in creative works by lesbians.

If you would like to know about other books we produce, or our Fiction Contest, write or phone us for a free catalogue. You can buy books directly from us. We can also supply you with the name of a bookstore closest to you that stocks our books. We accept phone orders with Visa or Mastercard.

Spinsters Book Company
P.O. Box 410687
San Francisco, CA 94141
415-558-9586

OTHER BOOKS AVAILABLE FROM
SPINSTERS BOOK COMPANY

✧

Bittersweet, by Nevada Barr $9.95

Child of Her People, by Anne Cameron $8.95

The Journey, by Anne Cameron $9.95

Prisons That Could Not Hold, by Barbara Deming $7.95

High and Outside, by Linnea A. Due $8.95

Elise, by Claire Kensington $7.95

Modern Daughters and the Outlaw West,
by Melissa Kwasny $9.95

*The Lesbian Erotic Dance: Butch, Femme, Androgyny
and Other Rhythms,* by JoAnn Loulan $12.95

Lesbian Passion: Loving Ourselves and Each Other,
by JoAnn Loulan $11.95

Lesbian Sex, by JoAnn Loulan $10.95

Look Me in the Eye: Older Women, Aging and Agism,
by Barbara Macdonald with Cynthia Rich $6.50

All the Muscle You Need, by Diana McRae $8.95

Considering Parenthood, by Cheri Pies $9.50

Coz, by Mary Pjerrou $9.95

We Say We Love Each Other,
by Minnie Bruce Pratt $5.95

Desert Years: Undreaming the American Dream,
by Cynthia Rich $7.95

Lesbians at Midlife: The Creative Transition,
ed. by Barbara Sang, Joyce Warshow
and Adrienne J. Smith $12.95

Thirteen Steps: An Empowerment Process for Women,
by Bonita L. Swan $8.95

Why Can't Sharon Kowalski Come Home?
by Karen Thompson and Julie Andrzejewski $10.95

Spinsters titles are available at your local booksellers, or by
mail order through Spinsters Book Company (415) 558-9586.
A free catalogue is available upon request.

Please include $1.25 for the first title ordered, and $ .90
for every title thereafter. California residents, please add 7.25%
sales tax. Visa and Mastercard accepted.